A PLUME BOOK

CALIFORNIUM

© Doug Brewer

R. DEAN JOHNSON grew up in Anaheim, California, and now lives in Kentucky with his wife, the writer Julie Hensley, and their two children. An Associate Professor at Eastern Kentucky University, he is Director of the Bluegrass Writers Studio Low-Residency MFA in Creative Writing program. His essays and stories have appeared in *Ascent, Hawai`i Pacific Review, New Orleans Review, Santa Clara Review, Slice, The Southern Review,* and elsewhere. This is his first novel.

ALSO BY R. DEAN JOHNSON

Delicate Men: Stories

CALIFORNIUM

R. Dean Johnson

A PLUME BOOK

PLUME
An imprint of Penguin Random House LLC
375 Hudson Street
New York, New York 10014

Copyright © 2016 by Robert Dean Johnson
Penguin supports copyright. Copyright fuels creativity, encourages diverse voices, pro-
motes free speech, and creates a vibrant culture. Thank you for buying an authorized
edition of this book and for complying with copyright laws by not reproducing, scanning,
or distributing any part of it in any form without permission. You are supporting writers
and allowing Penguin to continue to publish books for every reader.

P REGISTERED TRADEMARK—MARCA REGISTRADA

LIBRARY OF CONGRESS CATALOGING-IN-PUBLICATION DATA

Names: Johnson, R. Dean, 1968– author.
Title: Californium / Robert Dean Johnson.
Description: New York : Plume, 2016.
Identifiers: LCCN 2015042415 (print) | LCCN 2016000773 (ebook) | ISBN
    9780143128779 (paperback) | ISBN 9780143128786 (eBook)
Subjects: LCSH: Teenage boys—Fiction. | Family secrets—Fiction. |
    California—History—20th century—Fiction. | Domestic fiction. | BISAC:
    FICTION / Coming of Age. | FICTION / Family Life. | FICTION / Literary. |
    GSAFD: Bildungsromans.
Classification: LCC PS3610.O3725 C35 2016 (print) | LCC PS3610.O3725 (ebook)
    | DDC 813/.6—dc23
LC record available at http://lccn.loc.gov/2015042415

Printed in the United States of America
10 9 8 7 6 5 4 3 2 1

Portions of some chapters of this book previously appeared, in different form, in the
following publications: "Matter" as "Catching Atoms" in *Ruminate*, "Native Customs"
in *Paradigm Vol.1*, and "Two-Car Studio" in *Tribute to Orpheus*.

For Julie, Boyd, and Maeve.
For more things than I could ever say,
and more than I could ever hope.

SET LIST

CALIFORNIUM

[Opening Act]

In the dark, my popcorn ceiling looked like one of those old black-and-white pictures of the moon—all shadowy and imperfect and so real it seemed fake. It didn't make sense to suddenly be awake in the quiet of the house, and I knew my clock must be in single digits, later than late but still too early to be early. Then the voices came back. They'd hiss like waves at the beach and fade into the dark before I could make out what they were saying. That's what woke me up. That's how it all started.

For a second, I wondered if I was dreaming. But if it was all a dream, the voices would have faces or bodies; something would be chasing me through quicksand or across a field of wet grass and I'd have no shoes on, just soda bread strapped to my feet and a backpack full of bricks. Nobody dreams boring stuff. That's why the sheets were up to my chin while I stared at the dark side of the moon, waiting for I don't know what. The voices to come back, I guess.

Then it hit me: If it was half past infinity, why would there be any light at all on my ceiling? So I followed the glow across the room, down the wall, and to my door, which was mostly closed except for a crack just big enough to let in the light that was sneaking down the hallway.

I was ready when the voices came back, staring at my door, the hiss louder this time. "Go," a voice said. "You have to go."

Then, a different voice, softer, like air leaking out of a pipe: "Where can I go, Packy? Tell me."

"Home," the first voice said. My dad's voice.

"You know the trouble that'll bring."

"So you bring the trouble to me?" my dad said, louder, almost like he was in the room with me and not just on the other side of my door. "You can't be here in the morning. You know that."

"It's the last time, Packy. I promise."

"No, Ryan. The last time was the last time."

"Please," Uncle Ryan said. "I'll sleep in the garage. The kids won't see me."

Dad sighed the way he does when we're running late for church and I still don't have my shoes on and he's about to explode but knows he shouldn't. "Jesus, Ryan. Why do you do this to me?" It made me feel sorry for Uncle Ryan, the way his voice sounded like mine begging for just five more minutes of catch and my dad saying no.

I went to the door thinking maybe I'd tell Uncle Ryan he could sleep in my room. He could get up early and make one of his big breakfasts, like he always did when we'd wake up and somehow he was just there, in the kitchen, scones in the oven, coffee and tea and juice on the table, and him saying, "Happy Wednesday, Reece. How do you want your eggs?"

When I opened the door no one was there. At least, not where I expected. My dad and Uncle Ryan were farther down the hallway by the bathroom.

"Reece?" my dad whispered. "Go back to bed."

Uncle Ryan looked the other way, like something really interesting was happening just over there, by my parents' bedroom door.

"What time is it?" I said.

Dad stepped over to me—put a hand on my shoulder. "Doesn't matter. We're all done."

"Can I get some water?"

He thought for a second. "Okay. Fast."

The living room and dining room were dark, but light and the smell of coffee were seeping from the kitchen. My mom was there, leaning against the counter, arms crossed with a green cup in one hand. She had on her morning robe, all pilled and older than me and my brother and sister combined.

"Why are you up?" she said, and I told her about the water.

She filled a big, plastic New York Jets cup for me, said I could take it back to my room, and sent me out of the kitchen. Uncle Ryan's beat-up army jacket was slung across the back of a dining room chair. His keys were in the front pocket like always, so I fished them out and dropped them into my cup. A little water spilled over and I took a sip before stepping back into the dark hallway.

My dad and Uncle Ryan were by my door now, like maybe they were ready to come out of the hallway. "Good night," Dad whispered.

"Good night," I said to Uncle Ryan. He patted me on top of the head without looking at me, then nudged me into the bedroom.

■

I was up before my alarm, out of bed and through the house. I walked to the kitchen, and my mom was there in the same spot, wearing the robe, holding the same green cup. Like she hadn't moved.

"Get dressed," she said.

Uncle Ryan's jacket wasn't in the dining room and suddenly nothing about the night before seemed real. Maybe the voices were a dream. Maybe Uncle Ryan hadn't been in the hallway.

It wasn't until I was dressed and looking for my shoes that I saw the Jets cup on my nightstand. And there at the bottom, like a sunken ship, were Uncle Ryan's keys.

I slipped on my shoes and grabbed my backpack fast so I could go out to the garage, or wherever, and wake up Uncle Ryan before school. Maybe get him to teach me a new limerick my mom wouldn't want me to repeat.

The thing is, he wasn't in the garage. He wasn't in the basement, or on the spare sofa, or anywhere.

I ran to the living room window to see if his car was at the curb. It was.

"What are you doing?" my mom said. She was standing across the room by the chair where Uncle Ryan's jacket was supposed to be.

"Where's Uncle Ryan?" I said.

"He's gone."

I looked back out the window, made sure the car out front was a dark blue Oldsmobile, that it had the new license plates with the shape of New Jersey where the dash used to be, and that it had the dent by the front tire. "But his car—"

"He's gone," Mom said, louder this time. And that's when I noticed what was missing: Dad's truck.

I turned and my mom was still standing there. Her nose freckles weren't hidden beneath powder. Her hair, which should've been braided or swirled up neat like she was balancing a red Danish on her head, was down and splashing around her face and shoulders like hot lava. She wasn't rushing around, yelling at Brendan to wake up, telling me to go get Colleen, stepping around my dad while he made breakfast and she packed lunches and asking if he wanted leftovers or a sandwich and he'd better decide right now because she still had to get dressed and if he didn't want to drop the kids off at school on *his* way to work, everyone needed to get it in gear right now.

"Where's Dad?" I said. "Did he take Uncle Ryan home?"

She shook her head and walked into the kitchen. She sat down at the table, wrapped both hands around her teacup, and stared at the tablecloth.

I sat down across from her. "Mom?" I said, and you'd think it was the first time she'd seen me all morning the way she looked up at me. "Where's Dad?"

She slid one hand across the table. Without thinking, my hand slid out to meet hers halfway, suddenly wrapped inside and squeezed snug. "He's looking for Uncle Ryan."

Matter

The night before school starts, I write my first letter to Uncle Ryan, which is weird because I've never written a letter to anyone before. Not really, unless you count the postcards they made us send from outdoor education camp in fifth grade. And there was that note I got from Linda Donofrio in seventh grade, asking if I wanted to be her dance partner for the square dancing unit in PE, which I didn't because I was going to ask Regina Campbell as soon as I had the nerve, but I wrote back, *I guess,* because she was nice and I didn't want to make her feel bad. But here I am, spilling my guts out to Uncle Ryan, telling him how it feels to leave everyone behind in Jersey and move to a place I've never heard of and live around a bunch of people I don't know. I don't say how moving in the middle of summer was extra awful because it meant leaving my baseball team right before the play-offs, or how we got to California too late for me to join a new team.

Instead, I tell him how much I miss him and how on the way up the hill from the freeway there's a sign that says WELCOME TO

YORBA LINDA, LAND OF GRACIOUS LIVING. "Better be," my dad said the first time we drove by it. And maybe it will be. Our new house could swallow the old one back in Paterson. Colleen's room is so big she can keep her dollhouse right in the middle of the floor without tripping on it. Brendan's even got a weight bench in his room, which he thinks he needs now that he's in junior high and allowed to play football. My room's pretty much the same as it was back home; there's just a lot more carpet between my bed and the door.

I tell Uncle Ryan about all the overtime and extra Saturday shifts my dad's working too, because he says Rockwell has more money than they know what to do with. They pay machinists time and a half the microsecond you get past forty hours, double time on weekends. "It's good for all of us," my dad keeps saying, and I haven't said anything except how summer's gone and we didn't make it to a single ball game. I tell Uncle Ryan that's never happened before, which he probably knows, but that it's like the only places my dad goes anymore are work and church. *And what's fun about either of those?* I write, then think about it for a long time before adding the *Ha! Ha!*

■

The first day of school and the sky is one giant gray cloud. Only this is California so you know it's not going to rain. It'll burn off to some kind of blue and the guy on the eleven o'clock news will lie and say it was another perfect day. But either way, Mom's not letting me out the door without something for the rain that won't come. My Paterson All-Stars jacket from last year doesn't fit anymore and I don't have my back-to-school clothes yet, so she gives me my dad's old work jacket—a navy-blue, sharp-collared, cut-tight-at-the-bottom-so-it-doesn't-get-sucked-into-machinery machinist's jacket. There's a patch over the heart with my dad's nickname on it, *Packy*.

Mom says she's excited about all the new friends we're going to make at school. And that's probably true for Brendan and Colleen because little kids don't care what you're wearing or how you do your hair. Not like high school, where everything matters. Especially when you're new. That's why the All-Stars jacket would have been helpful, because then people would know how good I am at baseball and they'd like me right away.

When I get to the corner of our cul-de-sac, Keith's across the street, waiting on his front lawn for me. The first thing out of his mouth is "Packy? Who the hell is Packy?"

Keith's the one friend I've got, so if it were anybody else I'd think they were razzing me. My clothes are already out-of-style hand-me-downs from my cousins; the jacket just makes things worse. It's too big, all saggy in the shoulders and so long in the sleeves I'm cuffing them as we walk. But me and Keith decided neither of us were going to the back-to-school sales with our parents. We're waiting until after the first week of school so we can know what the cool people are wearing. Then we'll buy our clothes and make the right kind of impression on everybody. And without Keith, I wouldn't know who the cool people are.

■

The day we unpacked the moving van, Keith just appeared in the garage, his hair spiked and stiff so it looked like he could cut something with it. "Where'd you come from?" he said.

"Paterson."

"Pad-a-son? Where's that?"

"You razzin' me?" I said.

He laughed, a nice one like I'd told a joke, and said he didn't think so but now he had to know where people who said "razzin'" were from.

I folded my arms. "New Jersey."

"That's cool," he said and stuck out his hand.

I shook it. "Where'd you come from before this?"

Keith pointed back out of the cul-de-sac and across the street. "Right there. The house that looks like yours."

That's the thing about California. If you pay attention, you start to see how there's a pattern to things. My house is the fourth one in, right where the street bends and starts curving back around to come out of the cul-de-sac. But every fifth house is the same house. Sometimes it's painted totally different or the front door and garage are flipped to the opposite side, but it's the same house.

"You going to be a freshman this year?" Keith said, and I nodded. He was too. "Do you know who your neighbor is?"

"I don't know who anybody is."

Then Keith told me there were only two names to know at Esperanza High School. One was Astrid Thompson, the only sophomore ever to make varsity cheer, and now a junior. That, he said, is my new neighbor. The other name was some guy Keith had never heard of until last year, Marc van Doren. "But the guy's a senior, the lead singer of Filibuster, and he was a state finalist in the sixteen hundred last year. They did a little story in the paper and called it 'The Misfit Mile,'" Keith said, though he didn't know why they called it that. "I don't even know what he looks like. There wasn't a picture. I just know I've been hearing about that guy everywhere for almost a year now. Whatever formula he's got going really works."

■

Me and Keith both have first-period General Science. He sits in the desk behind me and leans forward during roll to say who's worth taking notes on. The classroom is crowded and you can tell it's a mix of underclassmen and upperclassmen. We're supposed to be looking at the guys, but it's hard not to notice girls wearing acid-green and neon-yellow tank tops. And plenty of them are perfect makeup, big bangs, and designer jeans that have you following the white stitches up their legs like little roads leading somewhere you really want to go. The guys are mostly Levi's jeans and T-shirts—*Star Wars,* Superman, and dirt bikes. A couple guys have short-sleeve shirts with their collars turned up. And some guys, like Keith, have those corduroy shorts with the *OP* on them that I thought meant Op, like Op-Ed from the newspaper, but then Keith said, "Are you stupid? *OP* means Ocean Pacific." Then he said he was sorry for calling me stupid since I'd been living near a whole different ocean and there was probably Ocean Atlantic stuff, but I don't think I've ever seen a little *OA* on a pair of shorts anywhere.

Before the bell rings, the teacher says real loud without yelling, "I'm Mr. Krueger, and that clock is seven seconds slow." He's looking at his watch and pointing to the clock on the wall. As soon as everyone is quiet and looking, the bell rings and Mr. Krueger gets this grin on his face. He taps his watch and says, "This is set to the atomic clock in Colorado—the most accurate clock in the world. *Your* watch may not be, so you'd better get to class early every day because we start at the real time, not the bell."

Behind Mr. Krueger, in the right corner above his desk, hangs a gigantic chart of the periodic table. "Everything that matters starts right here." He reaches back and pats the thing like it's a dog. "That's why it's behind my desk, the only place where I can never stand in front of it." Everyone's staring at him, and I'm thinking, *Yeah? What about when you stand up to walk over to the podium?* But then Mr. Krueger shoots out from behind the desk sideways, the metal wheels of his chair humming along the tile floor like a train on its tracks. He pops up at the podium, grinning again. "You learn this"—he points back at the periodic table—"and life here will go smoother than you ever thought possible."

Mr. Krueger lets us go seven seconds before the bell rings, and Keith stops me by the door. "We've got to get on it," he says, pointing at a poster taped to the wall. "The Howdy Dance is Saturday."

The bell rings and by the time we're to the stairs, people are everywhere, headed in every direction. Conversations are buzzing by, people laughing, people yelling to other people going the other way, some people already talking about Friday night and *Are you gonna go?* Then the lockers start opening. They're outside lockers, all along the classroom buildings and crammed into the breezeways, that *click, click, pop,* over and over again like a scratched record.

Keith's not looking at me when he says, "You've got Algebra next and Spanish before lunch, right?" He doesn't even wait for me to answer. "Remember, when they call roll, write down all the names of people who aren't freshmen. No freshmen, no matter what."

Keith's going to go over my list after school and tell me who to take fashion notes on the rest of the week. "And if you see van Doren," he says, "write down everything, even if the guy picks his nose."

■

The Wednesday after I met Keith, my dad dragged me out of bed early. "It's trash day," he said. "Remember? That's your chore now."

I had hot summer sleep all over me, and as I got to the side of the house, my hair was standing up on its own. On the other side of the fence, our neighbor was pulling his cans out too, the plastic grinding across the driveway like a plane taking off. Halfway to the curb with my first trash can, I heard, "Hey, trash buddy," and it wasn't the voice of somebody's dad. It was Astrid. *The* Astrid Thompson. Skinny, muscly, tan legs stretching out forever from her Dolphin shorts to her sneakers. Blond hair feathered into perfect wings, very *Charlie's Angels*. She also had a tank top on under a gigantic sweatshirt that had no collar. You might think that would look more like a potato sack than something cool, except the sweatshirt was hanging off to one side so one tanned shoulder stuck out like it was saying, *You should see what else is in here.* I couldn't dream a girl that beautiful, you know? "I'm Astrid," she said.

"Reece," I said, wiping my hands on my pants and holding one out.

She took my hand for this little shake, and it was like dipping it into a sink full of warm water, each finger getting its own dose of soft and nice. She said my dad told her dad that I'd be starting at

Esperanza. "I'll be looking for you at the football games," she said, real serious. "You better have school spirit."

"I will. I'm very spiritual."

She laughed and went into her house.

Now I'm up a little early every Wednesday to make sure I'm not wearing something stupid, and then half the time I don't see her anyway. When I do see her, I have no idea what to say. I mean, what do you say to the most perfect-looking girl ever when you're taking out the trash, *Nice cans?* Actually, I almost did say that one morning because the Thompsons really do have these shiny silver cans with matching lids and no dents, but thank God I realized what I was saying as I was saying it and changed it midsentence to "Nice, uh, day." And even though it was pretty gray outside, Astrid said, "Yeah. It's gonna be," which just confirms how nice she is and what an idiot I am.

This is how I know Keith knows what he's talking about with clothes and everything. There's something like three junior highs funneling into Esperanza, so it doesn't matter who you used to be. If you make a good impression right away, two-thirds of the freshmen and pretty much everybody else will think you've always been cool.

"If you get it wrong, though," Keith said, "you're screwed for the next four years—no cool friends, no cool parties, no girls." No Astrid Thompson.

■

Almost no one is sitting in Mr. Tomita's Algebra class second period. There are letters and numbers along two of the walls. On the chalkboard, everyone's last name is listed with a letter and number next to it. A few people start walking down the rows and sitting down. I'm B-4, so I go two rows in and four seats back, which I think is right.

To be safe, I ask the girl behind me what she is and she says, "I'm an American of Japanese descent, just like Mr. Tomita."

The embarrassment rushes up my neck and spreads out across my face until she grins, like, *Gotcha*. "If your last name is Houghton," she says, "you're in the right place."

It takes me a minute to find B-5 on the chalkboard, then I say, "Are you Okuda?"

"Yeah." She smiles. "Me and my whole family."

Mr. Tomita starts taking roll and it goes quick since he knows exactly who to look at when he calls a name. I'm guessing which people aren't freshmen and writing names as fast as I can. When Mr. Tomita calls out, "Edith Okuda," she says, "Here," then leans forward and whispers, "Make sure you put me on your list as Edie, okay?"

At the end of roll, Mr. Tomita stands up from his desk and he isn't that much taller than he was sitting down. He has a wooden yardstick in his hand and says, "If you want to be successful, remember, when it is time to play"—and he swings the yardstick like he's hitting a golf ball—"play. Have fun." He's smiling and kind of goofy with his shiny bald head and glasses; then he snaps the yardstick to his shoulder like a rifle. Even though he's only about five feet tall, he's about that wide too, and solid. The smile slips away and his forehead wrinkles up serious. "And when it is time to work, work. Be serious." His face eases up and the yardstick drops down like he's putting a golf ball. "So when it is time to play, don't work. And when it is time to work, don't play." We're all nodding and this big old grin takes over his whole face. He shuffles over to the far left of the chalkboard, places the yardstick flat against it, and in three quick strokes has a perfect triangle. "So now, it is time to work!"

■

Third-period English is all freshmen, which is good since the guy behind me sneezes all through roll and gets me to answer to "Denise" because it sort of sounded like "Reece." Everybody laughs until the teacher tells us it won't hurt to be nice to each other.

After class, California starts feeling like California, so I'm at my locker dropping off my jacket. It's a bottom locker, which means I'm squatting, twisting around legs, and getting nudged and bumped, the lockers around me slamming shut and rattling like a chain-link fence. With my books, folders, lunch, and backpack in there, my jacket is a tight squeeze and it's hard to see which folder is which. They only give you five minutes between classes, and after getting here and then getting my combination wrong twice, then having to dig out the little card with the right combination, it feels like at least three minutes have burned by. Every folder is here and of course Spanish is the last one I get my hands on. My heart's knocking at my chest, and the whole world's gone quiet, like that instant of silence right before something hits you. Then, *fwap*, something really does hit me. A folder bounces off my head, light and not so bad. I've never been drunk, but this must be the feeling: *How did my own folder hit me in the head? How did it get on the ground in front of me when it's still right here in my hand?*

The sound of lockers and voices comes rushing in like the start of a record, and there's a guy standing over me saying, "Sorry about that, little man." He's skinny and tall, and he's got one of those crop cuts where your hair is flat and straight like the Beatles before they became hippies, but there's also this spot in the back of your head where it's chopped short and sticks up kind of random. It looks like a mistake. He's wearing a button-up gas station shirt with the name *Gus* sewn on it.

He asks me to hand the folder up and I've got no choice. It really may have been an accident, and besides, he's got a couple friends waiting around. So I hand it back up to him and he says, "Thanks, bud," and slams his locker shut.

As soon as "You're welcome, Gus" is out of my mouth, his buddies laugh and all three of them walk away.

■

I write down a few names in my Spanish class and me and Keith go over the list at lunch. He circles the names of people he thinks he's heard of. He tells me the whole thing at my locker is no accident; upperclassmen love getting top lockers because the things they drop can pick up more speed before they hit you. "You're lucky it wasn't a history book."

After lunch, we've got PE together with Coach Scheffler. All freshmen. When class is about over, we're hanging out in the locker room, waiting for the bell to ring, and all these guys in jeans and letterman jackets start walking in. Who knows how they got out of fifth period before everyone else, and who'd stop them? They don't look like high school kids. They're tall and wide, thick necks and massive thighs. Half of them have five o'clock shadows and it's only one thirty.

Most of them go straight into the varsity room, but as the bell rings to end fifth period, one of the biggest guys steps into the hallway. Everybody goes around him like he's a boulder in a river. Then he puts out his arm, the leather from his jacket crinkling, and wraps it around Keith's neck. "Here's our guy," he yells back into the varsity room. He wraps his arm around Keith's shoulder. "You want to help out the team?" Only, he's not asking. He's telling.

"You wait right here," he says to me. When he turns and walks Keith into the varsity room, I catch the name stitched on the back of his jacket: *Petrakis.*

A few minutes later, guys start coming out of the varsity room, one by one, carrying their helmets and wearing shorts and practice jerseys with just their shoulder pads. Petrakis is one of the last guys out the door and he slaps his hand down on my shoulder, telling me it was smart I stayed. He gives me the combination to his locker, which is where he's left Keith, and says if anything gets messed with he'll shove my head up Keith's ass and tie us to the flagpole.

The bell rings for the start of sixth period, but Keith doesn't say anything until we're outside walking. "If you get in trouble for being late," he says without looking at me, "just say you went to the wrong classroom."

I'm nodding and smirking, and because Keith looks more mad than scared, I say, "What's it like being 'the guy'?"

Keith, it turns out, is the guy small enough to fit into a varsity locker and still move around. Petrakis locked him in there and made him rub his shirt all over the back and sides to dust. "This is exactly what I'm talking about," Keith says. "First impressions."

"Was it roomy in there?"

He stops. "It's not funny, Reece. Tomorrow, you might be 'the guy.'"

I hadn't thought of that. "Maybe we shouldn't wear anything nice."

Keith rolls his eyes, and his head follows them up to the sky. "That's what I'm saying. If we'd been dressed cool, and not nice, this never would have happened."

■

On Tuesday, I take notes on all the people Keith circled—what they wear, how they wear it, and if other people say anything about it. Gus drops a pen and a ruler on me, except he's wearing a bowling shirt that says *Gary*. After PE, Petrakis grabs Keith again.

Wednesday, Gus/Gary drops an orange on my head and says he can't believe it rolled out like that. It's so stupid and I wonder why he isn't the one getting picked on with his weird name shirts and gray worker pants like my dad wears. I can't believe I'm going to have to take it from this guy for a whole year just because he's a senior and probably knows everybody and all I've got is Keith.

After PE, Keith steps into the varsity room as soon as he sees Petrakis. Petrakis smiles and says, "You're a team player, little dude. But you should know better than to come into the varsity room without being invited." Then a bunch of guys drag Keith to the showers, tell him they're sorry but this is bigger than all of them, and hold Keith still so they can wet him right on his crotch like he's pissed himself. I'm so scared watching it's like I'm Saint Peter, knowing it's too late to save the guy and scared they'll get me next: *That guy? I'm not with that guy. I have no idea who he is. Never seen him before.*

Keith won't even talk after that. He just heads to class, and who can blame him? I mean, if this is what they're doing to us the first week, how are we supposed to still be alive by Halloween?

On Thursday, a little English book crashes down on my knee. Not too bad. Keith waits at the varsity room door with sweatpants on under his PE shorts. Petrakis makes him dust another locker, but he puts Keith on the honor system and doesn't lock him in. When Mrs. Wirth gives me detention for being late to World History, I tell her what's been happening after PE. She says she can't imagine Coach Scheffler would ever allow that in his locker room. "But it did happen," I say, and she doubles my detention for smarting off.

On the way to school Friday, Keith says if I stop being his friend now I can probably save myself. When I tell him we're in this together he says, "Okay. Then we're buying clothes tomorrow no matter what."

Almost everyone is wearing school colors. Even Mr. Krueger has on a maroon T-shirt with gold letters that reads *Class of Bismuth*. He's grinning and looking pretty proud of it, but nobody gets it until he says that we have two people in here that are in the Class of Bismuth. "Is that eighty-three?" I say.

"Well done, Mr. Houghton." He takes two steps down the aisle of my row so he can look right at me. "What will your class be?"

It's eighty-six, but I know not to say, "Eighty-six." I look up at the flourescent lights for a second like maybe it will come to me; then I shrug and say, "I should know, but I don't."

"Radon," Mr. Krueger says and points to the chart at the front of the room. "It's quite dense," he adds with this tiny grin.

By lunch, we still haven't seen van Doren, but it's like he's everywhere. We've heard he's getting invited to run the Misfit Mile at indoor track meets in LA. Over the summer, his band Filibuster played a pool party that was so big they had an opening act. The pool had giant blocks of ice and so many cans of beer floating around that van Doren started the show off by walking across it without getting wet. The guy who threw the party, Ted Fischel, got kicked out of his house when his parents got home. Now everyone's calling the party Ted One because when a party is that great, there has to be a sequel. And as long as van Doren's around, Ted Two could happen at any time. Some people say van Doren's getting scouted by record companies. Some say he's getting scouted by UCLA. We look for his name on letterman jackets, listen for it in crowds, but we still haven't found him.

We have pretty good notes, though, and when Petrakis gives us Friday off for good behavior, I say it's a good sign.

"The only good sign," Keith says, "is when the people who matter are talking about us the way they talk about van Doren. That's when we matter."

Native Customs

This time last year my dad would always get home from work in time for dinner. Colleen would show him some Popsicle-stick doll she made in preschool and he'd act like he never knew someone could do such amazing things. Brendan would explain how even though it's not his fault Chad Beckerman caught the football with his face, he's sorry anyway. Dad would tell him to try and do better tomorrow, then ask me how the Yanks were looking for their next series in Boston or if those IRA guys were still on that hunger strike in Northern Ireland.

That's not how it is now. Friday night, hours after dinner, I'm on the bed in my room, filing baseball cards into shoe boxes— one for the American League, one for the National, and one that's all Yankees.

My dad knocks on my door and walks in, his work clothes still on. "Got anyone good there?"

I shuffle through them and hold up a Willie Wilson card.

"He's not too bad." My dad reaches out to grab it. His hand is scrubbed clean but it smells oily. There's still dark stains around the edges of his nails and fingers, the way a cartoon hand is outlined.

"Maybe I should hold it."

As he sits down in my desk chair, I flip the card around to show him the statistics side. Willie Wilson is a .300 hitter. He's been leading the league almost the whole year. "Look," I say, "he's better than 'not bad,' even if he isn't a Yankee."

"You're right," he says, only he doesn't laugh or even look at the card. His eyes are down at his hands and they stay there for a few seconds. I'm studying the card like there's going to be a Willie Wilson test or something; then my dad asks if I have time to grab the tweezers and a needle. Sometimes the lathe gives him these little metal splinters in his fingers and it stings pretty good. My mom can get them out, unless she's running an errand or busy with Colleen. When she can't do it, it's up to me.

It's not so bad. My dad's hands are thick and rough, and he tells me not to worry about hurting him. He winces a couple times, sucking in air through his teeth real fast, but most of the time he sits there quiet, one hand at a time under my desk lamp until we're done.

He doesn't stick around afterward to ask about school or see other baseball cards. He says, "Thanks," and heads downstairs to heat up leftovers.

I pull out my notebook from the desk and work on a letter to Uncle Ryan, tell him about Keith and Petrakis in the locker room and how this guy van Doren is kind of a ghost. When I start telling him about the Willie Wilson card and how even with all those hits and stolen bases he looks stupid in his sky-blue Kansas City uniform, it makes me mad. *Dad's been totally different without you around,* I write. *But it's his fault we're all the way out in California. And he's the one volunteering for all those extra Saturday shifts and overtime. I kind of want to say to him, "See what you did? Are you happy now?" But I guess he wasn't all that happy before we left, either.*

It's weird seeing that on the page. I've been thinking it; now I know it's real. And even though I can take it back by ripping up the letter, I don't. What's the point in lying about it?

∎

Saturday morning, Keith's at the front door fifteen minutes before he said he'd be. My parents aren't up yet because my dad needs to sleep in before his Saturday night shift.

I creep into the room, to my mom's side of the bed, and crouch down by her face. "Mom," I whisper and shake her shoulder.

Her hair is spread across her face, hiding her freckles and eyes. "What?" she whispers.

"Keith's here. We're going to buy school clothes."

"School clothes?" my dad says from the other side of the bed. "School's started."

"Get me my purse," she says. "It's on the dresser."

My dad rolls over. "You didn't buy his clothes yet?"

"He wants to do it himself."

I hand my mom the purse.

"When the sales are all over?" my dad says.

She sits up and blinks at the purse before peering inside.

My dad rolls back over. "I hope you know what you're doing," he says, and I don't know if he's talking to me or my mom.

■

Keith says Miller's Outpost will have everything we need, so we hop my back wall for a shortcut through the park. Since summer ended, they've turned the baseball diamonds into soccer fields and me and Keith walk around all the painted white lines. We could cut the corners since it's the littlest kids playing and they all bunch up around the ball anyway, but Keith says we shouldn't. People here are crazy about soccer and they might not like it.

Miller's Outpost is in a little shopping center with a Tower Records on the other end of the parking lot, sort of mirroring it, and a bunch of small stores running between them—cleaners and tax guys, nothing good.

We're the first people in the store, the place still smelling like powdered carpet deodorizer. The back left wall has shelves and shelves of blue jeans, all Levi's. Keith walks straight back there because we need 501s with the button fly. We each grab a couple pairs and walk over to the shirts. They've got the short-sleeve collared ones you wear with the collar up and the long-sleeve button-ups you leave untucked if you want to look cool. This is what we learned taking notes, stuff I'd never have guessed. We take turns picking out shirts to keep from getting the same colors and end up with six each—one for every day of school plus an extra for the Howdy Dance tonight. In the changing rooms I unfold the first pair of jeans and the price tag drops down in front of me. Then I catch the price on a shirt and suddenly my hundred bucks doesn't seem like a lot of money. Depending on how much tax is, my money's only going about as far as two pairs of jeans and maybe three shirts. How's that supposed to last the year, like my dad says it should, when it won't even get me through a week?

I walk through the double swinging doors without trying anything on and start looking for a sale rack. The big window banners that said BACK TO SCHOOL SALE since August started are all gone. Now they just have leaves everywhere and say FALL FASHION.

Keith comes over to me in jeans that go past his feet and a stiff shirt rising off his shoulders. "Does this look right?"

I shake my head. "Have you looked at the prices of this stuff?"

"Not really." He pulls a shirt off the rack we're standing by and holds it up. "Check this out—there's a little plastic baggie on here with extra buttons."

If nothing's on sale, I need time to think. Are a couple nice things from Miller's Outpost better than a whole bunch of crappy stuff from Kmart? "Let's go over to Tower Records."

"Now?" he says.

"Yeah. Let's see what Adam Ant's wearing on his album covers."

At least four different girls at school this week have said Adam Ant is a total babe, so Keith says okay to a quick look, just to make sure we're not forgetting anything.

We walk across the parking lot to Tower Records, talking about the other album covers we should check out for clothes because girls always like guys in bands. As we're coming through the door, Keith freezes and I nearly knock into him. Not ten feet away, just on the other side of the first row of album bins, there's a guy with a bleached Mohawk. A real Mohawk with the sides shaved bald and the huge stripe of hair down the middle. Guys back in Jersey never wore Mohawks. At least, not in Paterson. You might see a guy wearing combat boots and ripped jeans, or a sleeveless Levi's jacket with chains and patches all over it, but you never saw it all put together on a guy with massive arms and a white-as-snow Mohawk big and spiky enough to stab somebody.

Keith walks around the first row of bins, staring at the floor. He doesn't stop until he gets to the back of the store, where they keep the posters. My feet don't want to move at first; then they just go straight to the bin in front of me. The Mohawk's on the other side and I know better than to look up, but it's like an eclipse: You know you shouldn't stare straight at it—it's dangerous and there's a safer way to look—but that just makes you want to do it even more. I flip through three or four albums at a time, my head down and eyes up to see when it's clear. Finally, the guy turns toward the front counter and the Mohawk fans out for me like peacock feathers.

Keith's looking too, and when we see each other, I give him the *Get over here* look. He opens his eyes real big, which means nothing to me until I realize Mohawk guy has turned around and is staring at me. We make eye contact for a millisecond before my eyes dive back into the bin. And there's Adam Ant, black eyeliner and a thick white line painted across his face. A white-guy Indian/pirate.

The chains on Mohawk guy's jacket clink real soft as he steps to the bin right across from me and Adam Ant. When I move down the row to the *B*'s, Mohawk guy does the same thing, in the same direction. I wait a second, then look up, and his face is already there, waiting. "What are you looking at?" he says. It's not mean-sounding like you might think. He leans forward and looks down, the Mohawk bearing down on me like some giant buzz saw. "The Beatles?"

My eyes can't find words, just four hairy guys walking across a street, the one in front looking like Jesus in a disco suit. I look up. "Do you work here?"

"Nope. I just know my music." He closes his eyes and nods when he says it. "If you want my advice, don't be a trendoid and buy *Abbey Road*. Get *Revolver*." The Mohawk goes a little sideways and he squints. "I know you, right? From school."

I know it's only been a week, but if a guy within a mile of you has a bleached Mohawk and arms bigger than your legs, you're probably going to remember him.

"Are you van Doren?"

He shakes his head. "I'm Treat," he says. "You sit in my row, right? In front of the dude who's allergic to school?"

"In English?" I say. Treat nods, making the Mohawk cut at me. "Yeah, I sit right in front of the sneezer. Couldn't take my jacket off all week, you know, unless I wanted a snot shower."

Treat laughs like we're old buddies and checks out my jacket. "That's bitchin'. Is Packy your nickname?"

"Nah, I'm just Reece. The patch sort of came with the jacket."

"Salvation Army?"

"Hand-me-down."

"Well, it's a good one." Treat flicks his head toward the door. "You can't get bitchin' stuff like that at candy stores like Miller's Outpost."

"Not for a hundred bucks," I say.

"Totally," he says. "You could get ten of those for a hundred bucks at the Salvation Army."

"Really? They've got cool stuff?"

Treat nods, waits a second, then says, "You want to check it out?"

I do. I mean, not with this guy, but Keith's staring at a Led Zeppelin poster like he can't figure out how hippies with no shirts and supertight pants equals cool. "Okay," I say, "let me get my friend."

■

The Salvation Army store is in the old downtown. My dad says President Nixon grew up here when downtown Yorba Linda was the whole town. Now it's just a couple blocks of Joe Schmoe, Attorney-at-Law, and I. M. Lame, Real Estate Agent. No wonder Nixon left.

On the walk, Treat tells us he didn't get the Mohawk until yesterday after school. He'd have done it sooner, only his dad said he had to get a copy of the school dress code first and prove it would be okay. "If I came home with a Mohawk," I say, "my dad would cut off my head just to make it go away."

Treat busts up and we look at Keith.

"Well, if I ever cut my hair like that," he says and touches the back of his head, "which I never would, I'd tell my mom it was super important to me and then my dad would go along with whatever she said."

The Salvation Army store is big and high ceilinged like an old A&P. There's used furniture up front and racks filled with clothes from the middle all the way to the back. Treat says, "You guys need jeans, right?" He weaves through the furniture and shelves, splitting between people instead of walking around them. They all take a good look after he passes, and one old guy stares at him the way you do when Walter Cronkite says, "We want to warn you: The following footage is graphic."

Like at Miller's Outpost, there's Levi's 501s stacked on shelves along the wall, except these jeans look like laundry day, folded uneven, faded and fraying everywhere. Keith won't touch them. If he can't see the yellow size tag sticking out, he goes on to the next one. I've got three pairs over my shoulder to try on by the time Keith hooks a pair of dark blue ones by the belt loop and pulls them out. They look brand-new until they drop open to show a rip by the left knee.

"Bitchin'," Treat says. He snatches the jeans and holds them up high. "You can't usually get new ones with a good rip." He tosses them back before Keith is ready and they flop over Keith's face. "You'll have to wash the hell out of them to get 'em faded right, but that rip's perfect."

There must be a thousand shirts on the racks. Keith tears through them pretty fast, still only that one pair of jeans over his shoulder.

"You're not going to find any alligator shirts," Treat says, and Keith just stops where he is and looks at me. Treat flips through the rack and out come these long-sleeve button-up shirts. They don't have the thin stripes like guys at school are wearing; they're thick and dark and some have weird patterns and shapes you can't even find in a geometry book.

We both give Treat the *Are you serious?* look and he says these shirts aren't finished yet. "You have to tie them in knots and bleach them. Like this one," he says, and holds up a red paisley shirt with white blotches all over it.

"That's not an accident?" Keith says.

I take it from Treat. "I'll give it a shot."

It's weird trying on the clothes. The jeans are already worn in, not stiff like cardboard, and they aren't scratchy. Everything feels like it just came right out of my closet.

Keith steps out of the changing room in the ripped jeans and one of the long-sleeve button-ups, and it looks pretty decent.

Treat folds his arms and nods, the Mohawk shooting forward. "Yep. A little bleach and those will be totally punk rock. Now all you guys need is boots." He tears out across the store.

When Treat gets far enough away, Keith says, "Are you buying any of this crap?"

"I think so."

"None of it's new," he says.

"That's why it doesn't cost as much. And this guy's cool, isn't he?"

Keith looks over at Treat firing through a big bin of shoes. "I guess. He looks like one of the Plasmatics."

"You think Petrakis would ever stuff that guy in a locker?"

Keith squints at me because I've sworn never to bring that up again. "I didn't say I don't want to be his friend. I'm just not sure I want to look like him."

Treat comes back a minute later empty-handed. "Boots are the hardest thing to find," he says. "You have to get lucky."

I tell Treat I already feel pretty lucky with the jeans and shirts. He turns on this half grin and asks Keith if he likes the stuff he's got.

"I guess," Keith says.

The Mohawk shakes from side to side. "Look, you can go over to Miller's Outpost, get your school uniform, and look like every other freshman. Or you can be totally punk rock, be your own man."

Keith doesn't look real convinced, but he buys a bunch of stuff anyway.

When we're walking back toward the park, I ask Treat if he's going to the dance tonight.

"No way, man. I'm not buying into the system." He says he'll see us at school Monday and that he'll keep his eye out for some boots. He turns around, waits, waits, waits, then runs across all six lanes of Yorba Linda Boulevard and disappears down a side street.

Keith wants to go back to Miller's Outpost. I say to give it a week, to wait and see what happens at school. "I'll see what happens tonight at the Howdy Dance," he says. "After that, I can't make any promises."

In the park, the older guys are playing soccer now. They

look real sharp in their uniforms with their shirts tucked in and socks pulled up high. They spread out over the entire field the way they're supposed to. We could still cut the corners on the way to my back wall, because even with the coach yelling, a few of those guys can't resist drifting in a little. But this time, I don't bring it up. We just decide what time to walk to the dance and swear to each other that we'll wear the clothes we just bought.

New/Old Clothes

My whole life, the only reason to get dressed up on a Saturday night has been for confession. There's ice cream after if we're good, but the scratchy shirts and choking ties don't really feel like an even trade, especially with how long it takes Brendan to get through his list of sins. When he was eight, my mom used to catch him throwing rocks at birds. All the time. She's not a yeller, but she stays on you like a tick. Like you don't even know she's there until you turn around and can tell by the look on her face she just saw everything. Or enough. Then it starts: *Do this; don't do that; pick that up; put that down; get going, mister; don't you walk away from me; God helps those who help themselves;* and my favorite of all: *I love you, but if you keep acting like that, I'm the only person in the world who will.* It always gets me to stop what I'm doing wrong, or to get moving, or to straighten up and fly right. But not Brendan. She could bust him for throwing rocks at birds in the morning and then catch him doing it again in the afternoon.

One Saturday, Brendan's in the confessional going as fast as he can and leaving out as much as he can so he's not stuck with a rosary and a million Hail Marys. Then it stays quiet even longer than it normally takes for the priest to add up Brendan's sins, and finally Father Nash says, "And what about the birds, Brendan? Aren't you sorry about trying to hurt God's creatures?"

It scared him to death, and when Brendan told me about it later it was pretty clear he had no idea Mom had called Father Nash beforehand. Now he's in there every confession racking his brain for every little sin, even the ones he's only thought about. By the time he's done with his penance, my clothes are at war with me—the collar slicing my throat, the pants crawling over my thighs like I'm strapped to an anthill. It's worse than any penance a priest has ever given me.

So even though I'm dressed up for the Howdy Dance, it's my new/old clothes: faded jeans and the bleached red paisley shirt Treat found for me. When I asked my mom if my dad had any old boots, she came back with this ancient pair of black Converse All Stars and they seem to fit. Everything feels like warm sheets on a cold morning and yet I look different to me. New.

Keith says the dance is just the opening act. After this, it's football games and parties and formals. Then basketball games, more parties, and more dances. We don't have to get this perfect; we just can't mess up and start a chain reaction that blows the whole year for us.

At the dinner table, Brendan gets a look at my shirt and laughs.

My mom glares at him and he goes instantly quiet, shaking to hold it in.

My dad looks up and leans sideways in his chair to see what the big deal is. "Are these your new clothes?"

"They're new?" Brendan says and starts laughing out loud again.

Colleen's across from me and her head disappears under the table to see. "What's so funny?"

My mom reaches over and pulls her up. "Be a lady." She waits until Colleen is settled and looks over at me. "Do you like these clothes?"

My dad's in his machinist uniform, about to leave for his extra shift. My mom's in a housedress that's softer than a pile of kittens. Brendan's got grass stains on his tube socks. Colleen's pink play clothes are smeared with jelly.

My dad says, "You want people to think we're poor?"

"Pat," Mom says, "it's a style." She looks at me. "Right, Reece?"

"Yeah, it's pu—" I say, stopping myself just in time. "Puh-retty rockin'."

Brendan breaks into a new round of laughing. Mom looks at her watch and says, "You know, Pat, we may have enough time after dinner to make confession. Do you think anyone needs to go?"

Brendan doesn't make a sound after that, except to thank me for passing the butter, then the salt, and later a second serving of broccoli, which means he's laying it on pretty thick since he hates broccoli.

On my way out the door, Colleen says my new/old clothes

look neat. With my Packy jacket on, I get a curfew and kiss from my mom while my dad makes Brendan clear the table. It's not exactly a blessing, but it gets me out the door.

                                    ■

Me and Keith walk into the cafeteria and it's a different world. It's not just ribbons and posters like a junior high dance. The punch table is in a corral, a real wooden fence with a working gate and straw covering the tile floor. There's a red barn made out of cardboard boxes with a real deejay inside. And even though it's nighttime, nearly all the lights are off.

Keith's got on the ripped jeans he bought and some plain green T-shirt Treat found. He says he can't believe he dressed up to look like nothing, but it kind of doesn't matter what any of the freshmen are wearing. They're all standing along the walls and only talking to other freshmen. Out on the floor are clumps of people you know must be sophomores and juniors because they're all over the place, changing groups and people hugging or giving high fives because they haven't seen each other all week and *It totally sucks; I thought we'd have at least one class together.* They're sipping their punch and talking to each other relaxed, the way James Bond walks into a casino and fits right in.

Keith points at the barn and says, "There's your neighbor." Astrid's standing around with some other girls from varsity cheer. They're all wearing straw cowboy hats, Levi's, and Howdy Dance Committee T-shirts in maroon and gold, our school colors. Astrid wears everything better. Her shirt and jeans hug her body like a Christmas present that can't hide what's beneath the wrapping. And instead of a belt, she's got a red bandana going through the loops around her waist. Most of her hair is hidden in the straw hat, and even though the strands pouring out each side are tucked behind her ears, they're splashing onto her shoulders so you can see how long and blond it really is. She's perfectly symmetrical except for this big silver hoop earring in her left ear. You might think that would throw everything off, but every few seconds there's this flash of light from a tiny diamond in her right ear. Then the hoop shimmers and I can't decide which side of her face looks better with which earring because they both look so good at the same time.

Keith jabs me in the ribs. "Go say hi."

I swipe his arm down. "Yeah, right."

"Seriously," Keith says. "You're probably the only freshman she knows. Tell her you found her other earring."

Theoretically, I could do this: walk up to Astrid and go, *Hey*, and maybe she smiles and says, *Hey, yourself.* Then my stomach tightens and my arms ache like they've fallen asleep. It's not even real, and I'm a mess.

For real, though, Mr. Krueger appears in front of us. "Mr. Houghton. Mr. Curtis. You gentlemen are in my first-period class, are you not?"

"Yes," Keith says.

"Yes, you are not? Or, yes, you are?"

"We're in your class," I say.

"Good," he says. "Tell me, Mr. Curtis, what does *Fr* stand for?"

Keith looks stunned. Mr. Krueger said we'd get pop quizzes; we just didn't think that meant he'd pop up places and quiz us.

Keith throws his arms out like he surrenders. "I don't know. Freshman?"

Mr. Krueger rubs his chin and says, "I'll accept that as a valid answer, Mr. Curtis. On the quiz, however, you'll want to answer, 'francium.'" He claps us each on the shoulder. "Have fun, gentlemen."

"Jeez," Keith says as Mr. Krueger walks away. "He got one look at my clothes and labeled me an idiot."

"No, he didn't."

"Yeah, he did." Keith tugs on the ripped part of his jeans. "I'm going to check my hair. At least I can fix that if it looks stupid."

With Keith gone, it's easy to pretend I'm watching people dance and not looking over them to the other side where Astrid is. She's been standing there the whole time with her friends, her head tilting every so often, talking, listening, smiling, laughing. No one's asked her to dance, which makes sense, because who would have the nerve? My heart's gone hummingbird just thinking about being wrapped up with her in a slow song, my thumbs looped through the bandana on her hips, and then a voice whispers in my ear, "It sucks being cool, huh?"

Edie from Algebra is right next to me and I don't know how she got there. Or when. She's wearing blue jeans and a T-shirt with the sleeves rolled up, showing her arms, which are skinny but not bony. She's grinning like maybe she's been watching me watch Astrid, or maybe she's just happy to see me. I say, "Hi," and she says, "When it is time to work, work. And when it is time to dance, dance."

"Are you asking me to dance?"

She grabs hold of my sleeve. "Now is the time to dance!" She pulls me through pairs of people standing still at the end of a song. We're in the middle of the dance floor and the deejay says to get ready for "What I Like about You," and Edie does. She squares off in front of me as the new record starts hissing. "Do you know how to pogo?"

A guitar riff launches out of the speakers and Edie is airborne. Everyone is. They're bouncing up and down to the music, and as soon as Edie lands I take off with her on the next jump. It's not so complicated, you know, and near the end of the song I'm turning myself sideways in the air, hitting the floor, bringing my knees up then down, hitting the floor, scissoring my legs out and back, hitting the floor. Edie's laughing with each move, bouncing along with me and trying my moves herself.

When the next song starts, Edie's legs go stone-still, which is funny because it's "Shake It Up," by the Cars. Her arms start moving, though, and as the song picks up she flails them around and shakes her head side to side. I'm mirroring her the whole time, my arms swinging a little more crazily, my head shaking a little harder.

"You're good," Edie says as the song ends.

I'm breathing heavy, beads of sweat rising in my hair and tickling my scalp. "Thanks. You are too."

The next song comes up quiet, a synthesizer rising and a slow drumbeat. Neither of us move; then Edie sticks her hand in the middle of my chest and pushes me back a step. "Come on; I don't dance to slow songs."

We find Keith near the wall and I introduce him to Edie.

She shakes his hand, says how nice it is to meet him, and takes off to find her friends.

For the next half hour, Keith's bugging me to go find Edie and her friends so he can dance too. It's pretty easy to ignore until he says, "If you're not going to talk to Astrid, it'll look a whole lot better if you're dancing with girls instead of talking to me."

We find Edie with three other girls. Keith already knows two of them from his junior high. The third girl, Cherise, is someone Edie must know from her junior high. Cherise doesn't talk much, and between her long hair and the darkness, you can't tell if she's a fox or a dog, or something in between.

We all end up dancing in a circle so no one is really dancing with anyone, but it's fun. The only time anybody even touches is when one of Keith's moves goes wrong and he stumbles into somebody, which is fine since he apologizes each time and you can tell he's not doing it on purpose.

By the time the lights come on, we must have danced to ten songs, with little breaks for punch or the girls saying they'd be right back whenever a slow song came on. One of the girls from Keith's junior high asks if Filibuster is playing somewhere after the dance. "Yeah," Keith says, "van Doren's always got something up his sleeve."

The girls wait like maybe Keith actually knows something. Then the deejay crackles over the sound system that everyone rocked, and disco sucks, and it sucks if we leave the gym trashed like a disco, so it would pretty much rock if we all threw some trash away as we left. Keith grabs Cherise's cup and says, "We'll get them." Edie hands me her cup and Keith grabs the rest.

Two of the girls walk away, leaving Edie and Cherise. "Thanks for dancing with us," Edie says.

"No problem," Keith says.

Cherise gives Edie's arm a little tug and Edie looks at me. "Now is the time to leave, and when it is the time to leave . . . ," she says and waits.

"Don't dance," I finish.

"And when it is the time to dance . . ."

"Don't leave," I say.

Edie tilts her head sideways. "Ah, that's sweet, but I've really got to go."

We both burst out laughing, and Edie gives me a little wave as she steps away.

Keith's smiling until we turn and head for the closest trash can. "What was so funny?"

"It's a math joke."

"There's no such thing," he says, and then just stops and stares. For a second I wonder if Treat is here, but Keith mouths, *Astrid*. He forces the cups in his hand onto me, then turns around and walks away.

Astrid gets to the trash can right when I'm tossing in the cups. "We have to stop meeting like this," she says.

"Yeah," I say and nod once like that means something.

She smiles, drops in a stack of cups, smacks her hands together like she's dusting them off, and walks away, the bandana swaying as she goes.

Keith's waiting for me by the big exit doors. "She smiled at you."

"To keep from laughing."

"No." Keith shakes his head. "She saw you in your cool new clothes."

He must be razzing me. "No one said we looked cool."

"We talked to girls. We danced with girls." Keith squints the way he did when Mr. Krueger asked him what *Fr* stood for. "That's what we want, isn't it? The experiment is a success."

Hey, Neighbor!

One of the things I tell Uncle Ryan in the next letter is how having a huge friend with a Mohawk will probably come in handy at school, but maybe it isn't the best idea to let my parents meet him. *Especially my dad,* I write. *You know how he is when things don't go to plan, and I don't think he planned on me having weird friends.* I write about the Howdy Dance and feeling stupid in front of Astrid because Uncle Ryan's told me before that we all do stupid things sometimes. "Me more than anybody," he said once, and I remind him of that.

After that, it's just a bunch of crap about Brendan getting in trouble at school, and Colleen already loving her new teacher, and Mom saying the tomatoes here are terrible and having great strawberries and oranges doesn't make up for it.

I know what I want to write next, but I'm not sure if I should. In the newspaper the other day, there was a family special on baseball tickets to see the Angels. Even though they were playing

Cleveland, I told my dad it would still be great to go. He said he didn't have time and I said that if Uncle Ryan were here he'd make time. "Well, Uncle Ryan isn't here," my dad said. I probably should've shut up about it right there because when he says something without looking at you he's either not really listening or he's trying not to get upset. "It's not like it's against the law to have fun in California," I said, and that was it. I got an earful about how life isn't fun and games all the time and if I thought it was, all I had to do was take a look at Uncle Ryan and I could see how that turned out for him. He stopped right there, real sudden, and looked at me like I'd just called him out at home when everyone else in the world could see he was safe. "I didn't mean that the way it sounded." He waited a second, said, "Let's just not talk about Uncle Ryan, okay?" and then left the room.

Uncle Ryan used to get an earful sometimes too, my dad telling him there's a time to have fun and a time to grow up and isn't it about time he grew up? I figure Uncle Ryan doesn't need any more of that coming through me, so I leave out all the stuff about the ball game and what my dad said. *I wish you were here*, I write instead, *or that you could write back, but I'm pretty sure you can't*. I add a *Ha! But I'm going to keep writing you, if you don't mind. It makes me feel a little better, so I hope, somehow, these are getting to you and they make you feel good too.*

■

Monday starts with Gus/Gary knocking me sideways to catch the physics book that somehow flew out of his locker. I'm flat on the ground and he's standing there with the book, saying it was a close one, he *almost* got me. He's smirking, but he sticks his hand out to help me up, so I have to say, "Thanks."

In Algebra, Mr. Tomita gives us the last ten minutes of class to get started on our homework. My left foot's propped on the side rail under my chair, my knee sticking up and out into the aisle, and suddenly it tickles a little where the hole is, like a fly's walking across my skin. Edie's leaning forward, a blue pen in her hand, writing on me. It feels so good I pretend not to notice until she's done and it reads, *Statement.*

"You think I'm making a fashion statement?"

It's quiet a second until she whispers, "Just a statement."

I turn around and she's got an *I know the answers you have to look up* smile. "What kind of statement?" I say, and Mr. Tomita shushes me from his desk, staring until we make eye contact. His chin moves down just a fraction but he doesn't say anything. It's a warning. A minute later a folded paper crinkles against my arm. Without looking up, I reach back and grab it. It's a drawing of a guy in ripped jeans, an untucked shirt, and a jacket. There's one of those cartoon bubbles above for what he's saying, only he's not saying anything. There's just an exclamation point.

I make a question mark next to it and slide it back. The paper crinkles and swishes a little like Edie's smoothing it over, but it never comes back.

When the bell rings, I turn around. "An exclamation point?"

Edie picks up her books and starts walking for the door. "Don't worry about it."

"How can I not worry about it?"

"Just don't." She stops next to the door. "Come on."

She's going in the opposite direction from my next class, but I walk with her anyway. "Tell me."

"You tell me."

"What my fashion statement is?"

Her voice goes pretend serious. "Yes, Reece. What *is* your fashion statement?"

We stop by the staircase. Gobs of people are bobbing down the steps like a waterfall. A couple freshmen are trouting their way up, getting knocked all over the place, which is their own fault. Unless you're Treat's size, you've got to wait until most of the people coming down clear out, because not only are they merciless; they've got gravity on their side.

"I haven't really thought about my clothes as a statement," I say.

"That's kind of what they're saying."

"Nothing?"

"Uh-huh. A big exclamation point with nothing in front of it." She hands me the folded-up paper from her pocket and jumps into the stream of people heading up the stairs. "See you later."

I unfold the paper and it's just the same as it was, the guy in the ripped jeans with nothing to say. On the way to English, I fold it up and slide it into my back pocket, keeping it safe from I don't know what.

Treat's already in the classroom when I get there, and people are staring at him since they've never seen the Mohawk before. He nods at my new/old clothes and a couple people look over at me, probably wondering how I'm friends with this guy. It feels pretty good, so when Treat says me and Keith should meet him in

the Bog at lunch, I'm all for it even though I don't know what the
Bog is.

■

The Bog, Keith tells me, is the middle of the quad where there's
trees and shrubs in these big planters, really nice except they
water it constantly so it's always muddy. Upperclassmen get all
the spots around the edges, so freshmen get stuck in the Bog.

For the most part, the upperclassmen couldn't be bothered
with you at lunch unless you cut across their grass or sit too close
to the planters up against the library, the Senior Circle. But as
Treat's cutting across the quad in front of the Senior Circle, guys
in letterman jackets just stare at him.

When Treat gets to the Bog he throws up a hand. "What's up?"

"A preposition," Keith says.

Treat grabs Keith's shirt in back and yanks it up. Keith looks
like a dog waiting to get smacked and Treat says, "You don't tuck
that in." Keith doesn't even move, and Treat claps his shoulder.
"You gotta get the rest. I'm not sticking my hand down your
pants."

Keith tugs and pulls real fast, his shirt flying up like a mush-
room cloud until it settles back down, completely untucked and,
really, looking a lot better.

Me and Keith tell Treat about the Howdy Dance and then we
all talk about our old junior highs. Treat went to a private school,
uniforms and everything. "I finally told my parents to save their
money because if I had to go one more year I'd get myself kicked
out again."

He says it so relaxed it takes me a second to realize he said "again."

"That's balls out," Keith says.

"I guess," Treat says. "Listen, you guys should come to my house today after school."

"Yeah?" I say. "What's up?"

Treat laughs. "A preposition." He punches Keith on the shoulder nice and solid, which looks pretty painful, but Keith gives it a tight smile. "Nah, it'll be bitchin' is all." He snatches some paper from a guy sitting near us and draws a map. "Bring your bathing suits."

■

Me and Keith are pacing around the PE lockers, wondering if we should try and get out of going to Treat's since even in California you don't go swimming with a guy you just met. We're coming around the corner by the varsity room when the bell rings and Petrakis is there waiting for us.

"Come here, little dudes," he says. "You friends with that Mohawk guy?"

We both nod.

Petrakis glances at me and back to Keith. "You tell that guy if he wants to come out for football, there's still time. Got it?" He slaps Keith on the back, solid, and pushes him toward the door. "Now, get the fuck out of here."

When we get to the quad, Keith says, "I'm going."

"To Treat's?"

"Yeah." His head moves up and down a few times, fast and short. "I don't care if you go or not; I'm going."

"I'll go."

"Good," Keith says, "because that guy scares me," and I don't know if he means Treat or Petrakis. Probably both.

■

Me and Keith hop my back wall to cut through the park and get across Yorba Linda Boulevard. The hills start dropping off into the canyon on that side of the street and you can tell the houses are older because there's no pattern to them. Sometimes there isn't even a house next door, just a field and horse fence.

Treat's house doesn't look any bigger than mine, but it's all one story and spread out wide. We put our bathing suits on in the bathroom next to the kitchen and Treat leads us straight out the glass sliding door to the backyard. It must be forty yards to the back fence, only there's no pool. Right before the yard drops back into the hill again, there's a wooden deck about three feet off the ground with a big, octagon-shaped bathtub sunk in the middle of it.

"Cool," Keith says. "A hot tub."

Treat shakes him off. "Jacuzzi." He turns this dial in the back corner of the deck and the thing comes to life like a boiling pot of pasta. Here it is, September, seventy-five degrees out at three in the afternoon, the sun coming through the flat roof in checkers, and Treat climbs in.

"Isn't it a little hot for this?"

"Nah," Treat says. "This is the perfect time."

"For what?" Keith says. "Melting my contact lenses into my eyes?"

"You have contacts?"

"No," Keith says. "It's an expression."

Me and Keith sit down on the deck and let our legs dangle in the water. We tell Treat what Petrakis said about football and he laughs. "Who the hell wants to be a gladiator? No, thanks." He leans back, looks around the yard, then says did we know that the Indians who lived in these hills used to do rituals that purified the land and their spirits?

"It must not have worked," Keith says. "We got all their land."

Treat looks at Keith like he might rip off his head, then stares past him. "It brings inner strength. The kind of thing that affects everyone around you."

"How?" Keith says.

"Who won?" Treat says. "The Pilgrims or the Indians?"

"The Pilgrims."

"How often do you see movies about Pilgrims?"

Keith thinks about it a second. "Sometimes. Around Thanksgiving."

"Maybe. But you see movies about Indians all the time. You know why?" Treat doesn't wait. "The inner strength. It influences people."

"People in Hollywood?" I say.

"People everywhere."

Beads of sweat are sticking to Treat's face and shoulders, and with his Mohawk growing all misty with the steam rising around it, he looks mysterious and wise, like the face in the mirror in *Snow White* handing out all those facts and advice. Treat says in sweat lodges the Indians would sit around in the heat and confess their fears and hopes and all kinds of things and just let them rise with the steam. "They could let private stuff out into the world without being embarrassed. So anything we say in the Jacuzzi stays in the Jacuzzi until it becomes part of the air."

Keith looks at me, like, *Is this real?* and it must be because Treat keeps talking. "I want you guys to know I didn't go to the dance because I knew the music would be lame and it wouldn't be very punk rock. But after you guys told me today how you hung out with those chicks, I almost wished I went."

Keith bobs his head a little and so I do too.

"Okay," Treat says. "I confessed something. Now you guys have to climb in and confess something too."

"What if we don't have anything?" I say.

"You've got something," Treat says. "Everybody does."

"What if we really don't?"

"Then you have to think harder. There has to be balance for this to work."

Keith slides in and starts telling this story about some girl he made out with in the bathroom at his church. When I ask who it was, Keith says it was early in the summer, before I moved here, and somebody's cousin from another state. I ask who the "somebody" is and Keith says, "Somebody who doesn't go to our school anymore."

"Are you confessing or bragging?"

"Confessing," Keith says. "She was a seventh grader and I was about to start high school. I sort of took advantage of her."

Treat nods. "That works."

Keith grins and looks at me. "What's your confession, Reece?"

"You mean confession, like a sin? Because I don't think making out with a girl is a sin unless she doesn't exist."

Keith looks around the yard like he's admiring the petunias, and Treat says, "It doesn't have to be anything like that. It can be something you've never told anyone. Something you want to get off your chest."

I have stuff like that, stuff I wouldn't tell a priest. Stuff like fishing Uncle Ryan's keys out of that stadium cup the morning he disappeared, hiding them in my backpack, and then throwing them in a trash bin on the way to school. Or even writing the letters to him, since my parents don't know about that and they wouldn't like it. Or how writing the letters at my desk is how I first noticed my window is right across from Astrid's. Now I'm gawking every time her light clicks on, hoping somehow through the curtains I'll see her taking off her bra or just lying on her bed.

But there's no way I'm getting into any of that. "Hold on," I say and I'm down the steps, running through the yard, and yelling back, "I've got one." The water flies off my legs and most of the drippy stuff's gone by the time I'm in the house and fishing through the pockets of my jeans. Then I'm back on the deck, holding out the drawing of me with nothing to say.

"Who gave you this?" Treat says.

"Edie," I say. "One of the girls from the Howdy Dance."

Keith leans out of the water to see it up close. "You got a note? Sweet."

Treat shakes his head. "This is serious shit."

I set the note down and climb all the way into the water. "I know. I don't exist."

"What are you talking about?" Keith says. "You got a note. From a girl." He turns to Treat. "A cute girl."

"It's not a note," I say.

Keith looks back at me. "It is too. It's just in hieroglyphics."

"Okay. Then it's hieroglyphics for a guy who doesn't exist."

Treat's nodding, but Keith's shaking his head. "How can you be nonexistent if Astrid talks to you?"

"All she does is say, 'Hey, neighbor!' when we take the trash out. She even called me 'trash buddy' at the dance. That kind of sucks."

"It doesn't suck," Keith says.

Treat looks hard at me. "That cheerleader chick everyone thinks is so great is your neighbor?" Me and Keith both nod and Treat takes in a huge breath. "That does suck."

"How?" Keith says. "How can a cheerleader talking to you, the head cheerleader, ever suck? Unless you say, 'Excuse me,' and she says, 'There's no excuse for you,' and you say, 'I don't need an excuse; I got a hall pass,' and she says, 'You could've fooled me,' and then you say—"

Treat fires a stream of water right into Keith's face. "Okay, I get it." He looks at me. "Not that it's my style, because a cheerleader's opinion doesn't matter, but we're going with de facto power here—"

"De what?" Keith says.

"De facto," Treat says. "Not who we wish had the power, but who actually has the power. Cheerleaders have it. So that 'Hey, neighbor!' crap doesn't mean anything good. She has to talk to him just to be civil. But it's like making friends with the neighbor's dog. You pat him on the head and say, 'Who's a good boy? You're a good boy. Yes, you are,' but you're never going to take him for a walk."

Keith knows I don't have a dog and I'm pretty sure he's

trying to figure out if Astrid does. Treat must see it too, because he looks right at Keith and says, "What I'm saying is she probably doesn't even know Reece's name."

"She knows my name," I say, even though I'm not sure she does. The weekend before school started, Astrid was on the side of her house messing with her trash cans, sort of rearranging them. It gave me an excuse to hop up on the wall and ask if she needed help with anything.

She had a grocery bag rattling with beer bottles. She smiled and right then could have asked me to drink whatever was left in every one of those bottles and I would have said, *Bring me a straw.*

"You're a lifesaver," she said. "Can I put this in your trash? Some of my friends came over last night and brought beer without telling me." I came around and took the bag and she gave me the smile again, toothy and perfect, her head tilting to one side. "Thanks, neighbor. I owe you one."

I tell Treat and Keith all about this and they're both quiet, watching me like I'm the last guy to cross the finish line. "Crap. She doesn't know my name, does she?"

Keith shakes his head.

Treat's head doesn't move. He's thinking hard, and then he says, "The note's a good confession, Reece. It's one thing if you don't matter to a cheerleader. Who does? But if freshmen girls aren't seeing you—"

"I knew it," I say. "I don't exist."

"Theoretically," Keith says.

Treat looks over at him. "Hypothetically."

Keith watches the bubbles coming up and popping around

him for a second. "Well, theoretically, hypothetically, meta-phorically. I know I exist."

Treat shakes his head. "Not really. But we're only a couple weeks in. You guys still have time to make an impression like I did."

I glance at the Mohawk. "No way. My dad would leave an impression on my face if I came home with a Mohawk."

Keith raises his fingers to the surface of the water, letting the bubbles boil through them like he's controlling some witch's cauldron. "We could throw a big party. Like that Ted guy did."

"Sure," I say, "and invite all the people who don't know who we are."

Keith shrugs and keeps watching bubbles. Treat nods slow and steady, and it's like he's about to talk, only he doesn't. I've counted something like fifty bubbles before Treat says, "You guys are posers." He doesn't say it mean, like you might think. He actually sounds nice about it. "Your clothes are good. You just aren't legit." He looks at Keith. "Do you know who the Dickies are?" Keith laughs and says that's not a real band, but Treat's nodding, serious. "How about the Germs? Do you guys know 'What We Do Is Secret'?"

"We're keeping this secret?" Keith says.

Treat splashes him. "No. That's a Germs song."

I laugh like I knew that.

"I'll make you guys some mix tapes," Treat says. "That'll help."

"Make sure you write *The Germs* on it," Keith says and gets this funny grin. "So my mom will be afraid to touch it."

"Sure," Treat says, "because we know she'd have her hands

all over *The Dickies.*" He smiles and splashes himself in the face. "There," he says to Keith. "Now you don't have to do it."

As soon as Keith smiles, Treat closes his eyes and puts his finger up to his lips. Me and Keith are looking at each other, like, *Is something going to happen?* and then something does. The water jets click off. Without the motor running, you can hear the last bubbles on the surface of the water breaking open and fizzing like a giant glass of pop. Treat's arms rise above the surface, the water running off them in a steady trickle at first, then drips and drops. He has us raise our arms too, and we hold them there a minute until Treat opens his eyes and says, "Now, we are in balance."

It feels pretty good how nice Treat is even though he looks so fierce, but I'm not feeling the balance. I don't see how wearing my clothes and knowing any song by the Germs is going to make me look different to Edie or be able to talk to Astrid. When I say that, Treat nods like he knew all along there had to be more. "We need to find the balance in our actions and not just our thoughts."

"Sure," I say.

"The tapes will help. There's something else, though. Something I was saving until you guys seemed ready."

Keith leans his chin out like a dog begging for a bone. "We're ready."

Treat closes his eyes. "Everybody knows guys in bands. They exist on a whole different plane." He opens his eyes. "So we'll start a band. A punk band."

Keith's nodding. "I totally concur with Treat's theoretical hypothesis: I don't even know who van Doren is and I know him."

"Van Dorken," Treat says. "That's what everybody called him before he started Filibuster."

Keith says he's heard that too. It's kind of hard to believe, if you ask me. Not with the way everybody worships the guy. And even if it is true, I'm not van Doren. Our band that doesn't exist isn't Filibuster. "How will this change anything?" I say. "I'll go from being the guy nobody notices to the guy in the band nobody's ever heard of."

"Come on," Keith says. "A band!"

Treat reaches his hand out toward Keith, like, *Hold on.* "Listen, Reece." His voice is soft like Uncle Ryan's the time he saw me drop a fly ball and told me after the game it was okay, nobody's perfect. "Just imagine: The next time you see that cheerleader chick walking out to her car, you say, 'Can you give me a lift? I need to go jam with my band.'"

Treat waits. His hair and the clothes he wears to school already make him look like the lead singer of some kind of band. Keith nods slow and serious. I've seen a guitar and little amp in his closet, and he said he'd had a few lessons once. It almost makes sense, and even with the two of them staring at me, I can see Astrid's face, surprised and happy as I'm standing in front of her with some guitar clinging to my side. We're at the curb, next to our trash cans, and I start strumming a song for her. Only, I don't really know how a punk song starts, and now my guitar is a baseball bat. But Astrid smiles anyway and says, *Keep going, neighbor.*

"Okay," I say as Astrid's face goes away and Treat and Keith are right there, waiting. "I guess I'm in."

Emperor of Idiots

Me and Keith have this game we play called Berlin Wall. One time, after they'd started lighting up the soccer fields behind my house for night games, we noticed how those huge floodlights make night shadows. We bolted from the dark side of the brick bathroom building to the shadow of a pole. Then we went from the pole to the shadow of a tree, sneaking all the way to my back wall. "Who are we hiding from?" Keith said. "The East Germans," I heard myself say, and suddenly it all became clear: The people in the park were border guards; the cinder-block wall separating my backyard from the park was the Berlin Wall. Our mission: move from one shadow to the next, staying still and waiting for the guards to look the other way, then sprint for the wall. If we got up and over fast and smooth we were safe in my backyard, West Berlin. Anything else and we were caught up in barbed wire or worse, shot.

We haven't told Treat about the game because we know it's

kind of stupid and we're not sure whose side he'd be on anyway. Plus, that would mean he'd know where we live and might want to come to one of our houses. How do you explain your huge friend with the bleached Mohawk to your dad when he doesn't even like ballplayers with bushy sideburns?

■

Our first band meeting is Saturday morning in Treat's room. We sit on Treat's bed as he fires through a stack of cassette tapes and plays different songs for us. The guitars sound like low-flying planes with some guy screaming in short bursts about who knows what because the music's so distorted. We're just getting to the Clash, which actually sounds like real music, when Treat's mom says it's time to go. They're heading to Treat's grandma's house in LA.

If we still lived in Jersey, I'd run home to catch the Saturday *Game of the Week*. My dad would be waiting for me, trying to get Brendan to sit down for an inning or two and trying to convince Colleen the reason some balls are called foul balls is because of the funny way they fly through the air, like chickens. But my dad's at work, so me and Keith stop in the park to practice some new moves for the Berlin Wall game.

I've been reaching the wall three steps before Keith, slamming my back against the blocks, dropping my hands down, and locking my fingers just as Keith gets to me. His right foot lands in my hands and I pull up hard, launching Keith to the top of the wall. It's about our tenth try and Keith finally makes it to the top without dangling and needing a second push. He reaches back to pull me up, just the way we planned. But as Mr. Krueger said on our first lab day, "If everything worked out the way we had it in our heads, we wouldn't need to experiment." Right as our palms slap together, Keith slides off the wall, landing in the grass next to me and going into a crouch.

"Did they shoot you?" I laugh. "We're done for!"

Keith gives me a *shush*, his finger pressed to his lips until we both hear the voices on the other side of the wall. Some guy says, "I don't think this will work even with an extension cord."

"You're right," says a girl. Astrid. "The patio's the best spot."

Keith grins like we're real spies now. I'm wondering where Astrid was about five minutes ago when I fell off the wall like I'd been shot and screamed, "Freedom!"

"Yeah," the guy says. "That'll guarantee everything is level."

It stays quiet until we hear Astrid's glass sliding door thud and click shut.

Keith looks up at the wall. "Astrid's having a party."

"How'd you get that?"

"What do you think she was talking to that guy about?" Keith bobs his head. "She's having a party. Tonight."

I look up at the wall, three inches of scratchy cinder block between my yard and hers, between both our yards and the park. "Do you think she saw us?"

"No way," Keith says. "I dropped as soon as I heard the door." He smacks my chest. "My instincts are trained for that stuff."

"Well then, did she hear us?"

"Who cares," Keith says. "She's having a party. We can spy on it tonight and see how cheerleaders get down." He hops up the wall without any help from me, first time ever. "Treat is going to be so bummed, hanging at his grandma's while we hang with cheerleaders."

I hop up onto the wall next to Keith. "You mean gawk at them."

Keith taps his lips with his finger, fake serious. "Observe. We'll observe their behavior."

"If by 'observe' you mean slobber on ourselves while watching Astrid and her friends, then okay, we'll observe them."

■

Keith shows up at my house after dinner with his backpack on. We say we're going to study for the periodic table test that's coming up, which is partly true. We are having a test; we just don't know when. Mr. Krueger says not knowing when you'll be tested is the best way to learn. "Anybody can memorize something for one big day," he said. "You have to live it if you really want to learn it." He spun around in his chair like he was surrounded by it. Our first quiz hadn't gone so good. "Come on, people," he said. "Live it. I know it's hard when you've got to know it to live it, but you can't start living it if you don't try to know it." He looked down at one of the quizzes in his hand, then around the room nice and slow. "Someday soon I'm going to give you a sheet of paper with a blank table on it. You'll have to show me everything you know, and then I'll know if you've been living it or not. You can't fake that."

Up in my room, Keith unzips his backpack and pulls out the biggest pair of binoculars I've ever seen. "My dad used to find Skylab's orbit with these and we'd watch it."

"What did it look like?"

Keith adjusts the binoculars. "Nothing really. A blip." He holds the binoculars up to test them. "Except when it started falling back to earth and burning up. You could really see the smoke trail."

I hold up the flash cards I've made of all the elements. "We've got to make this look good. My mom could come barging in here at any second."

Keith takes one of the cards and looks it over. "Nice," he says and hands it back. "We're not really going to study, though."

"Why not? How long can we stare at a party that we're not actually at?"

It turns out, you can stare a pretty long time. The regular party stuff got boring pretty fast, a bunch of upperclassmen standing around holding beers, talking and not really doing anything, and Astrid didn't seem to be anywhere. Then the football players showed up and we started connecting some dots. Like, we know Petrakis is dating Kylie Smith, who does the announcements every morning during first period, but we had no idea what she looks like. Then this girl with short brown hair, about half the size of Petrakis, came up and gave him a long kiss. She tucked herself under his arm and has pretty much stuck there ever since. It's so cute my insides go cough-medicine warm every time I peer over at her.

The only studying we've gotten in is figuring out which elements are most essential for a good party. Keith says you've got to have aluminum because you can't crush an empty beer bottle on your head. We decide neon only works if you're old enough to go to bars, but silicon could work anywhere. "Especially on Kylie," Keith says.

"Nah," I joke, "on Sergio Ortiz."

It's funny, I think, because Sergio is famous for ripping off his shirt every time he scores a goal for the soccer team. But Keith's face is totally serious. "You know he likes to get all-the-way naked at parties, right?"

"What?" I shake my head. I've never heard that, but there's Sergio down in Astrid's backyard, his letterman jacket on a lawn chair and his shirt already hanging out his back pocket.

Keith nods and says it's okay, that it wasn't as gay as he thought at first since I didn't know. We're quiet for a minute, maybe two, before Keith picks up the flash card for tellurium. "This one is cherry," he says. "*Te* is almost *Ted*."

"It's too bad the atomic number is fifty-two and not two," I say. Keith just stares at me. "It would be *Te* two, then. Ted Two?"

"Sweet," Keith says. "Maybe our band will play at Ted Fifty-Two."

I laugh. "If we're ready by then."

About eight thirty I get Brendan in the room to test us on some of the flash cards. It's a perfect move because he'll leave us alone the rest of the night if he thinks we're really studying. Colleen wanders in too, but as soon as I give her a couple blank flash cards she leaves for her crayons.

A few minutes after Brendan leaves, a band starts setting up on Astrid's back patio. From my room, we can only see the front edge of the drums, and it's hard to tell who's messing around with the guitars and amps because the back porch light makes everyone a silhouette at first. A skinny guy with a crop haircut is winding the cord around the microphone stand. When he stands all the way up, the park lights make him 3-D. "That's Gus/Gary," I say. He's wearing jeans and a stupid tank top that looks like a British flag, and he's saying, "Check. Check. Check," into the mic. I guess he got to come to Astrid's party because he's helping the band.

People start crowding around the porch and Keith's got the binoculars out, saying any second the whole band will come walking out the glass sliding door. But they don't. A couple guys who were just standing around pick up guitars and start twanging them a little. Another guy climbs behind the drums and thumps the bass a couple times. Gus/Gary is still at the microphone when a frumpy-looking guy in a plain white T-shirt steps up next to him. Everybody cheers and Gus/Gary puts his arm around the frumpy guy and says into the mic, "Thanks, you bastards."

Everyone cracks up and then Gus/Gary pulls the frumpy guy closer and says, "Ted!" A roar goes up and people start chanting, "Ted, Ted, Ted." Ted throws his arms up, his belly flops out of his shirt, and Gus/Gary shoves him into the crowd. Everyone keeps chanting, "Ted, Ted, Ted."

"Holy shit," Keith says. "*This* is Ted Two."

Gus/Gary shakes up a can of beer and pops the top, sending a stream of suds over the crowd. The guitars scream, the drums roll, and Gus/Gary throws the can over everyone, out into the darkness of the yard. He yells into the microphone, "Fuck you; we're Filibuster!"

The whole backyard roars like they've elected a new pope, and Keith pulls the binoculars down and grabs my arm. "Holy shit. Filibuster!"

"Van Doren's band?" I point at the lead singer, at Gus/Gary, even though Keith's looking through the binoculars again. "*That's* van Doren?"

"Guess so," Keith says. "Van Doren's the lead singer."

It's amazing. Gus/Gary still looks like Gus/Gary, but he's van Doren now and he's all over the patio, pogoing, pushing the people at the front of the patio, pushing the other guys in the band, swirling his head, swirling his whole body. The music zooms like race cars flying by, and the only word I can make out is *fuck*, which seems to be every other word. The song lasts about a minute and a half, then just stops. Everyone erupts into cheers. The people in front slap hands with the guitar players, but when they reach for van Doren's hand he gives them the finger. Then there's a *tap-tap-tap* from the drummer. The next song starts, and it sounds like the first song.

"These guys are *awe*some," Keith says.

They're not awesome. I mean, it's not like I expect them to sound like Billy Joel or the Bee Gees, but Uncle Ryan used to listen to Pink Floyd and the Rolling Stones, and even with all those guitars and the weird lyrics you can tell those guys know what they're doing. It is cool how the guitarist in Filibuster plays with one hand and slaps people's hands with the other. And the bass player is leaning back, his head up at the sky all peaceful, like he can't even hear the sonic boom coming out of his amp. Van Doren's bent at the waist now, leaning out toward the crowd, both hands hugging the mic. His body is perfectly still, but his head thrashes in a blur and he spits out every word like a cat with a hairball.

The backyard is a hurricane. There's a mass of guys circling, all in the same direction, bouncing off each other, kind of light at first, then faster and harder. Some guys spin while they circle, all of them smashing into each other randomly. Even a couple girls are in there. Not Astrid, though. She's off to the side with some of her cheerleader friends, bobbing her head a little to the music. Her hair is pulled into a sideways ponytail, like maybe she's ready in case she decides to jump into the hurricane too.

By the fourth song, me and Keith are swirling around the room and crashing into each other. It only goes for about a minute, and just when we're getting tired, the song ends. We catch our breath; then it all starts up again.

As the last song ends, with Keith holding his arms up in the air like all the cheers coming from Astrid's backyard are for him and me spinning in my desk chair, holding two pencils in the air like I'm a drummer, my dad comes booming through the door without knocking. "Are they done?"

Keith drops his arms but his legs are still spread out funny from the pose. I spin the chair back to the desk and shuffle the flash cards. "I think so."

My dad walks straight over to the window and looks down at Astrid's yard. "I wonder if Alex knows about this." He turns to me. "Is this one of those punker bands?" I can't believe my dad even knows those words. "Do you know these guys?"

"I don't *know* them. I've heard of them."

My dad shakes his head and starts walking out of the room. "Well, I wish I hadn't heard them. But if I do again, I'm calling the police."

Keith doesn't have to tell me how bad it will look to be the guy whose dad breaks up parties. But he does anyway. "You need to signal Astrid somehow."

"Sure," I say, "but what's the signal for *Keep it quiet, my dad's a jerk?*"

Twenty minutes later, when the guys from Filibuster start coming back onto the patio and picking up their instruments, I run downstairs to the living room. My parents are on the couch, looking relaxed for once. Mom's hair is down and she's leaning into my dad's shoulder while they watch TV. It's the way they used to look every weekend back in Jersey.

I don't have a plan, so I just blurt out, "You can't call the police. It's Saturday."

"It's scaring your little sister," my dad says. "She thought we were under attack."

In my head, there's a squadron of electric guitars flying over our house. I grin a little because it's got to be a joke. "Come on."

My dad isn't smiling. "Have you seen these punkers on the news? They're violent." He looks at my mom, who nods, then back at me. "That's not music."

When Treat played the Clash for us in his room, the cassette case had a picture of a guy smashing his guitar, and there were songs listed like "Spanish Bombs," "Clampdown," and "The Guns of Brixton." But these are just high school guys. They're Astrid's friends.

"Reece," my mom says and sits straight up. "Do you know these kids?"

"I don't know. Not really."

A rattle and rhythm of thumps force their way through our living room wall.

"I'm calling," my dad says.

"Wait," I say. "It's the weekend."

"It's almost ten o'clock," my dad says. My mom puts a hand on his arm and he looks at her. "Well, I can't just let them keep going all night, Eileen."

"Maybe," I say and don't know why I'm saying it, "I can talk to them." I look at my mom and she looks at my dad.

His chest heaves once, a big, thinking breath. "If you go over there and tell your friends to quiet down, I won't call the police."

"Okay," I say and head for the stairs to get Keith.

"Now," my dad says, stopping me at the first step. "Right now."

■

It doesn't feel real walking through Astrid's side gate, through the dark, past the trash cans and two guys going the other way. It's Yankee Stadium half an hour before the first pitch—the nerves and excitement about what could happen—and each step closer to the backyard sends an achy tickle up my legs.

I come around the side of the house right next to the patio, right next to the band, and everyone's packed tight in the yard. It's between songs, so the hurricane isn't swirling. There are so many people around the patio whose faces I've seen, even if I don't know their names. Then I can't believe it, but I see other freshmen—a couple people from student government and some football players who are hanging out near Petrakis. It's only about five people from the entire freshman class, but it makes me feel stupid. They got invited to a party that I didn't even know about, that I still wouldn't know about if I wasn't playing on my back wall like a ten-year-old.

And here are these guys already bonding with the right people, already exactly where Keith says we need to be. But I'm never going to be varsity this or vice president that. So do I have to pull a van Dorken, flip people off and shove them around so they can smile and give each other high fives for getting abused? Who wants to be the emperor of idiots?

Van Doren leans into the mic, says, "Let's do this motherfucker," and the guitars, drums, and hurricane all start at the same time. People like Astrid, who just want to stand, are on the other side of the patio, and it takes me the whole song to squeeze over there. The next song starts right away, and van Doren sings, "The fucking queen and / the fucking king / fuck all the fuckers / fuck 'em clean."

Astrid's hair swings back and forth with a rhythm you wouldn't think a song like that could have. She's wearing a sleeveless sweater and pink pants that are so tight all the way down to her ankles they must have grown on her. She's worn the pants to school before, but now, this close, I can see the stitches running down to little zippers at the bottom of each leg. Her arms are skinny but with just enough muscle that they're not scrawny, still summer brown with tiny blond hairs shining from the patio light. I tap her shoulder with my whole hand and it's hard and tight and soft and hot. Everything at once.

She looks over her shoulder to the crowd at first; then she sees me.

"Hey!" I shout.

Her whole body turns to me. "Hey, neighbor. I'm glad you came."

"Really?"

"Yeah," she says. She grips my arm kind of serious and leans in close, her breath warming the whole side of my cheek. "Have you had any beer?"

The only beer I've ever had in my life are the sips Uncle Ryan gave me once on Thanksgiving and once at the shore on Labor Day. I shake my head and she says, "Good. Promise me you won't drink, okay?"

I nod, then shout through the waves of music, "There's something I have to tell you."

She lets go of my arm and turns her ear to me. I cup my hand and lean in close. She smells like flowers and something else, not sweat or anything gross, something natural, almost sweet, and I've got that drunk feeling again, like when van Doren first hit me with a folder, but in a good way this time. "My dad is thinking about maybe calling the police if the band keeps playing."

Astrid pulls away and looks around the yard, then at her watch, which is pink with polka dots all over the face and only the number twelve at the top. She must be able to read it, though, because she nods and says, "Go tell your dad I'm sorry and that I'll take care of it, okay?"

"I'm sorry. He's really being a—"

"It's okay." She looks toward the side of the house where I came in, then back at me. "Just hurry up and go tell him."

By the time I'm back at my front door, a police car is creeping down our cul-de-sac, blue lights twinkling off my dad's truck, but no siren.

My parents are still on the couch, acting like they haven't moved a muscle. I leave the front door wide-open, the blue light pulsing off it: "You didn't even give me a chance."

My dad sits up straight and looks at the door.

"Why didn't you wait? Astrid said she'd take care of it."

He looks at my mom, then at me. "I didn't call them, Reece."

"Come on, Dad, I'm not stupid."

He walks over to the window and my mom says, "We didn't call them."

"Oh, right, Mom, they just appeared out of thin air."

Before my mom has a chance to say anything, my dad's in my face, his finger an inch from my nose. "You do not talk to your mother like that."

"I'm just saying—"

"Apologize right now."

I do, and my mom nods slow and understanding, saying it's okay.

Keith comes to the bottom of the stairs and my dad tells him it's time he headed home.

Even though you could throw a baseball from our front lawn to Keith's, my dad says we need to watch him walk out of the cul-de-sac and across the street to his house. Astrid's on her driveway, talking to a couple of policemen. She doesn't look upset like you might think; she just keeps agreeing and saying, "Okay, I will. Okay, not a problem." And maybe, if you're Astrid, it's not a problem. She's not the one whose dad just ran off everyone who matters.

I want to hop my back wall and run to Treat's, plop down in the Jacuzzi, and ask what the Indians did when everything started changing and everything that was important to them was disappearing.

Back in my room, it hits me how no matter what the Indians did, they couldn't stop it. They lost everything. It's so depressing, and staring at Astrid's empty backyard—the cans and bottles shimmering a little from the park lights—doesn't make it any better. I take a good look at the cinder-block wall, pull out my notebook, and start a letter to Uncle Ryan: *Greetings from East Berlin* . . .

War Drums

Sometimes back in Jersey, when my brother and sister were too little and my dad still liked to have fun, we'd go to Yankee games. One time, on a Sunday afternoon, Uncle Ryan went with us and said he had a surprise for me after the game. He took me and Dad around the outside of the stadium where the elevated subway tracks are. There's no gate or anything there, just these blue metal doors with no handles on them. Uncle Ryan said that's where the players come out. He pointed across the cement to this fenced-in parking lot with all these Corvettes and Cadillacs and said that's where the Yankees park their cars. "All we have to do is wait," he said, "and we can get all the autographs we want."

"Even Bobby Murcer?" I said, because he was my favorite. I think because his name made him sound like a kid and because my dad said he was supposed to be the next Mickey Mantle.

"You bet," Uncle Ryan said.

My dad said it might take awhile and my mom wouldn't like

us getting back so late. Uncle Ryan said he didn't mind wait-ing, that it was the least he could do since Dad bought the tick-ets and paid for the beer. "If you need to get going, Packy," Uncle Ryan said, "I can wait with the kid. We'll take the train home."

My dad didn't look so happy about any of it, but then Uncle Ryan said, "Come on, Packy. Look how excited the kid is."

It's true too. I was all smiles and jiggly legs while they were deciding, and I didn't need to beg because Uncle Ryan was doing it for me.

Finally, my dad said, "We'll all wait." He let out a big breath and looked right at Uncle Ryan. "I don't know why I let you talk me into these things."

"Because you're a good father," Uncle Ryan said and gave Dad one of those sideways hugs. "And not too bad of a big brother, either."

By the time the blue doors clicked and rattled open from inside, most of the crowd was long gone. Maybe thirty people had stuck around, and everyone rushed forward. A couple secu-rity guards stepped out and told everyone to make way. A minute later, the players started trickling out a few at a time. They looked so different in their jeans and button-up shirts, leather jackets and sport coats. Everyone rushed the really famous guys first, clump-ing around until they got an autograph and then peeling off one by one to clump around the next guy.

When Bobby Murcer came out, some kids yelled, "Bobby, Bobby!" and clumped around him. He towered over them, smil-ing and signing hats and balls and anything else they shoved in his face. Dad handed me a program and a pen and Uncle Ryan gave me a little shove. "Go on, Reece."

I stood at the edge of the pack, getting bounced around while people shoved past me. Bobby's hair was slicked back, black and still wet from the postgame shower. His left hand, so huge, just glided across everything he signed, a little swirl at the end before the pen popped up and he'd sign something else.

Pretty soon, I was the last one standing there. Bobby Murcer reached down and took the program out of my hands without me saying a thing.

"You want me to sign this, Slugger?"

I nodded.

"Can I use your pen?"

I nodded again, but he had to take it from me because my hand didn't move. Then he crouched down in front of me and everything else went away—the noise from the elevated tracks, the last of the people yapping to the last of the ballplayers. Dad and Uncle Ryan could have walked off and I wouldn't have known. The whole world was Bobby Murcer's face, his aftershave lotion hitting my nose sharp and clean, his eyes right on me. "What's your name, Slugger?"

"Reece."

His hand glided across the program. He clicked the pen closed with a flick and held everything out to me. I tried to grab the program, but Bobby tugged it back a little. He smiled the way Dad would when I'd tell him about all the good things I did at school. "Don't be afraid, son," he said. "I'm just a ballplayer." Then he let the program go.

Way before we came to California, the Yankees traded Bobby Murcer to San Francisco. I kind of lost track of him then, but I held on to that autograph. I don't know why. I mean, he wasn't the next Mickey Mantle. He wasn't even a Yankee anymore. He was just Bobby Murcer. One more nobody in California.

■

Monday morning at school, rumors about Ted Two are flying everywhere: Filibuster played until almost midnight; the cops busted Ted for minor in possession; van Doren crowd surfed onto a squad car to distract the police when Sergio Ortiz streaked out of the backyard and ran home.

Before Algebra, Edie's all over me: Did I hear about Ted Two? Did Filibuster really play? And she knows van Doren wasn't on top of a police car, was he, but was there some guy in a suit there to sign Filibuster for a record deal?

At least three girls have said they'll vote for van Doren for homecoming king if he promises to actually go to the dance. A girl in my Spanish class said Ted was cute, and her friend, who should have said, "Gross," or "You're so high," just said, "Yeah. Sort of."

Everybody's talking about the party. About Ted and van Doren. Nobody's getting it right.

At lunch, me and Keith are in the middle of the Bog where it bends and faces the Senior Circle. Astrid's over there, relaxed and talking to her friends and guys who either dress cool or are wearing a letterman jacket. She won't have to move once and by the end of lunch thirty different people will have circled around until it was their chance to swoop in and talk to her.

Treat's eyes are huge when he comes up to us. Did we see

the party? It was right next door to me at the cheerleader chick's house? Did I see the cops? Did they really get Ted? Why didn't I say anything about any of this in English third period?

"Because it's crap. If you believe any of it, I've got a bridge to sell you."

Treat laughs. "Is it in Brooklyn? I could use a bridge in Brooklyn."

We bust up. Keith just grins, then says, "There's no such thing as the Brooklyn Bridge, right?"

"Are you an idiot?" Treat says.

"No," Keith says real serious. "It's like Grant's Tomb, right? Only a sucker would buy it because it doesn't exist." He looks at me.

"There's a Grant's Tomb," I say.

"Keith?" Treat says. "Do you know who's buried in Grant's Tomb?"

Keith looks at us both real suspicious. "King Tut?"

Treat roars. "Awesome. And where do you think Grant's Tomb is?"

"You're going to tell me it's not in Egypt, right?"

"It's in New York," I say.

Keith folds his arms. "No wonder you know. You're from there."

"Jersey."

"Same difference."

"Okay," I say, "then how does Treat know?"

"I don't know. But none of that matters. Everyone is talking about Ted and van Doren like they rule."

Treat stops smiling and laughing. "That's true."

A couple guys right across from us have been telling everyone who walks up that the slam pit at Ted Two was so brutal some guy got his jaw broken.

"Who?" I yell over to them.

"Some guy from another school," one of them yells back. "Probably El Dorado or Villa Park."

Keith rubs his jaw. "Why is that cool?"

"It's not," I say.

"Yeah, it is," Treat says. "It's totally bitchin', even if it is bullshit."

"It doesn't make sense," I say. "The party wasn't *that* great. And Ted didn't do anything except get pushed by van Doren."

Keith nods to Treat. "He wasn't even dressed cool."

A minute goes by without anyone talking. We're just standing here, staring at the ground like maybe the answers slipped down into a crack in the asphalt. I'm thinking, here it is the third week of school and the only time anyone notices me is to ask if I hang out with the Mohawk dude. *Does he really have a tattoo of Geronimo on his chest? Is he part Apache or part Cherokee?*

"We really need to start the band," I say. "For real."

Treat gets a grin so big it's like he's got extra teeth. "Bitchin', but it'll have to wait. Lyle is making me rake leaves today after school."

Me and Keith look at each other, like, *Lyle?*

"My dad," Treat says.

"What if we help?" I say.

"You can't. Not the way I have to do it."

Keith looks at Treat real funny. "You got a blower? That's how our gardener does it."

Treat shakes his finger at Keith. "Lyle and Margaret do not stoop to such destructive devices. I've got to use an all-natural rake." He puts his hands out in the air like he's describing the vision of some distant universe. "Made wholly from the fallen limbs and branches of sequoias. Held together with dried kelp that washed ashore in Santa Cruz."

"Does that mean no?" Keith says.

"Yes," Treat says. "It means no. I've got the leaves; then we're tearing out the summer garden, tilling the soil for fall planting, turning the compost, building a—"

"Compost?" Keith says. "Like, your trash?"

"Like, potato peels and coffee grounds," Treat says. "We fertilize the garden with it."

Keith starts laughing. "So you guys eat your own trash? Remind me never to come over for dinner."

Treat folds his arms and they puff out huge. "Don't worry about it."

"What about tomorrow?" I say, and Keith looks at Treat with me.

Treat stares back at us, then says, "Yeah. You guys ready to do this?"

"I don't know," I say. "But if van Dorken can do it, maybe we can too."

Treat slugs me in the arm. "Nice, Reece. I like the way you're beating those war drums." He puts a hand on my shoulder and one on Keith's and pulls us in for some kind of a huddle. "We are so in balance, guys. We're gonna be legends."

■

Before bed, I sit down at my desk and write another letter to Uncle Ryan. I'm telling him how exciting it is to be in a band, how epic this is going to be. Astrid's patio light is on, and the more I write, the more real the band becomes—the three of us standing on that patio with a backyard full of people staring at us; Astrid off to the side, smiling just at me and then, what? No music comes into my head. No lyrics. I'm not even sure where my hands go on the guitar that's just drooping at my side. Astrid looks really confused and the little surges of excitement in my chest drop into waves of nervous in my stomach.

I'm lying in bed, the letter sitting on my desk, when my dad walks in. He doesn't notice it, or anything really. He's looking at the carpet when he says something about Mom needing to leave early and so I'll have to make my own breakfast tomorrow. Back in Jersey, my dad made breakfast almost every day. Only when Uncle Ryan showed up would he let someone else do it, I guess because he's the one who taught Uncle Ryan.

"No problem," I say, and he starts turning around to walk out. "Hey, Dad. Was Uncle Ryan ever in a band?"

He stops and turns back to me. One side of his mouth rises into a grin and he looks at me. "How did you know?" he says. "It was before you were born."

"I didn't know. I was just wondering."

"Oh," my dad says, and his eyes go back to the carpet. "They were pretty good."

I sit up in my bed, like, *Okay, tell me more.*

"They did a lot of covers." He looks up and says, "You know what a cover is?" I nod and he continues, "That got them some jobs at weddings and a couple bars."

"Wow. Why didn't he keep playing?"

"Well," my dad says. "He was so young then and they weren't making that much money." He looks back at the carpet. "And your grandfather gave him a hard time about it."

Grandpa Houghton was so nice, at least what I remember of him. "Why?"

My dad shakes his head. "Oh, your uncle liked all those English bands like the Animals and the Rolling Stones and, well, Grandpa grew up in Ireland." He says this like it makes sense, like that completely answers the question, but I just shrug. "It was a different time," he says and steps to the door.

"How?"

My dad takes a deep breath and then lets it out. "Your uncle and your grandpa didn't always get along."

"Because of the band?"

"I can't explain it right now, Reece." He looks up, his eyes sort of red but not like he's angry. "It's time for bed," he says, then closes the door before I can ask anything else.

Two-Car Studio

Tuesday morning I can't wait until English to talk to Treat, so I make Keith come with me to his locker before school even though I haven't even told Keith what's going on yet. Treat comes walking up alone, this green satchel slung to one side. It's canvas, kind of beat up, and has a star and *US Army* painted on it. "What's up," he says and looks at Keith, "besides a preposition?"

I slide one of the backpack straps off my shoulder so it's hanging just on one side. "Well, I was thinking that Keith's got, what"—I look at Keith—"those three guitar lessons and a little amp?" Keith nods. "And I've never played anything. How do we make a band out of that?"

Treat doesn't move or even look in my direction. Keith looks stunned, the same way he did when I told him Madison Square Garden isn't really square and definitely isn't a garden. "What about Treat's Mohawk?" Keith says.

"I know," I say, "that helps. But I've got nothing. No instrument, no money." I look at Treat. "The only way my dad's going to be okay with this is if we play all Frank Sinatra songs while donkeys fly over a frozen hell."

"A frozen hell?" Keith drops his backpack off his shoulder and lets it fall down until it's sitting on his feet. "Donkeys flying isn't enough?"

Treat steps around me and starts opening his locker, the dial spinning fast and the door popping open. "First off, we're not doing covers. Maybe some Black Flag. Maybe. But Frank Sinatra? Are you kidding me?" He slams his fist on the locker next to his and the rattle makes people nearby look over like maybe there's going to be a fight. "We're going to play what we feel."

I nod and step closer to Treat. "Okay. I feel nervous."

"Good," Treat says. "Nervous has energy. It's the next best thing to anger."

Keith holds out his arms like he's soaking wet. "Look at me. I'm wearing a used shirt some guy probably died in. You know why?"

"Yes," I say.

"Because you begged me to is why."

"I know, Keith."

"You can't quit before we start."

"Nobody's quitting," Treat says. He's calm and pulls two cassette tapes out of his satchel. He hands one to each of us. "It has begun."

Keith glances at his tape. "'The Germs and Other Afflictions.' Sweet."

Treat's left the label on mine blank. "It's the same five songs on both tapes," he says. "But this will get you started on song ideas, and I'll make you guys a better tape when I've got more time."

I take the tape.

Keith's happy again, stuffing the tape into his backpack. "What are we going to call ourselves?"

Treat puts his satchel in his locker and shuts the door with a quiet click. "Good question," he says and turns to face us again. "Let's brainstorm all day. Write down whatever comes to you on the wind and we'll vote on the best ones after school."

"Sweet," Keith says.

Treat points the Mohawk right at Keith and corrects him: "Bitchin'." He turns it to me. "Remember, whatever you come up with needs to sound cool and look killer when you write it." His face is so wide-eyed and excited he looks more like a kid on Christmas than this fierce Mohawk guy nobody will look at directly. He waits until I nod, says, "Okay," then does a half spin and takes off.

I take a step but Keith doesn't move. He stares at me like he's asked a question, so I answer: "I said, 'Okay.'"

He nods, says, "Okay, good," and we start walking to class.

■

While Mr. Krueger's talking atoms, I'm scribbling band names in the margins of my notebook: *Mohawk Jacket, Mohawk Jock, The Mimes,* and *Mime's the Word.* Then I start thinking about where I am, you know, what's on the wind: *Atomic Anarchy, The Splitting Adams,* and *Gone Fission.*

After class, Keith looks my ideas over, then shows me what he did: no names but a really good sketch of a tour bus.

In Algebra, more names arrive on the wind: *The Variables, The Unknown,* and *Solve for X.* Mr. Tomita is talking about prisms, so as soon as I write down $V = Bh$ I'm back at it with *Volume!, Volume = Base x hate,* and *Prism Bound.* My head jumps to fourth period, Spanish, and I get a head start with *Los Punks, Vamos Loco,* and *¿Habla Anarchy?* It's going really good until class is about over and it hits me how the margins of my notebook paper are crammed with ideas and the middle of the page is blank except for that one formula. I peek behind me, and Edie has a full page of notes, formulas with prisms and pyramids, really complicated-looking stuff, and sharp drawings. She smiles. "What?"

"Nothing," I say.

She leans closer and whispers, "It's my new shirt, isn't it? You can't take your eyes off it."

Edie's wearing a plain white button-up, except it doesn't button all the way up. It's not like Edie's got much of anything to show off, but now I see these speckled white puka shells I've never noticed before because I've never really noticed anything below Edie's neck. And suddenly I really can't take my eyes off her because her skin looks smooth and tight and there's this hint of a lacy bra just peeking out, and even though Edie probably doesn't need a bra, it's still a bra.

"Yeah," I whisper. "I've never seen a white shirt before. It's so exotic."

She grins and leans back. Then I hear Mr. Tomita clearing his throat. He's at the board, chalk in hand, solving a problem and staring at me. "Mr. Houghton, should I move the chalkboard to the back of the classroom?"

"Sorry."

"Should I move Miss Okuda in front of you?"

Everybody laughs and Mr. Tomita raises on his toes a little and bounces, which is his way of laughing without laughing. "That's okay," I say.

"Good," Mr. Tomita says. He looks at the clock at the back of the room. "Now, it is almost time to go." A couple people thump their books shut. "But"—Mr. Tomita is bouncing on his toes again—"until it is time to go, it is time to work." He goes back to carving away at the board and for the last five minutes I take real notes.

On the way to the stairs after class, Edie says, "What were you writing?"

"Some band names for a friend."

"Who?" she says.

"Keith. He's thinking about starting a punk band."

We stop at the staircase. Edie pulls her folder and book into her chest and squints at me, all Superman X-ray vision. "Are you in the band too?"

"Kind of."

She tugs my math folder out of my hand and writes *Innocents,* only she spells it Inno¢, like money. She puts her phone number underneath and hands the folder back to me.

"You want me to call you if we use the name?"

"No." She rolls her eyes the way she does whenever she's waiting for me to get the answer she's had for five minutes. "Call me if you need help with the notes you didn't take today."

"Okay, thanks," I say. "I'll tell the guys about the name, too. It's cool."

"I know," she says without even grinning. Then she jumps into the stream of people heading up the stairs.

■

We meet in Treat's garage after school. It looks cramped at first with boxes stacked everywhere and a VW Bug right in the middle. The Bug doesn't seem old like you might think. It's shiny and has that plastic smell, new and fresh and tasteless. Even the boxes around the garage are in good shape, not ripped and coming apart with old baby clothes or Christmas lights spilling out. They're perfect two-foot squares, sealed with clear tape and as solid as bricks. Treat says they're computers. Not the kind you see in movies where they're as big as trophy cases and light up like skyscrapers. Treat's dad helps design and build them, and he sells them to stores too. That's why Mr. Dumovitch can have a ponytail, because smart people always have freaky hair. When you think about it, Albert Einstein looks as punk rock as Johnny Rotten. And the only difference between Adam Ant's hair and Thomas Jefferson's is the color of the ribbon they put around their ponytails.

Mr. D is fine with us practicing in the garage as long as we stack all the boxes along the two walls that are connected to the house. I'm thinking it's to keep us from breaking something. Treat says it's to soundproof the room.

Treat opens the door to the Bug and says, "I'll get this out of the way."

"You can drive it?" I say.

"I've got my permit," he says.

Keith looks in the passenger-side window, then up at Treat. "How old are you?"

"Old enough to know."

"Know what?"

Treat leans on the roof of the car to get closer to Keith. "Know where to hide your body if you ask too many questions." He smiles and Keith does this chin-scratching, squinty-eyed nod, like, *Yes, that's exactly what I thought.*

I run my hand along the curvy back fender. It's so smooth and waxy the metal feels soft. "Where'd you get it?"

"My dad's had it since college," Treat says and climbs in. "It's still pretty cherry because as soon as he got a good job he stopped driving it."

"Why'd he keep it?"

"I don't know," Treat says. "Sentimental shit, I guess." He fires up the engine and it sounds like a baseball card when you strap it to your bike so the spokes hit it—loud and trilling and sputtery. "Somebody get the garage door."

With Keith backing away from the car and heading over to the door to the house, I walk to the garage door. Just as I'm about to start pushing it open, the door moves on its own and I almost fall over. With the car's engine zinging and the springs on the door creaking and popping, I'm as confused as a rookie in an all-star game. Then I look back at Keith standing by the door to the house, his finger on some little box on the wall and laughing at me like he's the Great Oz.

Once we start stacking boxes along the two walls, we get this rhythm going where I hand Treat a box, he spins and places it on the wall, then turns around and Keith's handing him the next box. Treat's twisting and placing so fast the shaved parts of his head start beading up and the Mohawk sags a little. He climbs up on the wall, four feet high now, and says, "You guys got any band names yet?"

"How about the Tix?" Keith says. "With an *X*. Or Fluff Knuckle?"

"Yeah," Treat says without turning around from the box he's slamming into place. "If we wanted to tour with the Village People."

I hand a box up. "Sometimes girls like stuff like that. Like if we were called Innocents but we spelled the last part with a cent sign?"

Treat slaps my box up against another one. "No."

"Wait," I say. "Do you get it? We don't spell it out all the way—"

"I get it," he says. He starts walking along the box wall he's built, rubbing the shaved parts of his head, getting his hand right up to the base of the Mohawk before sliding it back down to his neck. "Punk is about going against that candy store shit. Punk walks right up to the cops, knocks the doughnut out of their hands, and says, 'Oh, and one more thing, Officer Swine. Fuck the po-lice.'"

Treat walks back to the middle, stops, and stares down at us. He's already half a foot taller than me and I've got a couple inches on Keith, and with four feet of boxes beneath him and the Mohawk reaching up to the rafters, I'm not sure if we're supposed to bow or clap or what.

Before I talk, I put my hands in my back pockets and pull my head back. I think I saw this on an album—maybe it was Mick

Jagger—but it looked kind of cool. "So, punk is about saying, 'Fuck the Man'?"

Treat folds his arms, which only makes them bulge out bigger, and gets this little grin on his face.

Keith nods. "How about Fuck Knuckle?"

"Almost," Treat says. He counts bands off on his fingers: "The Sex Pistols, Black Flag, the Clash, the Dead Boys, Buzzcocks." He waves Keith up for the next box. "Think like that."

It takes a few more boxes for us to get our rhythm back; then the names start coming: the Convicts, Screaming Mimes, Second Thoughts, and Kurfew with a backward *K*. Treat says the names sound better, but he just isn't seeing them on album covers. We take a break and Treat brings out a Dead Kennedys sticker to show us how the initials *DK* look like a tomahawk the way they're pushed together with the stem of the *K* extra long like a handle.

"My dad loves Richard Nixon," Keith says. "How about him?"

Treat looks at the rafters. "Dead Nixons?"

"Tricky Dick?" Keith says. "That's his nickname."

Treat shakes this off. "Sounds too much like Soft Cell, and that's just one step above disco."

All week in Science, Mr. Krueger's been talking about how combining two things doesn't make them half of one and half of the other; it makes a third, totally new thing. "Dick Nixon," I say. "We leave out the *c* and push it all together, d-i-k-n-i-x-o-n."

"Diknixon," Treat says. "But with the *N* capitalized right in the middle."

I can see the name coming out of his mouth as he says it. The Mohawk starts moving up and down, Treat smiling and saying faster, all one word, and angrier: "Dik-Nixon. DikNixon. DikNixon!"

A smile creeps across Keith's face. "It's good," he says. "It's got the word *dick* in it."

■

As me and Keith walk home, we feel good about being DikNixon. All those guys playing soccer in the park, who knows they're soccer players when they're not in their uniforms? Who can tell if you're in Math Club or Spanish Club when you aren't at the meetings? But when you're in a band, people know. They know it exists because of you, and if you quit, it goes away. That's huge.

At home, all I want to do is talk about DikNixon, but I can't. My parents don't need to know, Colleen's too young to understand, and Brendan couldn't care less if it doesn't have anything to do with football. So here I am, geeked up in my room and just writing the name in different ways on notebook paper until I've got the word *Dik* angular with the *D* and the *K* shaped like two arrows, the *I* in between them: >*I*<. Then I stack it on top of *Nixon* with all those letters the same height and it looks right. I draw it careful and slow on the notebook I use for letters to Uncle Ryan, right next to the *NY* of a Yankees logo I drew, only bigger. Now it's official. I draw it on my English folder, then Spanish, and then I see Edie's number, swirly and blue across the top of my Algebra folder.

My heart's pounding—full-count, bases-loaded, bottom-of-the-ninth pounding—and in a second I'm downstairs in the kitchen, dialing. The phone hums and crackles and hums and crackles and then, in mid-hum, clicks. This tired-sounding "Ha-lo" comes through the line. With my best church voice I say, "Hello, ma'am, this is Reece Houghton from Edie's Algebra class. Is she home?" There's a mishmash of talking and the only word I can make out is "Edie!"

The phone crackles and thumps a little, there's this shuffle of footsteps, and did Edie just say something in Japanese? Then I hear, "Reece?"

"Yeah."

"What's going on?"

It's weird how clear she sounds, like she's right next to me, and even though I've never been to Edie's house I can see her standing next to the phone in her kitchen, leaning against the counter.

"Who was that?" I say.

"My grandmother." Edie has this way of talking while she smiles, especially if she's making fun of you, and I hear her face doing that. "Are you just calling to see if I gave you the right number?"

"No. We got a band name."

"Cool," she says, and she says it cool: not excited like she won a prize but long and smooth, like each *o* really matters.

"Yeah. Only, we didn't go with yours because Treat wanted something more punk rock." Just as I'm saying this my mom walks into the kitchen and starts pulling things out of the cabinets. My face and chest flash hot like I've been caught looking at panty ads in the Sunday *Times.*

"That's okay," she says. "What name did you pick?"

I look at my mom. Her hair is still done up, her nose freckles still hidden beneath makeup, but she puts on an apron over her work clothes. She's going to be here awhile. "Dick Nixon," I say just above a whisper.

Edie laughs. "Richard Milhous Nixon? For a punk band?"

"It's how you write it," I say.

And just as Edie says, "How do you write it?" my mom says, "Who are you talking to?"

"In English," I say.

"Reece?" my mom says.

I cover the phone. "Someone from school."

She nods and starts washing off potatoes.

"Oh," Edie says like I just told her the earth was round. "So you're not going to write it in Japanese characters?"

I know her arms are folded now and she's smiling like she's tough. "Characters?" I say. "They're not letters?"

"Not really. It's complicated."

"Oh. Well, this isn't complicated. It'll still look cool, though."

Edie laughs, a nice one, not like she's making fun, and then neither of us says anything. I'm staring at the floor tiles, listening to Edie breathe. Then it hits me: There isn't any other sound. My mom's at the cutting board, potato peeler in one hand, a potato in the other, only she's not peeling. She grins at me and mouths, *A girl?*

I shake my head no and she looks down to start peeling. "Have I met this person?" she says out loud.

"Is that your mom?" Edie says.

"Yeah."

"I have?" my mom says.

I glare at her and cover the phone. "Not you."

Edie says, "Tell her I said hi."

"My friend says hi."

My mom keeps whittling away at the potatoes. "What's your friend's name?"

"My mom says hello," I say.

"What's she do?" Edie says.

"Reece?"

"Manages some office," I say.

"What kind of office?"

My mom clacks the potato peeler down on the cutting board. "Reece?"

"I don't know," I say to Edie.

My mom's eyebrows rise. "I asked you a question."

"It's nobody," I say. "Just a person from my math class."

My mom gives me the *Now, was that so hard?* look before picking up the peeler and returning to the potatoes.

"Man," I say into the phone and don't hear anything back. "Hello?"

"I'll let you go," Edie says.

"That's okay. Dinner's not ready yet."

"Well, then I'll let me go. I need to get back to my homework."

"Oh, okay. I'll see you tomorrow."

"Sure," she says. "In math class."

The phone clicks and I've barely got the receiver back on the wall before my mom's rattling things off without even looking at me: How I'd better not *ever* talk to her like that again, especially in front of a friend, and do I think that was cool or something? Do my friends treat their parents like that? I stare at her and think, *Nothing*

I do seems cool, and yeah, Keith and Treat are worse. Only, if I say any of that, I'll be doing dishes and peeling potatoes every night until I graduate. So I just take it, then say how sorry I am and how it won't happen again. That gets her because she's a mom, except she doesn't say it's okay like usual; she says she forgives me, which is different, because it keeps the guilt on me.

Back in my room after dinner, I'm stuck after two algebra problems and spend most of the time drawing the DikNixon logo again and again. Every time I look up at Inno¢ and Edie's number, I want to call her back for help, but now I can't imagine how to ask without sounding stupid.

■

I'm early to Algebra on Wednesday, hoping to get Edie's notes, but she doesn't get there until just as the bell rings. Mr. Tomita hops up right away with a big announcement about this accident he saw coming in to school today. It gets everybody leaning forward, excited and wanting to know everything. Edie even shushes me twice, so I shut up and listen like everybody else.

Mr. Tomita says the accident happened at the intersection of Imperial Highway and Yorba Linda Boulevard. And not only did he see the accident; he also heard some of the stories the witnesses told. "I don't want to say too much," he says, rocking back and forth, "in case one of you knows the people involved. I'll just call the two people involved Mr. X and Mr. Y." Everyone's nodding like that makes sense; any way he can tell us more is fine.

Edie lets out this annoyed sigh when Mr. Tomita starts in about how the cops made people stand on one of the four corners depending on what they thought of the stories Mr. X and Mr. Y had told. He draws it on the board so we can understand better how some people believed both, some believed X and not Y or Y and not X, and how some didn't believe either. "We already know how some people are always positive," he says, "and some are always negative. They are the easy ones to understand. It's the people who are a little bit of both that we seem to have trouble with." He bounces on his toes, and Edie's sigh makes sense to me now. This isn't a story; we're moving on to a new unit and Mr. Tomita is tricking us into learning.

After class, I can barely keep up with Edie as she walks to the staircase. She hasn't said a thing, so I finally say, "You never said if you liked our band name."

Without stopping or looking at me, she says, "It's interesting."

"That means no."

Edie stops walking. "If my opinion offends you, don't ask for it."

"Offend?"

She starts walking again. "Look it up."

"I know what it means."

"Good," she says, "because I'd hate to think you need *some person from your English class* to help you with that homework too."

"What are you talking about?" I say, but Edie doesn't answer, doesn't even stop. She hits the stairs early, slipping between people and knocking others sideways as she trots her way up and away from me.

■

Right after school, me and Keith pick up his guitar and amp and go straight to Treat's. Treat has the garage open and the Bug out on the driveway. Mr. Dumovitch has taped some old egg cartons on the other wall and garage door. He's thrown a cloth tarp over the floor and it makes the garage kind of soft and less echoey. There's some folding chairs set out and an extension cord too, and when we set Keith's amp down and lean the guitar against it, it looks right with the brown boxes towering behind.

"Bitchin'," Treat says. "Let's plan to meet in the studio every day by three thirty."

"Studio?" Keith says. "The Two-Car Studio?"

Treat steps up to Keith, the Mohawk reaching out over the top of Keith's head like a wave about to crash on him. "Any-where you create art is a studio."

Treat likes the logo with *Dik* on top of *Nixon*. He covers the bottom words with his fingers so just >*I*< shows. "People will recognize this after they get used to seeing it over *Nixon*. Pretty soon, all we'll need is the top part. Like how people know it's the Dead Kennedys just by seeing the tomahawk or the Clash when all they see is the guy bent over, smashing his guitar."

"I didn't know that," Keith says.

"That's because I was talking about cool people," Treat says. "Not you."

Me and Treat laugh. Keith walks over to the back wall of boxes. "What if we drew the logo real huge on these boxes?" He looks at Treat. "When we have the garage door open, people will see it behind us while we're playing."

Treat steps over to the wall and outlines the logo with his hand. "Yeah. We could pull a few boxes out to stand on too. That way we'll be taller than the crowd in the driveway."

They both look back my way and out the garage door like there's a hundred people standing on the driveway.

"Hello?" I say. "We have one guitar, no drummer, and no micro-phone."

"Wait," Treat says and runs into the house. A second later he's back. He's got a bullhorn and sets it down on a chair, like, *Ta-da!*

"Are we going to protest drummers?" Keith says.

I tap Keith in the chest with the back of my hand. "No, it's like *Starsky & Hutch*. We're going to try to get them to come out of the studio with their hands up."

Keith picks up the bullhorn and says, "Just drop your drum-sticks and come on out. We don't want anyone to get hurt."

Treat shakes his head. He flips on the amp, picks up the gui-tar, and walks it over to me. "When I say 'four,' start strumming really fast and keep strumming until I hold up my fist."

He grabs the bullhorn from Keith and says, "One-two, one-two-three-four!"

I fling my hand down, smacking it against the guitar, and as it comes up, each string punches a finger. The amp fires out this whin-ing, deep *twang-twang*, like a hundred nuns playing acoustic guitars.

Treat leans back and holds the bullhorn to his mouth, point-ing it at the rafters. "You don't care / that I don't care / and I don't care / that you don't care." It sounds like Treat's screaming from the other end of a tube you have up to your ear. It's mixing with the music and vibrating in my chest. "No one cares that we don't care / so all we do / is stare, stare, stare / all we do / is stare!" Treat's arm flies up, his fist tight, and I stop just like he said. The last *twang*s crackle out of the amp. My hand is throbbing, red and hot, but I hold it up in a fist like Treat's.

Keith falls into a chair. "Holy shit. That sounded real."

Treat sits down in another chair, wrapping his arms around himself with the bullhorn sticking out the side. "See?"

I do see. I see people on the driveway, crowding around, pogoing all over the place, crashing into each other. Treat's jumping around and singing. Keith's on a box, strumming away, his eyes relaxed and cool. I'm up on a box too, my hands on the guitar in all the right places. And Astrid's in the front of the crowd, her hair tied back with a big bow that's more cute than pretty, her arms over her head, fingers snapping to the song. It's not sexy like I want it to be, but she looks good. Then Edie appears. She's wearing that white shirt and the puka shells, standing perfectly still, even with everyone bouncing all around her. She's glancing at Treat and Keith and everyone else but keeps looking back at me, her arms wrapped around a folder and pulled up to her chest and that *I know something you don't know* grin across her face.

"What do we do next?" I say.

The Anti-Mickey

Thursday in Algebra I'm taking real notes because Edie isn't talking to me. I'm working on the DikNixon logo in the margins too, making ones that match the one on my folder. When class is over, Edie grabs the folder and taps the logo. "So *this* is how you write it?"

I nod.

She hands back my folder, and her smirk appears. "Are you sure that's English?"

We walk together and I tell her how it's supposed to work, people seeing the logo so much they'll start to know exactly what it means even without the *Nixon* part.

"Where?" she says.

"I don't know. Around?"

"Okay." She starts for the stairs. "See you . . ." she says, and waits until she's a couple steps up before yelling back, "around."

■

Friday morning, it looks like a ticker-tape parade hit campus overnight. There's squares of notebook paper everywhere and I'm about to grab one when Keith says, "You're not going to pick up someone else's trash, are you?" It makes me wonder if it's some kind of joke they play every year to mess with freshmen, so I don't pick anything up. We just go to class.

In Algebra, Edie is almost completely back to being Edie now. She says hi to me as I sit down and even smiles. Her hair is all up, shiny and kind of pushed forward. As cool as it looks on her, for some reason my eyes go to her neck because, I don't know, I can see so much of it now. It's not like girls are posing in *Playboy* to show off their naked necks, but you don't always see a neck all smooth and soft and exposed like that. It's weird that it can look that good. I mean, it's just Edie's neck.

While Mr. Tomita is confiscating confetti from people who are showing it to each other, she slips me a note:

(Check One)

☐ *I am going to the football game tonight*
☐ *I think I'm too cool to go to the football game tonight*
☐ *I think, therefore I am (and I am going to the football game)*
☐ *I'm not a >I<, but I play one in my band (and I am not going to the game)*

Me and Keith have to be at the Two-Car Studio right after school for band stuff, but I could still probably make the game. Astrid will be there on the sidelines. Plus, Edie will probably be there with her friends, so I could sit with girls and not look like a total loser. And it's not like my dad is going to surprise me with tickets to a baseball game tonight or something. He'll get home late, say he has an overtime Saturday shift, and go to bed early. So I make a new choice and check: *I thought, therefore I am (going. If I can get a ride).*

After class, Edie tells me Cherise's parents are giving them a ride and to have a good weekend if she doesn't see me at the game. Most of the confetti is gone now; just a couple pieces, wrinkled and dirty, are swirling around people's feet as they rush to class. Astrid's at her locker, her back to me, wearing varsity cheer pants, which are maroon and tight and a trap: The stripes hug her legs and curve so perfectly around her backside you can forget how long you've been obviously staring at her. I'm ready when she turns around, just about to flash my eyes forward like they've been where they're supposed to be the whole time. But her head is down, a piece of that confetti in her hand, and then she's looking up and tapping another cheerleader on the shoulder.

There's no way the confetti is a trick if Astrid's looking at it, so when I get to English I ask Treat if he's seen it, but he hasn't. Mrs. Reisdorf starts class saying we need to put any slips of paper we've found away, and to stop talking about whatever it is. "We don't know what it is," somebody says, and Mrs. Reisdorf says then that's all the more reason to stop talking about it and to open our books to 463 for the author introduction to *Our Town.*

•

Keith has confetti in his hand on the way to lunch. "Look," he says, bug-eyed as he hands over the paper.

It's just a line of typed words, but they're not from a typewriter. Each letter is made up of all these dots, which is weird, but what's even weirder is what it says: >I< *Nixon is back.*

"Did you do this?" I say.

Keith says his dad doesn't have a dot-matrix printer at home. We figure Treat must since his dad makes computers, but when we get to the Bog, Treat says, "Did one of you guys do it?"

All three of us are grinning and looking at each other like somebody is going to admit it. Then Edie comes marching up, a piece of confetti in her hand. "Why didn't you tell me about this?" she says.

Some guy near us holds up the confetti he was showing his friends and says, "Do you guys know what this is?"

Edie turns and looks at the guy like he's an idiot. "Duh. You've never heard of the band DikNixon?"

Treat grins and as soon as the Mohawk starts nodding, the guy says, "Yeah, DikNixon is awesome." His friends nod too, like they've been listening to DikNixon for years. "I just didn't know if this meant they're coming back here."

"They are," Treat says. "So get ready."

When the guy and his friends go back to talking to each other and Edie leaves, I ask, "Seriously, who did this?"

"Does it matter?" Treat says. "It's done. It's working."

Keith's still watching Edie as she walks away, and it takes

him a second to realize we're watching him watch her. "What?" he says.

"We need to jam tonight," Treat says. "Don't lose focus."

It sounds so cool, so exactly what I want to tell Astrid the next time we're taking out the trash together. I almost forget we don't have drums, or a bass guitar, or anything else. "We need instruments."

Keith scratches his chin. "Yes. A fine point."

Treat looks out of the Bog toward the band room. "We could 'borrow' some things."

A cartoon of Keith rolling some big drum across campus in the middle of the night flashes in my head. Then it's me in the confessional, asking if it's a sin to steal instruments for the punk band you started so people will think you're cool and this cheerleader will start liking you in ways that you hope will have you back in the confessional every week for doing things with her that, if you're honest, you won't be sorry about. "No," I say to Treat. "That would make us a gang, not a band."

Treat nods and grins and says, "And DikNixon is not a crook."

I'm laughing right away and Keith is quiet. I almost want to tell him it's a Watergate joke just so he'll say, *I thought Watergate was a dam.* But Keith's still got his hand on his chin, still thinking, and then he says, "Here's what we can do: I'll tell my dad the band needs to practice at our house. Then we'll bring Treat over, and as soon as my dad sees the Mohawk, he'll buy us anything we need if we promise to go somewhere else."

Keith looks at Treat, then me. No grins. No punch line.

"Would your dad really do that?" I say.

"Oh yeah," Keith says. "He's afraid of anyone whose hair is longer than a flattop."

Treat says he has no problem being scary if it'll help the band. After that, the plan just fuses together. Keith will ask his dad to drive us to the football game tonight. We'll meet at his house. Treat will be Treat. We'll go to the game, get a ride home, Treat being Treat, and on Saturday we'll meet at Treat's house to make up a shopping list for Keith to take back to Mr. Curtis.

When I get to my locker after lunch, van Doren is there talking to one of the guys from Filibuster. "All I know is, I've never heard of these guys."

"Me neither," the other guy says, "but do you think they're coming here? Like Black Flag did at Katella?"

Van Doren doesn't even look at me as I slide down and start opening my locker. He hands the other guy a book and says, "After that riot? They'd be scared to let Barry Manilow do the morning announcements at Katella."

"Well," the other guy says, "DikNixon is going to be somewhere around here."

"Hooray," van Doren says, flat and low, like someone just told him he'd been drafted. He's so annoyed, he forgets to drop anything on me.

■

I get to Keith's early. He's just out of the shower, ripped jeans on and a towel around his neck. "I can't figure out a shirt," he says.

I don't have anything maroon to wear to the game, so I'm wearing my red paisley, spotty and bleached and totally punk rock. Keith doesn't have any maroon either, but he's got a closet full of red T-shirts from vacations: Maui, Taos, Vail, Disneyland, and Disney World. "Wear Mickey," I say.

Keith holds up the Disneyland shirt. "Treat will kill me just out of principle."

I grab it. "We'll rip the sleeves off and cut some slashes in it."

Keith rummages through his desk for scissors. "But it'll still be Mickey."

"It'll be Punk Mickey."

By the time the doorbell rings, we've sliced Mickey up good and put a Mohawk on him with a black marker. We fly past Mr. Curtis on the staircase and let Treat into the front hallway. He's wearing his best holey jeans and a spiked dog collar. His black shirt shows through his sleeveless Levi's jacket and his combat boots are shined up, blacker than ever. "What's with Mickey?" he says.

Keith looks at me and I say, "It's the Anti-Mickey."

"Bitchin'."

Mr. Curtis steps between me and Keith and stops. "Well . . . ," he says and doesn't move for a second. "You must be Treat." Mr. Curtis sticks out his hand.

Treat grabs it so fast and hard their hands pop. "Nice to meet you, sir."

"Yes," Mr. Curtis says. "You boys pile in the car. I'll go grab my keys."

Me and Keith grin as we lead Treat through the house to the garage. Even with the "sir," we know Mr. Curtis must be running to the kitchen to ask Keith's mom, *Have you seen this kid? Are we okay with this?*

Mr. Curtis has one of those new Buicks with the square head-lights, the seats squeaky and crunchy and smelling like dress shoes. And everything moves with the touch of a button. Really *Star Wars*.

Keith starts in on his dad right away about the band and how we're ready to start practicing, how my garage is way too crowded while their house is perfect because we could practice late and I'd just be a block from home.

From the backseat, I can't tell how Mr. Curtis is taking it. He's wearing these pilot sunglasses, his mouth steady like he's keeping his eyes on the road and barely listening. Then he says, "What about your parents, Treat?"

"What about them?"

"Would they be worried if you walked home late at night?"

"Nah."

Mr. Curtis keeps staring straight ahead. "Not even with all the news about kidnappings and child molesters?"

Keith looks at his dad with his eyes bugging. "What are you talking about, Dad? What child molesters?"

"I'm just saying, his parents may not be comfortable with him walking home alone at night."

"Nah," Treat says. "They think people are basically good inside, so stuff like that doesn't bother them."

Mr. Curtis nods and smiles. "Well, they sound like good Christians. Strong in their faith."

The first time I met Mr. Curtis, he said, "So your family moved all the way out here on their own? They sound like good Christians, letting the Lord guide them like that. Strong in their faith."

"We're not Christians," I had said. "We're Catholics."

Back in Paterson, everyone was Catholic. That, or Jewish. Just because you didn't see a guy in church didn't mean he wasn't Catholic. My uncle Ryan hadn't been to church since Grandpa Houghton's funeral, but every Christmas Eve, while everyone else went to midnight mass, he sat home with a glass of wine and watched the pope on TV from Rome.

When I told Mr. Curtis I was Catholic, he said, "You could think of Catholicism and Christianity as different things. A lot of people do. But a lot of people would say they're essentially the same thing. That's what I think. We're both followers of Christ, Reece. We'll all be saved come Judgment Day."

"My parents aren't Christians," Treat says. "They're Unitarians."

Mr. Curtis moves his head sideways a little. "You're a Unitarian Universalist?"

"I'm not." Treat laughs. "My parents are. I'm an atheist."

Mr. Curtis takes off his sunglasses and stares at Treat in the rearview mirror. I don't know what's keeping us on the road, though I'm sure Mr. Curtis would say faith. "Atheist?" he says. "Is that so?"

"Yeah, I don't believe any of that religion crap."

Keith can't look. He's staring out the window like there's something so amazing just over there, just on the other side of that other thing.

"Who do you think made the universe?" Mr. Curtis says.

"I don't know," Treat says. "I wasn't there."

"God made it, Treat. He made it for all of us."

Treat straightens up and nods, the Mohawk scraping against the roof lining. "Yeah. Right after we made God."

Even though the sun is pretty much hidden away now, Mr. Curtis puts his sunglasses back on. "Yeah," he says without sounding annoyed, like maybe he's on Treat's side. "You could see it that way. I don't, but some people do. Some people think it takes more faith to be an atheist than to believe in God."

"Thanks," Treat says.

"But what if Christians are right and atheists are wrong, Treat? Wouldn't it be a good idea to try and believe? Just in case?"

"I never thought of it like that before," Treat says. "Preventative maintenance."

We stop at a red light, the whole car quiet and everyone looking out the windows. The Buick hums to a kind of rhythm that's broken with a quiver about every three seconds.

"Bitchin'," Treat says out of nowhere. "Look at that boss 280."

We all look out the back window by Treat. There's an orange Datsun 280ZX behind us, its body molded into curves and low, flat hills.

Mr. Curtis says, "You like those Japanese cars, Treat?"

"I love the Z's."

"A lot of people think those cars are ugly as sin."

Treat says, "Doesn't the Bible say, 'Beauty is in the eye of the beholder'?"

Mr. Curtis grins. "Maybe in a roundabout way. But you're right. Some people might think they're ugly. But they don't see them the way an engineer does. Have you seen those Hondas?" He turns back around to check the stoplight, then looks at Treat in the rearview. "Ugly as sin. But that's a great little engine they've got there. And when they start making those cars look nicer, Ford and GM better watch out."

The light turns green and that Z shoots past us at the speed of light.

Mr. Curtis nods as the Buick pushes us back in our seats and pulls us forward. "Look at that. He doesn't carry half the weight of this boat."

Treat looks around the Buick. "Why'd you buy this?"

"Politics, Treat. My company has a lot of government contracts, so it wouldn't look too good if I pulled up in a hot little Japanese number."

"Oh, so you're a sellout."

You might think that'd make Mr. Curtis mad, but he laughs and pats Keith on the shoulder. "Sometimes you have to keep the people you work for happy to keep the people you *really* work for happy."

The rest of the drive, Mr. Curtis's hand rests on Keith's shoulder, which keeps Keith frozen and quiet until we pull into the Del Taco parking lot across the street from the stadium. "I'll be back at nine to pick you boys up."

Keith slips away from his dad and out the door. "Make it ten."

Mr. Curtis leans over, looking out the open door. "Nine thirty."

Keith leans in. "Nine forty-five."

Before Mr. Curtis can answer, Treat yanks Keith away from the door and says, "Nine'll work, Mr. Curtis. Thanks." He shuts the door and waves good-bye.

"Why'd you do that?" Keith says. "Now we can't hang out after the game."

"Exactly," Treat says.

Across the street is a park and Glover Stadium is maybe a

hundred yards in, the lights glowing over the trees, and people weaving their way through the paths like it's this giant magnet. "You know this is all propaganda," Treat says, "to get us used to uniforms and violence."

I nod real slow, like that makes complete sense and I totally agree. "Yeah, but we're stuck here now. We might as well go in."

"We're really going to the game?" Treat says.

"At least there'll be chicks," Keith says.

Treat throws his arms up. "Fine. But you're the sellouts. Not me."

The stadium is packed. Treat says he doesn't want a bunch of people looking down on him, so he pushes through everyone, stomping onto the bleachers and leading us all the way to the top.

I start scanning for Edie, but before I can even start to figure out what the back of her head might look like, there's Astrid on the fifty-yard line. Even from so far away, she's easy to pick out, her hair done up in maroon and gold ribbons, her white sweater glowing from the stadium lights. It's hard to focus on the game with her smiling and chanting and bending and stretching.

Keith's totally into the game—jumping up, sitting down, oohs and aahs. Treat's disgusted. He says we're really just Hitler Youth—everybody wearing the same colors, knowing the same cheers, and doing them on cue. "Look at everybody getting excited for blitzes and long bombs. There *will* be a World War III," he says. "And we'll be the ones who start it."

Just before halftime, the cheerleaders disappear and then, two by two, start reappearing in these skintight maroon leotards. "I'm going to the bathroom before it gets crowded," I say.

Keith stands up with me. "I'll go."

Treat's head turns so fast he nearly knocks Keith down with the Mohawk. "What are you, a girl?"

"Yeah," I say, and Keith shakes his head and sits back down.

It's crowded at the bottom of the bleachers, people heading out, heading in, some just stopped and talking. I'm up against the front rail as the whistle blows for halftime, only moving along about an inch a minute, my eyes on the field as the cheerleaders run out and start some routine, bouncing around and building things out of themselves. Astrid is everywhere, lifting other girls, spotting them, stacking them. Her boobs are smashed so tight in her outfit they don't move the entire time. It hits me that that's what they must look like when she's lying on her back. *When she's underneath you.* Then the whole squad drops to the grass and rolls over onto their stomachs. Astrid smiles, a sly red line of a grin, and my knees go soft and my heart knocks at the door like something's about to happen.

The routine ends and the cheerleaders come strutting back to the sideline, maybe five feet from me. Astrid's sweaty and glistening and gulping down water, and if I don't stop looking I'll have to hug this rail the whole second half. So I lean my head on the cold metal and close my eyes to let everything calm down.

"You gonna barf?" some guy behind me says.

"No," I say. "Just a little dizzy."

He leans in close to my ear so no one else can hear. "If you're gonna barf, get to the park. They can nail you here for being drunk at a school event, but not in the park. It's public property. Neutral. The DMZ."

I open my eyes, which are facing the ground, and see these

bowling shoes behind me—the number 10 stamped on each tongue with screaming faces penned into the zeroes.

The guy steps away before I can say thanks. His back is to me and he's wearing a hat, but not a normal one. It's a bowler, like English guys wear. I know because sometimes when Uncle Ryan was over at our house, he'd watch *Monty Python* until my dad would see it and tell him to change channels.

The guy keeps going up the steps and when he turns down a row I see who it is: van Doren. He's got suspenders on over a white T-shirt with a big red circle on it. There's a blue rectangle going through the middle of the circle and the words *Piccadilly Circus* in white. I know this isn't a real circus, but what else could it be? A pizza place? A punk band?

The stands are grouped with most of the freshmen way down the ends or up top, except for the freshmen football players and cheerleaders. They're near the middle, just outside some of the upperclassmen. Guys from the soccer team sit by girls from the soccer team who sit by girls in student government who sit by guys in student government. Some of the groups talk to the people in the groups next to them, kind of blurring things. Some don't.

Van Doren starts walking across the bleachers diagonally, stopping near some freshman pep-squad girls, then over with the soccer teams. He sits down for a few seconds, everyone stopping what they're doing and turning their heads to him while he passes out yellow flyers. Some guys shake his hand or slap his back before he climbs over a few bleachers to another group and starts all over again. If there were babies in this crowd, he'd be kissing them.

As I get back to our spot at the top of the bleachers, Edie

and her friend Cherise are sitting next to Keith. Edie's sideways, talking to Treat in the row behind her. And Treat, amaz-
ingly, is leaning down and listening to her, laughing and saying
stuff back. She glances at me, though she doesn't say anything.

I sit next to Cherise, who isn't talking to anyone. "What's up?"

"Nothing."

"Where are you guys sitting?"

She looks at me funny, like, how can I not see her sitting
right there. Then she laughs at herself and points a couple rows
down and across the aisle. "We've been right there the whole
game. Edie waved to you guys."

"She did?"

"You didn't see us."

"Sorry," I say. "It's been a good game."

"You think so?" she says. For the first time all night, I look at
the scoreboard: Esperanza—7, Katella—6. "We keep dropping
the ball."

"That's what I mean," I say. "Normally, we'd be killing these
guys by a lot more, and that's kind of boring."

"I guess," Cherise says, then goes quiet.

"I don't know if I ever told you my name," I say, and Cherise
looks at me. "It's Reece."

"I know," she says and laughs one of those girl laughs that's
real short and makes you wonder what it is she thinks she knows
about you.

"What?" I say and force a smile. "Is it because our names
rhyme?"

She waits a second. "Reece and Cherise. That's funny." She
laughs. "We could never get married."

"Yeah," I say and take a good, long look at her then, like, what if we were married? Cherise has wavy brown hair, kind of long, totally different from Edie's short black hair. It's pretty, even if it hides her face and she wears it the same way all the time. And like a lot of freshman girls, she's a little plain, kind of boyish and square, not real curvy the way juniors and seniors are. Edie has a boyish body too, but her face is different, real smooth skin and pretty cool eyes—and not because she's Japanese, more because her eyes are black and shiny and always, always curving into a smile, even when she's shushing me because she wants to hear what Mr. Tomita is saying about study groups.

At the end of the third quarter, Edie and Cherise get up to go back to their row. Edie smacks me on the shoulder as she goes past. "You know, she can't see you all the way up here."

"Who?" I say, but Edie keeps walking.

The rest of the game is Treat making more Hitler Youth comments and saying, "We should go. We can go back to Del Taco and get something to eat while we wait for Keith's dad."

"Not yet," Keith keeps saying. He's staring a few rows down and over where Edie and Cherise are sitting. When he isn't staring, he's all questions: Is Edie really smart? Is she smarter than him? Is she cool in Algebra? Where'd she go to junior high? Where does she live?

"Jeez," I say. "If you want her life story, ask her yourself."

"Okay," he says. "Can we eat lunch with her and her friends?"

"No way," Treat says. "How are we supposed to talk about band stuff, and guy stuff, in front of women?"

"Women?" I say. "It's just Edie. She's cool."

The Mohawk bobs a little. Treat looks over at Edie and Cherise. "Maybe. But not every day. And they have to come to the Bog."

Keith's smiling. "That's cool. Whichever days you say."

When van Doren gets over to Edie and sits down to hand out flyers, Keith turns his whole body to watch. Edie and Cherise and some other girls laugh and nod with everything van Doren says.

"What's he doing?" Keith says.

Treat leans forward, happy like a kid in front of a birthday cake. "He's nervous. All he heard at school today was *DikNixon, DikNixon, DikNixon.* I'll bet those flyers are for some gig they threw together about an hour ago."

"Then what are we doing?" Keith says.

Treat sits straight up. "Yeah. We need to keep the momentum."

■

The ride home is quiet, Keith and Treat staring out the windows and thinking about who knows what, and me wondering why Keith isn't putting the pressure on his dad about the band practicing at their house. The plan worked great on the way, but Mr. Curtis looks like he's happy to have Treat in the car now, like he's just one of the gang.

We pull into Treat's driveway, right behind the Bug, and Mr. Curtis says, "That belong to your family, Treat?"

"It'll be mine in about six months."

Mr. Curtis pushes down the parking break in a zip of quick metal clicks. "Mind if I have a look?"

Treat leaps out of the car. "Yeah, I'll fire it up for you."

With us all out on the driveway checking out the Bug, you'd

think Keith would start working on his dad again. He's not, though. He's shuffling around, his eyes on the concrete, rubbing his hand over the car while Mr. Curtis is talking to Treat like they're old buddies. "This a 'sixty-four?"

"'Sixty-five," Treat says.

"Gosh, she's in great shape."

"Cherry."

Mr. Curtis rubs his hands along the door handle. "You mind?"

Treat shakes his head and Mr. Curtis opens the door and sinks down in the seat. "What a classic," he says. "I had one in college."

I look at Keith. "Since we've been jamming in the garage, we have to leave the Bug out here."

Mr. Curtis looks at Treat. "Is that a fact?" Treat nods like it's a damn shame and Mr. Curtis starts tapping his lip with his finger. "We might have to do something about that."

Keith is blank, so I look at Treat, like, *Do something before he actually invites us to his house!*

Treat walks around the front of the Bug and climbs in the passenger seat. "Check this out," he says. "The radio works whether the keys are in or not." He turns the knob and drums pound through the speakers until a distorted guitar explodes and some lead singer starts screaming. Treat bobs his head with the music, the Mohawk crashing onto the dashboard every time it goes forward.

Mr. Curtis smiles at Treat and climbs out of the car. "All right, guys, we better get going." He thanks Treat the way your dad might thank a neighbor. "Real nice meeting you, Treat. You take care of that beauty."

Treat's out of the Bug and back on the driveway. "You got it, Mr. C."

On the way home, Mr. Curtis tells us our friend Treat is all right. "A lot of people might not think so because of that hair. I know I wondered at first. Or they might just see a shy kid screaming out for attention. That's what I see. A good kid." His eyes get squinty in the rearview as he smiles at me. And what can I do but smile back? "Yeah, you guys are a good influence on ol' Treat there."

Anarchy in Arkansas

Reece," my dad says. "Reece?" He's whispering and the sleep on my eyes keeps them closed. "Wake up, son. We've got a project."

I don't know where he's come from, when he got here, or how close he was until the weight of him lifts off my bed and I open an eye. The light coming through the window is a ghost, barely brighter than the dark of my room. "Throw on some clothes and come downstairs," my dad says, then walks out the door.

The smell of coffee creeps into my nose as I get to the kitchen. The milk and sugar are sitting by an empty mug. "Make yourself a cup and come out to the garage," my dad says. I'm only allowed to drink coffee when we get up early and do "man things," like hauling old beds to the dump or working on the car. He usually gets after me for using too much sugar or any milk at all. "You don't see Mr. Coffee using cream," he says, because that's Joe DiMaggio in those commercials and Joltin' Joe and Packy drink their coffee black, or maybe with a little sawdust.

The sky isn't sure what time of day it is—too black to be morning, too blue to be night. It's so cold, even for California, and I have to go back in for my Packy jacket, which is kind of weird since my dad's wearing one too. When I get to the garage, he's pulling out tool chests and setting them on the floor.

"What are you doing?" I say.

"We," he says and gets this fake grin, "are building a bar."

This is the kind of thing my dad and Uncle Ryan would do back in Jersey. They'd spend an entire weekend on some project they made up. My job was to get them beers from the fridge every once in a while. Sometimes, if I did it fast enough, they'd let me sink a screw or sand a plank. But now I'm supposed to play Uncle Ryan's part? "Don't you have to work today?"

"Not 'til nine," he says. "We'll get started today and work on the project tomorrow, too." He points at the biggest tool chest. "Circular saw."

I dig around in the chest with one hand, my coffee in the other, not even drinking it yet because that would make the warmth go away. I pull out the circular saw and he asks for the jigsaw. It's in another chest, so it takes me a little longer before I find it. "Got it."

We used to do equipment checks on the way to Yankee games: "Tickets?" he'd say. "Check." "Glove," he'd say, and I'd hold it up. "Check."

"Do you mean 'check'?" my dad says.

"Sure," I say.

"Then say 'check.'"

"That's stupid."

He looks at me and says nothing. And here's the thing about my dad: When he doesn't say anything to what you just said, he's mad or on the way to being mad, which is so not fair this time. I didn't drag him out of bed. And it's not my fault he doesn't have Uncle Ryan around for this pointless project.

"Wood putty?" he says. *Check.* "Hammer and nails?" *Check* and *Check.*

We put everything in one chest. My dad opens the garage door, saying all we need right now is the tape measure, a pad, and a pencil. Then, instead of getting in the truck, he walks across our driveway to Astrid's house.

"What are you doing?" I say.

He looks at his watch. "Don't worry, Alex is up."

Alex? I didn't know my dad ever talked to Astrid's dad. Has he been over there talking to Astrid's dad in front of Astrid? Did he bring me up in front of Astrid, like, *Little Reece will help out too on this project, Alex. It'll be cute to let him hammer a nail or two.*

My shorts are about a size too small, my shirt ripped and stained. My hair looks like who knows what. My pillow probably. "I can't go in there."

I start backing into the garage and my dad whisper-yells at me. "Reece!"

"Do this part without me."

My dad stops at the bricks on Astrid's walkway. "You need to hold the other end of the tape measure."

He's right. I take a deep breath and say, "Let me run and get a hat."

My dad takes a deep breath too and looks out at the cul-de-sac. "Hurry up."

I set my mug down to show him how fast I'll go. And I do. In an instant I've got on a hat, some jeans, and the City of Huntington Beach Water Treatment button-up shirt Treat talked me into that used to belong to a guy named Dat.

Mr. Thompson is at the front door, all smiles and handshakes, calling my dad Pat and saying, "Come in, come in." He looks me over and smiles at my shirt. Astrid's mom comes gliding out of the kitchen wearing this robe straight out of Japan, silky with weird plant patterns and those letter characters. Her hair is perfect, like she's hosting a dinner party, and you can see where Astrid gets it, you know? She hands my dad a cup of coffee without even asking him. My dad takes a sip and Mrs. Thompson says, "Isn't that nice, Pat? It's hazelnut."

"Hazelnut?" my dad says and takes another sip like he's thinking it over. "That is a nice surprise, Ashley." Then he looks at me, like, *Not a word*.

"Would you like some orange juice, Reece?" My chest goes warm like it's hugging her, because how does she know my name? Did Astrid tell her?

The living room and dining room are a snowdrift—white carpet, white leather couch, white curtains, and white pillows everywhere. It's so pure it makes the ivory-and-glass coffee table, the ivory-and-glass dining room table, and the ivory vases (with white flowers in, and etched on, them) look almost dirty.

"No, thanks," I say to the orange juice. Who needs that pressure?

Their family room is the same size as ours. Only, instead of an old couch with a new cover on it and a stereo cabinet with an eight-track player, Mr. Thompson has these cushioned red chairs with a little table between them. The little couch in the room is actually a little beaten up, but there's a pool table too. It's the nonwhite room.

Mr. Thompson asks if we can get a "complementary" wood. "White oak," my dad says and taps me to write it down on the pad. They talk about where the bar will go and how big it should be. We take measurements, and I've never been so perfect, doing everything my dad asks and doing it right the first time. I just want to get out of here before Astrid comes downstairs, silk robe and soft footsteps, messy hair and rubbing the sleep out of her eyes. It's what you'd want to wake up to every morning. But I don't want her to see me here, the official measuring-tape holder and Berlin Wall champion. The first time we're in that family room together, I need to be holding a guitar, or maybe a corsage.

We get out of there before anything goes wrong. My dad says he'll pick up everything we need after work. "We can get started building the bar tonight," he says, like it's some treat; then he leaves for work.

∎

Keith wasn't up when I knocked, so I told his mom I'd be at Treat's. It's earlier than we said, but Treat's happy to see me. He's got some ideas for my Packy jacket and shows me how to line safety pins up along the shoulder, like I'm a general in some punk army. We're totally into it, sitting on the floor with our backs against Treat's bed, putting the last pins on, when we hear the front door. Me and Treat grin at each other like it's Christmas morning.

Keith comes in the room and tosses a brown sack onto the floor.

"What is that?" I say.

Treat pulls something flat out of the bag.

"It's a car cover," Keith says. He sits down on the floor across from me, his back against the wall. "It's a gift for when the Bug's parked outside because my dad thinks you're a 'fine young man.'"

Treat stands up. "Yeah, right."

"You blew it," Keith says.

"*I* blew it? You didn't say dick after the game last night."

I wad up the sack and toss it at Keith. "He's right."

"What? I wasn't the one saying how cool Japanese cars are and going, 'Hey, check out my Bug.'"

"Look," Treat says. "Being an atheist should be enough."

Keith picks up the paper sack. "Not if you're an atheist with a cool car." He throws the sack at me but misses. Treat falls onto the bed, his whole upper body keeling over.

"Are you really an atheist?" I say.

"I'm punk rock."

"So punkers are atheists?"

Keith stands up. "I'm not an atheist."

"You don't have to be atheist," Treat says. "It's more of an anti-religion thing."

"Atheist," Keith says.

"No." Treat sits up. "You don't have to have religion to believe in God."

Keith sits back down. "Okay, I guess I'm still in the band."

I hit Keith with the sack again. "The one-instrument band."

"We'll get instruments," Treat says. "We'll just have to do something else while we figure that out." He reaches onto his nightstand and tosses a pencil and a pad of paper onto the bed. "Let's write some songs."

Keith picks up the pad. "That might be good."

We're in the room over an hour, mostly tossing the sack back and forth at each other because none of us really know how to write a song. Treat finally says we can go off later and each write some songs alone the way the Beatles did.

So we go from writing songs to deciding the kinds of songs we want to write. Treat wants anti-religion songs. Me and Keith say okay as long as they're not anti-God. We also figure we should have an anarchy song like "Anarchy in the U.K.," but it can't be "Anarchy in the USA," since in the grand scheme of things we don't really want that. "Maybe 'Anarchy in Arkansas,'" Keith says, and we agree since none of us have ever been there.

"See," Treat says, "we're in good shape. We've got a guitar, an amp, a bullhorn, and some songs on the way."

I pick up the car cover. "And this, to hide all our equipment under."

"No." Treat snatches it from me. "It's better than that. I asked and Lyle won't let us draw our logo on the boxes, so we'll draw it on this instead."

"That'd be bitchin'," Keith says. "We can take it with us to gigs, too."

Treat's eyes are getting big and he hands one end of the cover to Keith so they can stretch it out and get a good look. "It'll take some time to get the logo on there," he says. "We're going to have to get together tomorrow, too."

Keith says he's in even though it's a Sunday, and how can I say no to that, a two-thirds majority? "Me too," I say.

■

In the garage Saturday night, my dad does most of the cutting, leaving the boring stuff for me: measuring the wood, marking where the cuts should go, stacking the cut wood, and cleaning up sawdust.

When it's just support beams left to be cut, things no one will see, my dad sets me up with the wood already clamped to a vise and propped up on scrap pieces so the saw blade won't cut the worktable. The goggles are scratched all over and milky in the corners. It's amazing how once they're on they don't seem all that bad. For the millionth time my dad shows me how to use the circular saw, two hands and look ahead of your cut so you see where you're going and not where you've been. He's over my shoulder, saying, "Be careful," when I squeeze the trigger and drown him out with the whir of the saw.

The cut will only be about two inches long, but the beams are thick. The blade spits out a line of sawdust and the wood heats up, making the whole garage smell like a campfire.

We get going pretty good, me cutting and stacking the beams, my dad tossing the scrap and putting the next beam in the vise. We only need six but it goes even faster than you might think because our system is perfect.

"These look great," my dad says. "We'll get everything sanded tomorrow after church and then treat the wood."

"I can't," I say. "I'm supposed to go study with Keith."

My dad unplugs the circular saw, winding its cord around itself. "You can study on your own tomorrow night."

"But I need to study with Keith. We have flash cards and everything."

He unplugs the extension cord and starts winding it. "You have a test Monday?"

"Maybe," I say and look my dad straight in the face since I'm not lying. "Mr. Krueger gives surprise quizzes on the periodic table, and then there'll be a surprise test. We have to be ready for it at any time."

He nods and puts the cord away. "So you're not going to the arcade?"

"What arcade?" I say.

My dad starts sweeping the floor. "Your mother's making her corned beef for dinner tomorrow." This is his way of saying it's okay for me to be gone on a Sunday, just as long as I'm back in time for dinner.

■

On Sundays back in Paterson, sometimes Uncle Ryan and Aunt Mary would come over after church. Uncle Ryan would walk across the front lawn with a bottle of wine in his hand, and he'd yell, "Happy Sunday," to the first person he saw. We'd watch baseball or have a catch, and my mom and Aunt Mary would cook a bunch of food. If me and Brendan had a game or a puzzle going, Uncle Ryan would say, "Mare, I'm going to join these gentlemen in their recreation. Tell Packy his presence and two glasses of wine are required."

When we went places, it was usually some restaurant my mom wanted to try. And if the weather was nice, we'd go all the way down to Seaside Heights. Aunt Mary and Mom would find a bench on the boardwalk, happy just to talk and stay out of the sand. Dad and Uncle Ryan would take all us kids down to the beach for Wiffle ball. You never knew how long we'd be down there, but you'd know it was time to go when Uncle Ryan said, "Who thinks they can beat me at air hockey?" He was usually good for a game or two before my dad gave out a handful of quarters and said, "Half an hour. And keep an eye on your sister."

On the way to dinner, Mom would send me into whichever bar Dad and Uncle Ryan had snuck into so I could tell them where to meet us.

It'd be pretty quiet until Uncle Ryan got to the restaurant. Then he'd order a beer real loud and pretend to complain about the food. "Have you felt this bread? Mickey Mantle never owned a bat this hard."

The waiter would act sorry and try to grab the bread basket.

"Hold on," Uncle Ryan would say. "Just get me another beer and I'll soften it up. Packy, you want another beer?" He wouldn't wait for my dad's answer, which always cracked me and Brendan up, seeing Dad get bossed around by his little brother. "Two more pints."

Dad laughed every time, and if he started making jokes too, we knew Mom was driving us home.

Toward the end of dinner, when Uncle Ryan went off to the bathroom, Aunt Mary would get me to go through the pockets of his army jacket for his keys. Sometimes, Dad told me to do it before Aunt Mary did. That was the only time Uncle Ryan ever got mad. "I can drive," he'd say. "How do you think I get home from work every day?"

"It's a wonder," Aunt Mary always said, and suddenly Mom would be all over me and Brendan and Colleen: "Hug your aunt and uncle good-bye."

In California, no one comes over after church. My dad makes a huge brunch for everyone: bacon, eggs, sausage, potatoes, toast, tea, coffee, juice, and blood pudding sometimes too. The real stuff. He used to get so happy making everything because when he was a kid, the oldest boy still living at home made the Sunday brunch. "My dad taught me," he'd remind me and Brendan, "and then I taught your uncle Ryan before your mother and I got married." "We know," we'd say, and then he'd tell us more stuff we already knew, how someday I'd learn too and then it would be my job to teach Brendan. He'd get all happy when he said that stuff, like it was going to be better than going to Disney World. But now he just gets it done like it's one more chore, like it's no different from our Sunday dinners, which are always ham and cabbage, or corned beef and cabbage, anything and cabbage, or mystery stew and soda bread. Basically, every flavor of boring you can imagine.

■

Keith's at the door before I'm done with brunch, so I stuff some bacon in my mouth and say I'm full. I grab my backpack and throw my jacket on. The new pins make it look more punk, more like I'm in a band, and once we're outside I thrash my hair around with my fingers until Keith says it looks like an explosion. That's when it's perfect, when you can't tell how it got the way it is or where it's going. Treat's out on the driveway with the Bug as we come down his street. He puts his finger up to his mouth when we get close and waves us into the Two-Car Studio. "Lyle and Margaret are getting in touch with the earth," he whispers. Me and Keith look at each other and Treat says, "They're meditating." He smiles like we're supposed to laugh, then shushes us when we start to.

The car cover's spread out on the floor with little black dots of permanent marker outlining the >I< logo. We start scratching away with markers, coloring it in, and every once in a while we hear chanting or a chime, like some tiny version of the bell they ring at mass.

We're starting in on the *Nixon* part when Mr. and Mrs. Dumovitch open the door from the house. They're wearing sweatpants and sandals and these shirts that look like they're made out of potato sacks.

"Looks good so far, guys."

Me and Keith harmonize for the only time ever. "Thanks, Mr. Dumovitch."

Treat's mom asks if we're going to do everything in black.

"Do we have any red?" Treat asks.

"I don't know," she says. "Did you look?"

"Kind of."

"Kind of?" she razzes him.

"Well, I was trying to be quiet, Margaret."

"All right," Treat's dad says. "Let's just calm down." He takes a good look at the car cover. "Where did this come from?"

"It's a gift from Keith's dad," Treat says. "He supports us having a band."

Mr. Dumovitch takes the rubber band out of his ponytail and fluffs his hair out. With his beard and long hair and potato-sack shirt, he looks like Jesus. "What's going on, Treat?"

"Nothing. We're just trying to make a difference, and it isn't easy."

It's quiet until Treat's mom is back with a red marker. She hands it to me and says, "Uh-oh, are we having a moment?"

Treat won't look up. "No."

"Treat," Mr. Dumovitch says. "Just talk straight. Remember what Dr. Andy says?"

Mrs. Dumovitch says, "Talk to us, sweetie."

Treat keeps scratching away at the car cover, harder and faster, giving me chills the way it squeaks. "We don't have all our instruments for the band," I say. "We had a plan to get some, only it didn't go like we thought."

Mr. Dumovitch strokes his beard like he's thinking. "What do you need?"

Treat looks up. "A bass, amp, drums, microphones, distortion pedals. Just everything."

Treat's mom puts her arm around his dad. "My brother has a bass."

"That's right," Mr. D says, and they both smile. "Remember how he'd leave it in his living room for Carol to see when they were dating?"

Mrs. D rolls her eyes. "Oh yeah," she says and does her fingers like she's quoting herself, "his 'jazz quartet.'"

"Too bad the band broke up before Carol had a chance to see them," Mr. D says, and Mrs. D covers her mouth like it's so funny she can barely stand it.

"Treat," Mr. D says, "I'll call Uncle Arvil about his bass. Will that help?"

Treat stays hunkered down with the marker in his hand. No answer.

"You boys must be getting hungry," Mrs. D says. "I'll have some fresh hummus ready in a bit."

Me and Keith thank her, and Mr. and Mrs. D go back in the house.

With Treat not talking anymore, me and Keith start quizzing each other on the periodic table: "What's *Ar*?" I say.

"Arkansas?"

"On the periodic table?"

Keith grins. "An element."

I laugh because I really don't know the answer. "We really need to study."

"We will."

"You have to promise," I say. "It'll look pretty bad if we spend all this time"—and I do my fingers like Mrs. D—"'studying' and flunk the test."

Treat stays quiet squeaking away at the car cover until the hummus is ready and we go inside. The pita bread is soft, the hummus smooth, and with so many good flavors my whole mouth has to work to make sense of it all. There's olives and peppers and other stuff too, everything so much better than anything that's waiting for me at home. Mrs. D says to eat all we want, and I do, too much.

When I get home later, the smell of the corned beef about kills me. And no matter how annoyed my dad looks, I can barely touch anything on my plate.

Mr. Explosive Particle

Treat wasn't in English this morning, which is kind of weird considering he wasn't sick or anything yesterday. Maybe kind of mad for no real reason, but not sick. It's probably good, though, because at lunch Edie and Cherise find me and Keith in the Bog and we all eat together for the first time. Edie eats normal stuff, a sandwich and chips and some little carrots. Cherise's food looks like one of those plates your aunt puts on the coffee table at Thanksgiving: crackers, cheese, broccoli, and celery. She says she's a vegetarian and me and Keith look at her, like, *Why?* She starts talking about slaughterhouses and saturated fat, artificial colors and sweeteners, red dye number five and food additives. Keith's munching down his Fritos and says, "What about the napalm they use to keep the bugs off that celery?" That really gets Cherise fired up, and she says more in an hour than she's said all year.

Edie asks if we heard about the awesome show DikNixon played at the old train station in Fullerton on Saturday. Me and

Keith have no idea what she's talking about. "I heard it," she says and does this quick, sly smile. "I said it to myself, heard it, and then told everyone in first period what I'd heard." She smiles again and I could hug her for making us sound so cool.

Cherise says she heard about it too and told everyone in her third-period class and someone there said they'd heard about it in World History and now they can't wait until DikNixon comes here.

That makes me happy too. Not hug-happy with Cherise, but race-to-Treat's-house-right-after-school-happy. Which me and Keith do.

Mr. Dumovitch meets us at the front door and says Treat will see us later in the week. He doesn't say why or anything, only that Treat won't be back at school until Wednesday or Thursday.

"You think Treat's okay?" I ask Keith as soon as we're heading back up the hill and I know Mr. Dumovitch can't hear us even if he's standing next to the Bug on the driveway.

"He's probably dyeing his hair purple," Keith says, "and doesn't want us to see it until it's just the right shade of weird."

At the top of the hill, Keith says he'd better just go home; he's got some catching up to do in Algebra. I tell him that sounds better than the bar project I have to work on. Keith looks at me like I'm speaking Russian so I explain what the project is and how embarrassing it is that it's for Astrid's dad.

Keith slaps his own head. "You know how lucky you are? Her house?" He stops walking. His face has gone serious, no smirk, just eyes rounding and tight lips as he waits for me to stop, step back, and hear something big, like maybe he knows where Jimmy

Hoffa is buried big, or who really shot JFK big. "You should steal a pair of her panties."

"Are you insane?" I start walking.

"No, listen." He steps up next to me. "College guys do it all the time. A panty raid."

"But I'm not a college guy, you perv."

We stop and wait for a break in the traffic at Yorba Linda Boulevard. Keith has me trapped, so I have to hear him out. "It's not a perv thing. You just steal the panties, slip them into a folder, write *Top Secret* across it, and then bring them to her at school. Tell her some guys in the locker room were trying to sell them and you went crazy with rage."

"Like I saved her reputation."

Keith nods, tight-lipped. Still no grin. "Exactly."

The blur of cars passes and I give Keith a smack on the back of the head. "You're a total perv." Then I'm off, across five lanes of traffic, Keith right behind me, yelling, "The Wall! We must make it over the Wall!"

■

After dinner, my dad needs me to dig a metal filing out of his right thumb before we go to work on the bar project. It's on the bottom side, the bendy part below the knuckle where everything is tighter and even the slightest touch of the needle has him wincing. I'm being careful but he's jumpier than usual and we're getting nowhere. Suddenly, so fast it even surprises me, I dig in deep with the needle, pushing the metal just enough to get the tip of it with the tweezers. A groan and gust of air comes flying out of my dad like somebody punched him in the stomach. There's a lot of blood too, but it doesn't bother me. I've got that jagged little dagger in the tweezers and hold it up for him to see. His eyes are glasses of water about to spill, and he looks more tired than relieved, but that doesn't bother me either. I just think, *Good.*

In the garage, on the wall over the workbench, is a piece of notebook paper with the bar drawn in top and side views. It looks like a simple *L* from the top. The side views are complicated, though, with shelves and cabinets and a little sink. We measure and cut more wood the whole time, me doing the measuring and my dad doing the cutting. We're listening to an oldies radio station. Every time the saw stops screaming there's another "Teen Angel" or "Johnny Angel" or "Teenager in Love" whining about his poor, desperate life. Finally, I say I need to go take a shower so I'm ready for school tomorrow and my dad says that's fine, he'll finish up a few things and see me inside, but I don't see him inside. He's still going at it when I crawl into bed a couple hours later.

•

Tuesday morning, me and Keith get obliterated by our first periodic table quiz. There was simple stuff like the definitions of atomic weight and numbers, protons and electrons, neutrons, and what it means when things bond, and I think I did okay there. But there was also an actual table with some parts left blank and we were supposed to fill that in, and, well, now I really know what it means when people say they blanked out.

So it's kind of a relief to be back in the garage with my dad on Tuesday night, measuring and drilling little holes in the wood for the screws. He spent last night framing the spot in the counter where the sink will go and cutting all the cabinet doors to the right sizes. Now we just need to sand everything. Big surfaces with the power sander and a sanding board, corners and edges with little square sheets that get so hot they burn through and scald my fingers. We're hardly talking because my dad is clueless about baseball right now and there's no way I'm telling him anything about Astrid or DikNixon. Still, it's not too bad until he starts talking about work. He's making parts with the lathe for some satellite and he's kind of excited about it. Keith's dad works on the heat tiles that go on the space shuttles, which is better, only he doesn't make the parts; he designs them. Somebody else makes them, somebody like my dad. I go from feeling bored to feeling embarrassed for my dad. Then I'm annoyed that songs like "Return to Sender" say the totally opposite thing of songs like "Please Mr. Postman." How can anybody like this stuff? It's all so sad.

■

Treat's not at school Wednesday so I beg Keith to come by my house after dinner, and he does. He works in the garage with us for maybe half an hour, including the breaks he takes every couple minutes to let the sandpaper cool down. Then Keith dusts his hands off and says he's got a lot of homework.

My dad thanks him for his work and I walk him to the driveway. Keith's got good news: He told his mom how much Mr. Dumovitch was doing for us and she got all over his dad about it. Now his dad is taking him out this weekend to buy things for the band.

"Your dad didn't see right through that?"

"Probably," Keith says, "but he's not in charge."

Keith heads up the sidewalk and my dad steps out of the garage. We watch him walk all the way out of the cul-de-sac and across the street to his house. "That Keith's a good kid," my dad says.

"Yeah," I say. "He's a teen angel."

I don't mean it as a joke for my dad but he laughs, the first time in a long time, so I go with it, fake a laugh of my own, then ask if maybe we can change the radio station for a little while.

At first my dad tries humming along with Adam and the Ants and Madness. Then the Dead Kennedys come on. "Is that guy saying, 'Holiday in Cambodia'?" my dad says. He walks over to the radio and leans in like maybe that'll make him understand. "Who are these guys?"

I stare at the dials like somebody just asked me to multiply the atomic weight of hydrogen by the atomic weight of helium. There's no way I'm going to say the word *Dead* and then *Kennedys*, not one right after the other, not even in the same sentence, probably not in the same day. "It's just a punk band."

My dad clicks off the radio. "You got that right. Bunch of punks."

"It's just music."

My dad's shaking his head. "That's not music, Reece. I've seen these guys on the news with their army boots and hair standing up every which way. They scream just like that," he says, flicking his thumb at the radio, "and get everyone in the room crazy, running into each other. It's not normal."

I want to explain how it's antiwar and anti-imperialism and

really a good thing. That's what Treat says. But I can't imagine my dad seeing it that way, so we work a little longer in the quiet until we call it a night. My dad says it should all be dry and ready to install on Saturday, which means I've got to start figuring out some work clothes that don't make me look like a plumber or something.

■

Treat's back in English on Thursday, only he's at the front of the room until the bell rings, busy getting all the handouts and homework he missed. After class, he pats me on the Packy patch, says, "See you at lunch," and barrels out the door.

Edie and Cherise are in the cafeteria, the first time all week we don't see them in the Bog, and me and Keith are already sitting on the edge of the planter and eating by the time Treat gets to us.

"Hey," Keith blurts out with his mouth full of chips. "Where you been?"

Treat steps up in front of us, a little out of breath. "Nowhere." He pulls a couple cassette tapes out of his lunch bag and hands one to me and one to Keith: *The Nixon Tapes.*

"Get to know this stuff," he says. "Then write some songs for Monday."

"Is that what you've been doing?" Keith says. "Writing songs?"

Treat starts pulling food out of his bag. "Something like that."

"Maybe we should get together today," Keith says and Treat shakes his head. "Then what about Friday?"

"I've got plans." Treat takes a big bite of a sandwich with the thinnest, grainiest-looking bread you've ever seen.

Keith leans forward and looks at Treat. "I thought the band was our plan."

Treat stares Keith down without saying anything, his eyes bulging and jaw flexing while he chews.

"We'll get on it," I say and change the subject to *Guess who got in a fight with what's his name and do you know about the book report we have to do?*

I leave the tape in my pocket the rest of the day. The last thing I need is van Doren knocking it out of my hand with a book while I'm trying to put it in my locker and then the interrogation: *Is this DikNixon? Wait, are you DikNixon? What a joke.* But none of that happens. Right after school, he drops a pair of sweaty tube socks on me. Then he says, "I'm sorry." When I hand them up, he fires a fastball into the closest trash can. "What's the point?" he says and spins back to his locker. "Can somebody tell me? What's the point?"

Since he asked twice I figure I'm supposed to answer. "I don't know."

"Who does?" he says and slams the locker shut and starts walking away. "It's all bullshit. Complete bullshit."

■

Mr. Krueger has the periodic table quizzes in his hand Friday morning. "I had these ready to go yesterday," he says. "I've just been thinking about what to say." He peels one off the top. "According to one of you, and I'm sure a few of you agree, the definition of a proton is as follows: 'An explosive particle used often in the manufacturing of missiles.'" He leans on the podium. "I like *Star Trek* too. I know what a proton torpedo is. But if I had one, I'd shoot this person with it." We all laugh, because who else bawls you out like that?

Keith looks over at me like he got caught eating dessert before dinner, and Mr. Krueger keeps going. "I know my quizzes aren't easy, people. They're not supposed to be." He shakes his head, then nods, and it's hard to tell if he's agreeing with himself or saying no or just dizzy with all the information flying around in his head. "I could give you multiple choice and some of you would do well guessing, but science isn't multiple choice. The answers don't always present themselves." He slides the quiz he talked about into the middle of the stack. "I gave partial credit to 'Mr. Explosive Particle.' He has no idea what he's talking about, but he at least attacked the problem with creativity rather than leaving it blank. Better to try and fail than never try at all." He begins handing the quizzes back. "I won't be this generous next time. Charity is a rare and wonderful gift; don't come to depend on it."

My fourteen out of twenty on the quiz seems pretty good until I do the math. It's a C−. Keith, or "Mr. Explosive Particle," got a D. Instead of laughing it off, though, he gets serious after class. His dad said that once he sinks some cash into this band project, none of it better come between Keith and good grades. Keith says he needs the band, so now he needs the grades too. Right now, I don't know if my parents would even notice my grades, but I definitely need the band. And who knows what Treat needs. Hopefully the band too.

Solitary Man

Saturday morning there's bacon and eggs in the air, but it's all wrong because only my dad is up. It almost feels like one of those Tuesdays back in Paterson where I'd come out of my bedroom and Uncle Ryan would be there in the kitchen, a huge breakfast ready to go as soon as everyone woke up.

I'm wearing my best ripped jeans and Property of New York Yankees T-shirt, and my hair's done so it's perfectly messed up and my dad will think that's how I slept on it. "I'm not having anything," I say.

"Eat," he says. "I scrambled the eggs the way you like."

My stomach feels quivery, like the first at bat of the season, so I pick up the bacon. My dad sips his coffee and explains how we'll carry everything in so that it's laid out in the order we'll put it together. I nibble the bacon long enough that the eggs are still sitting there when my dad stands up. He looks down at them, sighs, and says, "Let's go."

Mr. Thompson's excited when we get to the front door, and he takes us straight back to the family room. Everything's cleared out and the floor feels spongy and reeks of new carpet. Mr. Thompson's going on about stain-resistant chemicals and my dad's nodding like that's the most amazing thing ever.

"I guess you won't know when Astrid has parties now," my dad jokes.

"Well, that's what neighbors are for," Mr. Thompson says, and they laugh. "Seriously, though," he says. "She always tells us."

Mrs. Thompson comes in the room wearing her silky robe, carrying a tray with cups on it. "Breakfast shake?" she says and holds the tray out to my dad.

He grabs two, shoving one into my hand without asking. "Thanks, Ashley. You're too good to us."

The stuff in the cup really looks like a shake, kind of frosty and thick, and it's nice until the smell hits you. My dad tips his back and powers the whole thing down in three chugs.

Mr. Thompson grins. "One of my fraternity brothers could do that."

"Do you like it, Pat?" Mrs. Thompson says.

My dad wipes his mouth with the back of his hand. "Oh yeah. You'll have to give Eileen the recipe."

"Oh, it's easy," Mrs. Thompson says. "Plain yogurt, skim milk, brewer's yeast, whey protein, soy, lecithin, and a little vanilla extract."

My dad nods, like, *Yes, I thought I detected a little vanilla extract in there.*

Mr. Thompson pats his belly. "I'm starting to get rid of this flat tire here. Diet and exercise."

"Honey," Mrs. Thompson says. "Why don't you help out today?"

My dad is straight-faced, nodding. "We could use an extra hand, Alex. If you've got time." He pulls out the plans he sketched and hands them over and you'd think it was Lou Gehrig's autograph the way Mr. Thompson takes the notebook paper so gentle, studying every last pencil scratch.

"Wonderful," he says.

"Great," my dad says. He wrinkles his forehead and nods the same way he does when Brendan wants to help change a spark plug or Colleen wants to pour her own milk.

We get started and Mr. Thompson has a hundred questions for every task my dad gives him, then re-asks a minute later. It gives me a chance to go slow and time things so that I'm installing a hinge or lining up a cabinet every time I hear a noise somewhere else in the house. I'm thinking, *If Astrid comes gliding into the room, I want her to know I can really sink a screw, you know?* Then I sink one at the wrong angle so it's not totally flush and my dad's all over me about staying focused. He looks at Mr. Thompson and at the exact same time they say, "Teenagers," like they're singing a duet. It's the only thing I've done wrong in an hour. I'm not the one who tried to attach a hinge, which moves, where a joint, which does not move, was supposed to go. And when Mr. Thompson put one of the cabinet doors on backward, my dad didn't get high-and-mighty on him. He just said, "Let me help you out, Alex. Those are tricky."

If Uncle Ryan were here, we'd have been done in half an hour and he'd be at the new bar, grinning and saying, "Let's test this thing out."

When my dad starts explaining to Mr. Thompson, again,

how we'll putty all the screw holes and he won't see the screws, and even shows him how he bought a shade of putty that matches the wood, I ask to use the bathroom.

"You'll have to use the one upstairs," Mr. Thompson says. "I just had tile laid in this one yesterday." He stops working and tells my dad about "this thug" who laid the tile, and my dad's shaking his head like it's such a tragedy.

It's quiet upstairs and Astrid's shut door is right across from the bathroom. I walk soft, listening for Astrid's sleep breathing and happy that even if I can't hear it I don't hear snoring, either.

The bathroom counter is a mad scientist's laboratory, only with makeup and lotion and perfume bottles spread across it. I'm letting the diet shake go where it belongs, looking down at a basket full of magazines. There's a *Tiger Beat* peeking out from the pile, but right on top is a *Cosmopolitan*. The woman on the front is staring so hard and so sexy it's like she sees me. Her earrings look like they're worth more than our house. And her dress has me needing a deep breath. It's not just that it's got no sleeves so you can see her creamy arms; the whole middle has been ripped out so you can see her belly button, and her cleavage, and her collarbone, and *Oh my God she can't be wearing a bra if I'm seeing all that.* Astrid reads this? What does it tell her?

I need to look somewhere else if I'm ever going to fit back into my jeans, and there, in the bathroom mirror, I see them: Astrid's panties. There's a bunch of them slung over the shower rod with matching bras—white lacy ones like you'd expect, and a maroon one to match our school colors. There's one pair of black ones, the stringiest and smallest, and my eyes blur for a second. My brain can almost put Astrid in them, and now the smell of lotions and potions wafting around the bathroom is like the soft parts of a girl you're not supposed to touch if she's not your girlfriend—her cheek and the back of her neck, her stomach and thighs. I still haven't put myself away, and there's no way I'm going to be able to now unless I do what my old confirmation teacher told us was "officially forbidden by the Catholic Church. But," he went on, "you should also know is scientifically natural and—now, this is my opinion here and not the Church's—nothing to be embarrassed about. Just be discreet." Then he told us what *discreet* meant.

I'm trying to be discreet fast. My breath goes shaky and loud, like holding a shell to my ear, and for a few seconds it's me and Astrid right there on the bathroom counter until a crack rings out. My heart launches from my chest and I'm stuffing myself back into my jeans fast, trying to zip up, and did I ever lock the bathroom door? What if Mr. Thompson walks in? Or Astrid? I peg-leg step over to the door to keep my dick from breaking in two and turning into hafnium. It's locked. Has been the whole time. Then I let go of the breath I didn't know I was holding and start washing my hands in cold water. This should calm me down, but Astrid's soap leaves a spicy perfume on my hands. And as I go to dry them on a towel slung over the shower rod, it hits me: This must be the towel Astrid used last night after her shower. It's been everywhere: *All. Over. Her. Body.* I'm inches from the black bra and panties and somehow the bra brushes across my cheek. The palm of my hand folds around one of the cups. The lace panties are scratchier than you might think and they weigh about a feather squared. And in the mirror, you can't even tell they're in my front pocket.

I have this vision of the panties slipping out when I'm leaning over to hold a bracket and the whole Thompson family looking at me like I'm some perv, which I must be because even before hanging them back up I know I'm going to let them brush across my cheek. They feel so sexy on my face and I don't know why but I want to smell them. I mean, who does that? Me, I guess, because I press the thin crotch against my nose soft and take a deep breath like I'm at the doctor's office. It smells like nothing, maybe detergent, and I let the panties glide across my cheek once more before hanging them up.

Now, as much as I wanted to see Astrid in her robe and pillow hair, if she's waiting outside the door, I don't know how I'll wipe the panty-sniffing look off my face. My chest and arms and legs are warm and tingly and my face is so flushed with school spirit that splashing cold water on it only gets me back to almost normal.

I take another deep breath and open the door. It's clear all the way back downstairs, where my dad is sanding out scratches on the cabinet door Mr. Thompson dropped when he was trying to install it. My dad doesn't give me anything to do and that's the worst. If Astrid comes downstairs now, I'm not sure how to look at her without feeling like I stole something; you know, like I saw the answers to the test before taking it.

We're cleaning up when the phone rings, and a second later Mrs. Thompson is jingling keys, saying she's off to pick up Astrid from Karen's.

■

After church Sunday, my dad lets us pick up doughnuts *and* makes a big Irish breakfast with all the meats and puddings. He brags about our bar project, so my mom makes Brendan and Colleen each say something interesting they did this weekend too, I guess so my dad can keep up with who we are.

In the afternoon, I get away to my room to start writing songs. Nothing comes at first and pretty soon I'm writing a letter to Uncle Ryan instead, bringing him up to date on the bar project and how it wasn't too awful, plus the band and how Treat says we're supposed to write songs about anarchy and injustice and consumerism and how the world won't listen. Then I ask if he ever did anything crazy for a girl without explaining what I mean by "crazy."

I'm back at it again after dinner and homework, trying to write songs. Nothing.

Astrid's light clicks on, so it must be after eight. She's less than fifty feet away, probably in a silky robe and definitely in lace panties. It's all I can think about, but I'm not going to get discreet. I don't want anything to happen with Astrid in my imagination anymore. If it isn't real, what's the point? And the only way to make it real is to bring DikNixon to life.

I go over to Brendan's room, the stink of sweaty socks hitting me as soon as my head's through his door. He's lying on his bed, looking at the pictures in *Sports Illustrated* (he never reads the articles).

"You know any punk songs?" I say.

His head drops over the side of the bed and he looks at me upside down. "You like punk?"

"Some. Do you know any or not?"

"Is Devo punk?" He sits up. "'Satisfaction' is a good song."

"That's a Rolling Stones song."

Brendan looks back down at the magazine. "I like how Devo does it."

I walk down the hall thinking how the Devo version of "Satisfaction" doesn't even sound like the original. How it's pretty much a different song except for the lyrics. Isn't that stealing? And why doesn't anyone care? I mean, they played that song all over the radio for a while; people must have thought it was okay. Next thing I know, I'm downstairs flipping through my parents' albums, wondering what DikNixon can steal. There isn't anything good, no Rolling Stones or Beatles. My dad won't listen to English bands because of the things he says the English did to the Irish. The only time he ever got red-faced at Uncle Ryan was when a Rolling Stones song came on the radio, and there's my dad, trying to change the station, and Uncle Ryan saying the only thing Mick Jagger ever did to the Irish was introduce them to soul, and then my dad laughed and said fine, just this one time.

Back at my desk, I've got some albums that have the lyrics printed inside the cover or on the sleeves. I reach over to my cassette player and pop in one of *The Nixon Tapes*. The music seems pretty good at first, an easy, thump-thump-thump beat and then guitars flying in like a plane landing. It's fast and distorted and every once in a while everything stops except the drums. The singers fire through the lyrics and change the shape of some words so it almost sounds like another language. I read through the lyrics of the albums I've got and copy down a few. They're not exactly punk, but at least they're real songs. I tuck the lyrics into a new folder with a >I< logo on it.

Astrid's light is off when I crawl into bed. Treat will probably have some better songs tomorrow, and I think about how good we'll look playing in front of Astrid, those lacy black panties hiding beneath her jeans while she sways to our music. I almost get discreet, but I fight it off by thinking about the periodic table. When that doesn't work, van Doren shows up next to Astrid, only he's not swaying. He's staring me down, looking kind of shocked and mad that we can be this cool. That works so perfect my hands start behaving themselves and instead I just feel kind of nervous.

■

I've got my lunch and my song folder with me at the Bog on Monday. Edie and Cherise are already standing there with Keith. Edie's sandwich, juice, apple, and carrots are laid out perfect on the bricks. Cherise has a plastic bag full of almonds and a can of V8 vegetable juice, with a straw. Keith's food is still in the bag, and he's talk-singing from a paper in his hand: "They don't respect you / won't infect you / all they want to do / is connect you."

"'Connect you'?" I say.

"Yeah," Keith says. "*Connected*. Like in *The Godfather*."

Edie grins. "What do you have?"

"Some things you can't hear."

She gives me an *Oh really?* smile. "Love songs about Astrid?"

There's a million people out there in the quad, and every one of them goes quiet right as Edie says that. Cherise takes a drink of her V8, her eyes getting big all of a sudden like the can is sucking back; then Treat comes trouncing up behind me, through the planter. He hops down, throws his arm over my shoulder, and looks at Edie, like, *Don't mind me.*

"You're getting embarrassed," Edie says.

"I didn't write any love songs. These are punk."

Treat gives me a nod and my face cools off.

Edie takes a bite of her apple. "What about you, Treat? What songs do you have?"

"Why?" he says.

"So Cherise and I can give you some feedback."

Treat looks at Cherise and you can tell she's thinking, *I never said that. I wouldn't make you do anything.* He rubs his hand around the Mohawk without touching it. "I don't have my stuff with me."

"Well"—Edie turns to me—"I guess we're stuck with your love songs."

"They're not love songs."

Treat pulls a sandwich from his bag. "Let's see one, Reece."

I flip open my folder and pull out the most anti-love song I've got. Treat snatches the paper and looks down. He's perfectly still for a few seconds except for his eyes scanning up and down; then his lips move a little but no sound comes out. The four of us stare at him like something's about to happen, and something does. Treat starts humming and he's getting the tune right. His voice rises, fast and loud, like he's angry, and he punks-up the lyrics, "I'll be what I am-uh / a soli-tary man-uh."

He repeats the last line, like, three times, louder and faster each time. Then, he grips the paper tight and looks up at us. Edie and Cherise clap. He looks at me. "This is boss, Reece. What's it called?"

"'Solitary Man,'" says my mouth; *by Neil Diamond*, says my head.

"Bitchin'. It's totally punk rock."

Keith nods. Serious. "That really is good, Reece."

Edie looks at me kind of surprised, not happy surprised or mad surprised, just surprised. "Keith's is good too," she says, "right, Cherise?"

Cherise nods and wipes nothing from her lips. "Yeah. You guys are gonna be good."

Treat looks over everything in my folder, bouncing his head and moving his lips. He hops up on the planter and punks-up every song, tromping over shrubs and staring straight down at the pages. "Walk like a man-uh / talk like a man-uh / fuck this and fuck that-uh / fuck it all the fuck out of the fucking brat-uh." He isn't singing so much as talking out the lyrics. Everyone's watching, so everyone sees Vice Principal Marshall rush past us and step right up into the planter. He grabs Treat by the back of the jacket. "Let's go, Dumovitch. My office."

Treat turns his head to see who it is, grins, and yells, "I am not resisting arrest! I am not resisting arrest!"

Mr. Marshall pushes Treat a little to hop down and start walking to the office. He grabs the papers in Treat's hand but Treat won't let go. It's not like Treat's trying anything; Mr. Marshall hasn't exactly asked for the pages, but suddenly the whole quad is going "Oooooh." Mr. Marshall gets so mad he lets go, holds open his hand to show Treat, and says, "Hand 'em over."

Treat holds the pages up, then lets them slip out of his hand and float down, back and forth like a pendulum, until they scratch to a stop on the pavement. Mr. Marshall scrapes them up. "Bad move, Dumovitch." He points to his office door with the pages. "Get moving."

Military-Commercial Complex

Treat's suspended two days for vandalizing the planters and swearing. Mr. and Mrs. D aren't mad about the swearing, though they still called Mr. Marshall and said Treat would be happy to spend his Saturday weeding all the planters on campus, which Mr. Marshall thought was a great idea.

After school Tuesday, Treat's got the Two-Car Studio open when me and Keith get there. He must've spent half the day putting together all the stuff Keith's dad bought us. Keith's guitar is on the left with its amp and a new distortion pedal. Treat's uncle's bass and a new amp are on the right. And there's a little Roland drum machine on its shiny new box in the middle. Treat said you can't always make a drummer do what you want, so the drum machine is fine for now. The three folding chairs are in a half circle next to the instruments, the bullhorn on the middle chair, and the car cover is pulled tight over the wall of boxes behind, a three-foot-tall >I< centered over the foot-tall *DikNixon*.

Treat leads us in and the Mohawk mixes with the logo and the instruments and it all looks so real. It's like how Mr. Krueger says sometimes things work out even when the original plan blows up in your face. "A happy accident," though Mr. Krueger says there are no accidents, just incidents.

"Does Mr. Marshall really have a Hot Wheels track in his office for whipping people?" Keith says. Treat tells him no, no track, no stick, no paddle. Not even a ruler. "Then what'd he do to you?"

"Nothing."

Keith drops his backpack next to a chair. "Come on, nothing?"

"He actually said he was sorry he had to suspend me." Treat steps around Keith and flips on the bass amp. "He filled out some paperwork, told me to have Lyle call with any questions, then made me sit in the office and do my homework until school let out."

"That's it?" Keith says. "That's like going to the doctor's office."

Treat picks up the bass and hands it to Keith. "Yeah, I got bent over."

We laugh as Treat hits the button to close the garage door.

"I'm bass?" Keith says.

"Don't worry," Treat says. "Sid Vicious played bass."

I pick up the guitar and flip on the amp.

Treat starts humming the tune for "Solitary Man," and as me and Keith start figuring out how to make the guitars sound something like that, Treat gets the drums going.

It takes forever, a lot of things sounding okay on their own and then just awful when they mix together. I've heard "Solitary Man" a million times when my mom cleans house with the stereo on. The guitar doesn't sound anywhere near right. But with Treat getting all the lyrics punked-up, when we turn on the distortion pedals and play faster it sounds pretty decent with everything whirring and echoing. The song doesn't sound the same twice in a row, but Treat says that's okay. "Punk isn't formulaic like corporate rock. It's got synergy."

We do a version of "I Am, I Said," and Treat's yelling at the top of his lungs, "No one heard at all / not even the chair!" He kicks over some chairs and Mr. D comes out, eyes bugging, until Treat says, "It's okay, Lyle, just part of the song."

"All right." He looks around at the chairs, sideways and flipped over, me and Keith smiling real polite. "Just remember what we do with real anger."

Treat throws his arms out and looks around the studio at the chairs and the amps, then holds up the crumpled lyrics. "Use it creatively."

Mr. D holds his hands up and folds his fingers together like he's praying. "Good. And be careful around the computers."

We work on a few more songs until Treat opens the garage door for some air. The sky's bled way past orange and purple and settled into black.

"We better get going," I say.

Treat walks us out onto the driveway. He pulls a couple patches out of his back pocket. "Here, Reece. You're DikNixon's official songwriter now."

One patch has *TSOL* and the Statue of Liberty's head on it.

"Sew it on your jacket," Treat says.

"Are these guys on *The Nixon Tapes*?"

"Yeah. They do 'World War III.'"

Keith takes the patch in his hand. "T-S-O-L. Tell Satan, Ouch Lady?"

Treat shakes his head. "True Sounds of Liberty."

The other patch is simple, just GBH on it, and Treat waits while Keith strokes his chin. "Guitar, Bass, and Harmony?"

Treat laughs. "Grievous Bodily Harm. They're on *The Nixon Tapes* too."

"Nice," Keith says. "So when are we going to play a show?"

"Gig," Treat says.

"Fine. When are we going to play a gig? Because everyone says we're coming and if we're going to get invited to Ted Three—"

"Ted Three?" Treat says. His lips pucker up for a second and he says, "Why not Woodstock Two?"

Keith glances at me and you can tell he's thinking about the bird who hangs out with Snoopy, so I start giggling.

Treat pushes my shoulder back. "You going to make a hippie joke?"

"About Woodstock?"

"Fuck you, Reece. Your parents were probably *for* the war."

Keith says, "World War Three?"

Treat folds his arms and leans against the Bug. "Your dad's an engineer, right, Keith? He probably wishes Vietnam was still going on so he could make more missiles and shit."

"What are you talking about?" I say.

"The military-industrial complex, Reece. The balance of terror. Mutually assured destruction. The end of the world." He looks over at Keith. "Your dad doesn't share those tasty treats around the dinner table, does he?"

Keith shakes his head.

"I thought we were talking about Ted Three," I say.

"I have no idea what we're talking about," Keith says. "Military-commercial complex? Woodstock? I thought Woodstock was a bird."

Treat holds his face tight for a second longer, then bursts out laughing. He steps over and slaps Keith on the back. "A bird. That's so bitchin'." He tells Keith what Woodstock really was, about the peace and love, and about the people running around naked and how it went on for days.

"What's that got to do with Ted Three?" Keith says.

"Do you know when Ted Three is?" Treat says. "Or where it'll be?"

Keith shakes his head.

"Exactly," Treat says. "It may never happen."

"But people want to see us. Maybe we can play a party or set up—"

"We will," Treat stops him. "This is happening."

"We really need to get going," I say. Treat says *fine,* he'll clean everything up, he always cleans everything up. So, of course, we say we can help and he says he's kidding, that he doesn't have school tomorrow like we do.

■

We can see the glow of the park as we're walking up the hill out of Treat's neighborhood. These nights are the best, people practicing on the soccer fields while we sneak our way from the shadow of a tree to the shadow of the bathrooms, trying to time it so the East German soldiers on the parade grounds don't see us on our secret mission.

When we get to the first shadow in the park, behind a light post, I say, "Have you got your cyanide tablet?"

"No," Keith says.

"No?" I say and point at the soccer players. "What about the mission?"

Keith shakes his head and walks right out into the light. "Edie thinks we should play soon. In front of real people."

"Edie? When did you talk to Edie?"

"We've got a band," Keith says. "We should play a show."

We're alongside one of the fields now, the soccer players steaming in the cold air. "We will," I say. "Two weeks ago we had nothing. Now we've got a name people know, instruments, some songs. It's happening."

Keith stops, grins at me, then takes off running. He slides through the wet grass, stopping perfectly behind a light post, and whisper-yells, "Take cover."

I drop and crawl over to Keith faster than my little sister can run.

"Here," he says and forces something into my hand. "I stole this from their headquarters, but I'm a dead man. *You* must deliver it to Agent Okuda."

I look down at a folded-up note, and there's Edie's name written so big I could have read it without the park lights.

"She's expecting this intelligence at your morning logistics briefing."

"Algebra?"

Keith smiles and takes off for the wall, catching it with both hands and flinging himself over, disappearing into my backyard. When I get to the top of the wall, Keith's already through the yard and opening the side gate.

I catch up to him on the sidewalk in front of my house, holding up the note. "Why did you give this to me? Just give it to Edie yourself."

"I don't want to keep it in my room. My mom's a snoop."

The note feels heavy, maybe two or three pages. "Do you like Edie?"

Keith looks at his house, then back at me. "I don't know. She wrote me a note and told me to write back. Maybe she likes me."

"Maybe," I say, even though Edie's way too smart for Keith. It's probably good he's doing this by note, you know, so Edie can be nice about things and it won't ruin everything the way it does when one friend likes the other and it's not mutual and everything gets out of balance and uncomfortable.

"Don't read it, okay?"

"I won't," I say. "Just don't get weird on me."

Keith's head snaps to his shoulder a couple times and his eyes round into Ping-Pong balls. "I'm never we-we-weird." He smiles and salutes me. "And now, for something completely different." He turns on one heel and goose-steps up the sidewalk toward his house.

Up in my room, I unfold the note slow and careful, making sure to notice how Keith has folded it originally. There's two pages of writing with little drawings in the margins: a little bear, some DikNixon logos, and a square-looking swan with markings around it like it's the blueprint for how to build a swan. It says *Origami 101* on top and I start feeling bad for Keith. He's trying pretty hard and it might be really embarrassing when things don't turn out. And it's not like me and Astrid. Astrid's older and popular and doesn't really know me, so I can't exactly take it personal if she never likes me. But if we were in the same grade and hung out together a lot, and then everybody in the world found out how much I liked her and she rejected me, that'd be the worst. Just thinking about how this could wipe Keith off the face of the earth makes my stomach hurt.

I start folding the note back up without reading anything. A few words stick out the way you see someone you know in a crowd—*do, think, cute, hot*—and it's hard not to stop and read the whole thing. But I promised, you know, and you've got to be loyal to the people who are closest to you, even if you think what they're doing might not be the best idea. Even if it means you have to sort of help them do the thing you think they shouldn't be doing. That's what friends are supposed to do.

■

On the way to school Wednesday morning, Keith makes sure I've got the note. He helps me safety-pin the TSOL and GBH patches to the shoulders of my Packy jacket.

In Algebra, I plop the note down on top of Edie's book. "That's for you."

She says, "Thanks," without looking up from her homework.

"It's not from me," I say and sit down sideways in front of her.

"I know." She flashes me a quick smile.

When the bell rings and Mr. Tomita starts in at the board, I hear the note crinkling open. Edie giggles a couple times, quiet

ones that don't make it up to Mr. Tomita; then there's more crinkling, the little quick ones from paper getting folded and smoothed
at the creases.

After class, Edie asks me about the new instruments we have,
not what they are—she already knows that—but how they sound.
"Good," I say as we get to the stairs. "I mean, we're still trying to
get it all together."

"You'll have it together Friday, when you play on the back
of a truck at San Diego State."

I get it. "How'd you hear about that?" I say.

"My cousin goes to school there. She's going to tell me all
about it this weekend."

"Wait. Do you really have a cousin at San Diego State?"

Edie shakes her head. "No, she goes to UC San Diego, but
SDSU is the party school. More believable." She smiles and
hands me a note with Keith's name on it. "Can you deliver this?
Cherise has to eat in the cafeteria today."

"Why?"

Edie sighs. "Will you please just give it to Keith?"

The note is a perfect square and Edie has made a flower out
of the *i* in *Keith*. "If you open it," she says, "I'll know." She taps
the note. "The top of the *i* is on a different fold than the bottom.
You'll never be able to line them up."

The letters are neat and swirly and the folds come together in
a diagonal across the front, a tiny white line on the white paper
separating the flower from the stem. I can't believe she's spent all
this time on a note for Keith.

"I won't read it."

"Good," she says, and we stand there for a second longer while the stairs empty out. "Call me if you need help on the homework."

"You can call me too."

Edie shakes her head. "No, I can't. You're the boy."

Her face doesn't crack a smile as she turns and heads up the stairs, and I can't tell if she's razzing me. Would only a boy need help on math homework? Is she not allowed to call boys no matter what it's for? What else is she up to?

The note is thick, at least three pages pressing against my thigh all through English and Spanish. It's killing me not to read it, because no matter how embarrassing whatever it might say is, Keith would trust me with it. I mean, when I told him that sometimes Astrid lies out in her backyard with her bikini straps undone so she doesn't get lines on her back, I didn't deny it when he said, "I bet you pack your mule every time you see that. I would. Guys have to do things like that or we'll die." And if I ever lose my mind and tell him about everything that happened in Astrid's bathroom, he'll be on my side about it. So maybe that's why I don't read the note, because Keith will tell me if something big is up.

■

At lunch, it's just me and Keith in the Bog. He reads the note before taking a bite of his sandwich, his eyes scanning the page, lips shaping some words and stretching into a smile for others. Then he stuffs the note into his pocket and looks up at me. "Do you think Treat's been acting funny lately?"

"Treat?" I say, and Keith nods. "Has *Treat* been acting funny?"

"Yeah," Keith says. "I mean, has he been staring anywhere at lunch or looking at anyone a lot but not saying anything?"

"I don't know. Treat always acts funny."

"Yeah. I guess for him to act funny he'd have to not act funny."

Keith sits back on the planter, really giving it some thought, really acting serious, and that's it. We start talking about a million other things after that: homework, tests, how Petrakis never messes with us anymore, and how van Doren only drops books near my head now, never directly on it. Things are getting better at school and it's all because of Treat, which is what I'll tell Uncle Ryan in the letter I write later tonight. I won't tell him that nobody knows tomorrow is my birthday. I guess I'm holding on to that like a fifth ace, or a pen that's really a gun, or a note from a cool girl. Or maybe I just don't want anyone making a big deal of it. Things really are getting better, but it doesn't mean I'm ready to celebrate. After all, for things to be better that means they had to have been pretty bad in the first place, and you can't just all of a sudden forget that. At least I can't, no matter how hard I've been trying.

Flatbed Truck

Before I left for school today, my dad was still in the kitchen, work clothes on, car keys in hand. "Happy birthday," he said. "We'll celebrate tonight." I said, "Okay," and he looked at my mom. She nodded once, like it was okay for him to leave now, and then one of those Mona Lisa smiles came over her face, and that's how I knew the whole thing was rehearsed. I appreciate it and all, but I wish it didn't seem so fake.

School, at least, feels normal until I get to English. There's a circle of people around Treat before the bell rings. He's telling everyone that after Mr. Marshall sat down behind his desk Monday, he uncrumpled the pages to the song lyrics and couldn't talk until he'd read them twice.

"I told him, 'I know my First Amendment rights. I can write lyrics no matter how punk they are.' And you know what he did?" Treat pulls the exact same crumpled-up pages from his back pocket. The pages in my handwriting. "He gave them back to me and said, 'Fine. But you keep the swearing to yourself.' So I took them and said, 'I'll try hard as hell to keep the god-damned swearing under control.'"

Everyone laughs and a couple people sneak a peek at the desk to see if Mrs. Reisdorf heard. Her pencil never stops moving, checking off last period's assignment, but there's a smirk on her face that she usually saves for when we read our own work out loud.

"Did you really say that?" Penny Martin asks because she isn't afraid to ask anything of anyone, not even Treat.

"Yeah," Treat says. "Right before I asked him to jam with my band."

A couple people laugh and Mrs. Reisdorf comes out from behind the desk, saying the bell is about to ring so we need to get to our seats.

"That's boss," the sneezer whispers to me as he sits down.

"Yeah," I say. "Totally unbelievable."

■

Me and Keith are already in the Bog, halfway through our sand-wiches, when Treat gets there. "Where're your little girlfriends?"

"They're in the cafeteria," Keith says.

"They're not our girlfriends," I say. "Where have you been?"

Treat looks around and grins. "Promoting the band."

Keith wipes his mouth off with his hand. "What does that mean?"

"Making up stories," I say.

"No." Treat holds up a finger. "Letting people think what they want."

"Yeah?" Keith says with a mouthful of sandwich. "Like what?"

"Some people think I told Mr. Marshall to fuck off. And some people think I got arrested for attacking Mr. Marshall in his office."

"No way," Keith says and smiles.

Treat nods and peers into his lunch bag.

Petrakis comes up to us and stands next to Keith. He's wearing his dark blue Levi's 501s and the T-shirt all the football players wear: *The Future Is Now: Esperanza Football, 1982.* "Gentlemen," he says.

Keith steps aside without saying a thing and Treat squints at Petrakis.

"Hey," I say.

He holds a hand up, like, *That's enough,* and turns to Treat. "I heard you're in a pretty bitchin' punk band. Is that true?"

Treat crosses his arms, crumpling his lunch bag between them. "Does the Ayatollah Khomeini have a beard?"

Petrakis thinks about it a second. "I knew it. Are you guys playing anywhere soon?"

Treat stares at him and it's hard to tell if he isn't answering on purpose or has no idea what to say.

"Friday," I say. "We've got something going on."

Petrakis looks at me, kind of surprised I'm in the band. "Sweet. Where?"

Treat comes back to life. "Why?"

Petrakis turns to Treat. "Me and my friends want to check it out, see you fuck a few people up in a slam pit. Like the time you did that backflip off the stage at the Palladium."

The Mohawk moves up and down and Treat laughs a quick "huh."

"Yeah," Keith says. "That was an awesome night."

Petrakis looks at him, like, *You're in the band too?* And now we need to make this real or he's not going to believe anything we say.

"We're going to be in San Diego on Friday," I say. I look off to the side like I'm talking to the ground, the way they do the undercover drug deals on *Starsky & Hutch* where you don't make eye contact because only a cop would make eye contact. "We're parking a flatbed truck in a parking lot at SDSU and playing until the cops make us leave."

"Ah, man," Petrakis says. "That sounds awesome, but we've got a game. What about Saturday?"

Treat shakes his head. "If we're not in jail, we're working on some new shit Saturday."

Petrakis get this sly grin; then he looks over at the Senior Circle and you know he's feeling the pressure, talking to freshmen this long. He shoves his hands into his jeans pockets and takes a couple steps. "Let me know when you've got a Saturday show. I'll bring some of my boys."

"Sure," Treat says. He waits for Petrakis to turn and step away; then he flicks his hand out a couple times like he's brushing Petrakis off. Some people nearby give that an "ooooh," but Petrakis keeps walking like it can't possibly be about him. Treat turns to me and whisper-yells, "What the fuck is this SDSU stuff?"

I tell him about Edie and her cousin, and he likes it. But now I'm wondering what Treat said about *his* band. "Did you tell people you're in DikNixon?"

"No," Treat says. "Just a band."

Keith is suddenly miserable. "We can't go to the football game now, can we? We're supposed to be in San Diego."

I look at Treat. "You know when everyone hears about the SDSU show from Edie, they're going to connect those dots to what Petrakis knows and—"

"DikNixon lives!" Keith says. So happy now.

Treat flicks my TSOL patch. "We're gonna need a lot more songs. Soon."

Just as the bell's ringing to end lunch, Edie comes up to me, right past Keith and Treat, and shoves my shoulder back. "Somebody just said, 'The Mohawk guy's band is playing at SDSU.'"

Cherise has come over too and they're both looking at me, waiting for an answer. I smile. "It's kind of a long drive, so you guys might want to wait until we're playing closer."

Cherise nods like that makes sense, but Edie's got that look in her eye, the one she uses when we're comparing homework answers and mine are different. "You know what this means?"

Cherise looks at Treat and actually talks. "Everyone's going to know you're DikNixon."

Treat lifts his arms and makes peace signs with both hands.

Cherise crosses her arms and sort of smiles, then looks at Edie. "Are you guys ready for this?"

"We're gonna be," Treat says.

Edie brushes atoms off my shoulder. "You better be."

On the way to our lockers, Treat tells Cherise and Edie it's too bad they can't come down to SDSU. It sounds so good I'm thinking what it would be like to say that to Astrid. Then suddenly we're playing the same party with van Doren and Filibuster and Astrid is all over me between sets. I'm nothing but happy until Edie shows up in my head saying our set didn't sound anything like Bad Brains but it looks like we have them. It's a punk rock joke, which Edie wouldn't really make, but imaginary Edie and real Edie are both right. If we don't sound like we know what we're doing when we do play for real, they'll call us names or throw things or, worse, rush the stage and throw us off. There's no coming back from a meltdown like that, and just the thought of it makes a bolt of pain shoot through my stomach.

■

When the whole class is good, sometimes Mrs. Wirth lets us slip out of World History a couple minutes early since it's the last period of the day. It's amazing how campus is the quietest place in the world two minutes before the bell rings, before people come flying out the doors like it's the Kentucky Derby.

My backpack's nearly filled with homework when the wave of noise and people starts. No one's gotten to my row of lockers yet and, *bam*, a book hits me in the thigh. It doesn't hurt because it's this tattered little paperback, *Fear and Loathing in Las Vegas*. But like an idiot, I look up to van Doren's locker even though he's not there.

"Over here."

I turn around and van Doren's walking across the grass behind me.

"I hear you got a gig Friday night."

Even though my backpack is set to go, I keep crouching there, looking up at him. "Uh-huh."

He snatches the book from me and stuffs it into his back pocket. "Wonder Bowl?"

"What?"

Van Doren opens his locker. "Yeah, that's what I thought."

"We're playing in San Diego," I say. "I'll let you know when we play around here."

"Not necessary," van Doren says. The last bell rings and he pulls some sunglasses from his locker and slips them on. "I'll know before you do." He closes the locker soft and takes off across the grass, disappearing into the mass of people spreading out from the open doors.

■

We work on another Neil Diamond song after school, "Forever in Blue Jeans." I've changed it to "Forever in Ripped Jeans," just in case Treat or Keith might have heard it before. We get it punked up pretty good; then Treat wants to start in on another song. He says we need to work right through dusk and dinner and home-work. Maybe even sleep. I say I can't. Keith is all over me about commitment and hard work, and Treat's nodding until I lie and say it's my little sister's birthday.

"So?" Keith says.

It's not like I wouldn't rather be here, but I can't get away with missing my own birthday even if I haven't wanted to cele-brate much of anything lately.

Treat throws his hands up. "Blood," he says. "It's everything." He pulls a patch from his back pocket and hands it to me. It's a Dead Kennedys tomahawk, just the *D* and the *K* fused together yet somehow looking really threatening. Really simple. Really cool. "Go," he says. "And start sewing these on."

I've been unpinning the patches on my jacket every night and hiding them in the pockets until morning. I don't know if I'll ever be able to get away with making them permanent, but I can't think about that now. "Check," I say, and I'm gone.

∎

My dad gets home from work when dinner is just about over. He's excited, even smiling a little, and eats real fast to catch up. My mom brings out this chocolate fudge cake, which gets Brendan happy, and Colleen's bouncing in her chair because she loves blowing out candles. It's a weeknight, my dad in his work boots, my mom's hair up and freckles still covered in powder. It doesn't feel like my birthday even with everyone singing to me and smiling. I let Colleen help me blow out the candles. When we're done with cake, my mom sets three normal-size boxes next to me on the table and one big one.

Brendan taps the big one. "You'll never guess what this is."

"Brendan!" my mom says. "Shush."

I get a new batting glove for my right hand from Brendan, and one for my left from Colleen. My parents get me two checkered button-up shirts that they probably paid too much for. "I noticed you like these kinds of shirts now," my mom says.

I try to imagine them bleached out and looking decent. "Thanks."

Brendan shoves the big box in my face. "Now open this one," he says, and the table shrinks in on me. Brendan and my mom lean forward, smiling. Colleen stands up on her chair and puts her elbows on the table. Even my dad sets down his cup of tea and leans forward.

It's too light to be an Atari or some other kind of video-game system, and it's not like my parents have heard of that stuff anyway. They don't usually go in for gifts that cost a couple hundred bucks, especially if they don't improve your hand-eye coordination, teach you your ABCs, or at least warm your toes *and* keep them dry.

For a second, I wonder if it's something Uncle Ryan bought for me a long time ago and told my dad to save until I was a freshman, or fifteen, or something like that. I rip through the paper, more excited than I mean to be, to a plain white box that's kind of flimsy with the paper off. The tape is just plain old Scotch—not the long, impossible-to-tear-without-ripping-the-box skinny stuff that companies use on things that are really worth something. The box pops open no problem. There's tissue paper, but I can see dark blue through it with swirly white letters spelling out *Yankees*.

"It's authentic," my dad says as I hold it up, a shiny blue, satin jacket. "We had your aunt Mary pick it up for us by the stadium and mail it out."

"When?" I say.

My mom smiles. "We've been working on this since school started and we had to give you your father's jacket."

She looks so proud of herself that I have to look down because I can feel how blank my face is. I trace the big letters with my fingers, try to think of something to say. "It's got the real stitching."

"That's what I told your aunt," my dad says. "Don't get one of those cheap, ironed-on deals. We want the real thing."

I still can't look up. "It's really nice."

"Put it on," my dad says.

I stand up and slide it over my shoulders and down my arms, slick until my hands break through and the cloth at the end of the sleeves grips my wrists snug. Each blue button snaps together with a solid pop, and the cloth around the neck goes just to my collar, not too high, not too low. The letters are stiff and glowing across my chest, and it looks so official that for just a second, it has me. I'm thinking of a night game in Yankee Stadium with my dad, me leaning over a railing and asking Bobby Murcer to sign right on the *Y*.

My mom leans back in her chair, hands together, that proud smile still on her face. "It really looks good on you."

Brendan grabs the right shoulder. "Look," he says. "It's even got the official Yankees patch." The Uncle Sam hat on top of a bat with *Yankees* across it is stitched perfectly to the shoulder.

"Cool." I walk around the table to give my mom a kiss and my dad a hug.

"You like it?" my dad says like he's not so sure.

"Yeah." I glance at him but it won't stick, so I start gathering up the other boxes. "I've always wanted a Yankees jacket. It's perfect." I leave the jacket on, to sort of prove how much I like it already, and say I can help with dishes after I run this stuff up to my room.

Colleen's gone back to searching her mess of cake for any icing she might have missed, but Brendan looks up at me like I'm crazy.

My mom shakes her head and my dad says, "It's your birthday. Don't worry about the dishes."

"Thanks," I say. "I better get up there. I've got a load of homework to get to."

In my room, I hang the Yankees jacket in my closet and sit down at my desk. My Packy jacket is on the back of my chair, the patches and safety pins in the pockets. I get to work and everything goes fine until the last couple algebra problems. Those are always the hardest, the ones that aren't just number 23; they're 23a, b, and c. And if you get 23a wrong, you're screwed for b and c. It's not like Mr. Tomita won't give you full credit if you get everything done but those last few, but I figure, why not call for help when someone has offered it?

At the top of the stairs, I hear the water running and the clang of pots and pans. Probably my mom. I go back to my room to wait her out. My homework is pretty much done, so I get out my notebook. The Yankees logo looks funny now, and I could use my jacket as a model to make a different one, but instead I make a new DikNixon logo, the >*I*< part bigger and better than the *NY*.

In my new letter to Uncle Ryan, I'm wondering how I'm supposed to be punk rock and also wear a Yankees jacket. *I know you know what I'm talking about, because I remember my dad always giving you a hard time when you'd wear your army jacket since you were never in the army. I was just a kid and I knew it was really a John Lennon jacket, and cool. How could my dad not know that?* I tell Uncle Ryan that the only guys at school who actually wear Dodgers or Angels jackets don't really play ball. Or talk to girls. Or end up at good parties. And it's not like my dad's taking me to a game anytime soon. *Not with his work and without you here to make him do it*, I write. *So where do I wear this thing?* I stop writing after that because it's making me mad just thinking about the jacket. I even start feeling a little mad at Uncle Ryan, you know, because without him around, my dad doesn't do so good with things that are different. But like I said, I don't write any of that down.

The kitchen is empty and dark now. Even though it's still before ten o'clock, it feels funny calling Edie this late, especially when she picks up, real polite. "Okuda residence."

"Miss Okuda," I say. "Now is the time to talk."

She doesn't laugh. "How was practice?"

"Good," I say. "We're practicing again tomorrow night."

"I know. Cherise and I are coming over to watch."

"You are?"

"Yeah," she says, like, haven't I known about this for weeks? "We're going to walk over with you and Keith after school."

"Really?"

"Really. I talked to Keith about it earlier when he called."

It's weird thinking of Keith calling Edie. What would he say to her? Band stuff, probably. "Okay. I guess I'll see you tomorrow at school."

"And after," Edie says and leaves it kind of up, not exactly a good-bye. I guess in case I want to say something else. Only, I can't think of what else to say, and it stays quiet until she asks, "Is that what you were calling about?"

It's like one of those questions you see on a game show where the answer is right there, and you know the person knows, but they go retarded because of the pressure: *Name a fruit whose skin you can eat: Watermelon. Orange. Banana. Guh!*

"Yeah, that's why I called."

"Okay," she says and waits another second. "Now is the time to say bye."

"Yeah," I say. "Bye."

Only, Edie doesn't say "bye" back; she says, "Good night." It tickles my ear, runs down to my feet, makes me warm everywhere like when you're a kid and your mom tucks you in, only better because it's not your mom; it's someone who doesn't really have to do it.

I don't touch the last algebra problem, don't even look over to see if Astrid's light is off. I pull my desk chair closer to the bed, turn the light out, and climb in. In the dark, my hand slides up the desk chair and onto the rough cotton of the Packy jacket. My fingers work into the front pocket, tracing over the letters on each patch, reading them like Braille: *TSOL, GBH,* and *Dead Kennedys*. It makes me happy the way acing a test does, how you know you did good even before you turn it in, how you could've done it half asleep and gotten it perfect.

Lyle the Fascist

Me and Edie are walking to the stairs after Algebra, after I've given her the note Keith wrote last night even though he talked to her on the phone, even though we'll see her at lunch and after school.

"Can you do me a favor?" she says.

"Not another note."

Edie grins. "Why, are you tempted to read them?"

"How do you know I don't?"

"I'd know." She pats the one in her back pocket. "But I'm going to see you guys at lunch, so why would I hand off a note?"

"Well, yeah."

Edie looks behind us like maybe we're being followed. "I just need you to promise not to tell Treat about us coming over after school. Okay?"

She nods like I've already agreed, then turns to go. It happens so fast that as I'm reaching out to make her wait, her shoulder flies by and I catch her hand as it swings back. She stops and turns back, her eyes huge spheres. "What is it, Reece?"

Her hand is so soft and light to the touch I'm not even sure if I'm actually holding it. "I can't not tell Treat," I say. "He doesn't do so good with surprises."

Edie squeezes my hand, a quick one that lets off without letting go. We *are* still touching. And now the warmth wraps around my fingers. Edie says something like "Please, as a favor," and I must ask, "Why?" because she's talking about how she wants to tell me and she will tell me but she can't tell me right now. She keeps squeezing my hand, like a tiny massage, until I say, "Fine."

The whole walk to English I'm sort of wondering why Treat can't know and why Keith is still getting notes. Mostly, though, I'm wondering why my hand feels like it's glowing. My eyes are who knows where until some girl at her locker comes into focus. She's wearing a warm-up suit with school colors, tight and stretchy. It looks good so I keep looking, like it's a sunset, and now she's looking back. Our eyes are locked; I know because her head follows me. Then this little grin pulls up the corners of her mouth and makes me feel great all over, definitely better than a little hand glow.

It's so smooth, almost normal, until I think: *Wow, who is this?* Then it's like I've woken up late for school. *Astrid? Astrid! I should say something. Or do something. Or something.* And I do. I throw a hand up in the air the way Uncle Ryan used to do. "Happy Friday."

Astrid's eyes slide back and forth real smooth, her mouth a tight grin until she says, "Happy Friday." Then she shakes her head, the grin still there, and I don't know if that means I look potential boyfriend cute or just puppy cute.

∎

After school, Keith's all over Edie on the walk to Treat's: How did her day go, how did the discussion of *Huck Finn* go in AP English, and was her history test as easy as she thought it'd be? She's answering everything with smiles and jokes. Cherise walks next to me and she's pushed her hair back behind her ear more times than she's looked up or said a word to me.

"You should get one of those hair thingies," I say.

She turns, looks me in the eye, and says, "My mom says they pull your scalp and weaken your follicles." Then she goes back to chaperoning her feet.

"Okay." We walk on for five, six, seven more sidewalk squares. "So, do you like punk?"

"Maybe," she says to square nine. "I don't think I know what it is."

As we head across Yorba Linda Boulevard and down the hill to Treat's, I list every punk song and band on *The Nixon Tapes*. Cherise is shaking her head no to everything. "Wait," she finally says and pushes her hair back. "I might know 'Anarchy in the U.K.' Who's that by?"

"The Sex Pistols," Keith says. "Unless my mom's asking. Then it's the *Sax* Pistols."

Edie and Cherise crack up and Keith leads us up the driveway and knocks on the Two-Car Studio. The garage door opens and Treat's there by the button, studying some notebook paper in his hand.

"We need to get a couple more chairs," Keith says.

Treat looks up, his eyes locking on Edie and Cherise. "Perfect," he says, but not in a good way. He opens the door to the house and it slams behind him.

"He may not come back," I say.

"Isn't he getting chairs?" Edie says. Keith shakes his head and Edie looks at me. "Somebody should go get him."

Keith sits down in the chair by his bass and starts getting it out.

"Fine," I say to Keith. "If you're too scared."

"What? I'm getting things ready."

Treat's room is at the end of the hallway past his little sister's room, the door with band stickers and a fake parking sign that says NO PARKING / EXCEPT FOR TREAT. He pops his head out before I can knock. "Why are *they* here?"

"Keith said they could come."

Treat shakes the Mohawk. "I don't care who brought them. Why are they here? Does one of them play drums? Does the other play tambourine?"

Even though he's razzing me, I imagine Edie holding a tambourine and wearing fake cat ears and a tail like Josie and the Pussycats. Cartoon Edie looks at me and tilts her head like, *Meow? What's so funny?* I start giggling.

Treat opens his door all the way, his arms folded to their hugest. "What?"

I explain about Josie and the Pussycats and Edie in the cat ears. Treat grins. "That's stupid. Cherise too?"

"Sure. And Keith," I say, and we both laugh. "You coming out?"

He shakes his head.

"You know we need to practice in front of real people. And they're cool. Edie won't say anything bad."

"What about Cherise?"

I roll my eyes. "She won't say anything at all. She never does."

Treat steps into the hallway. "One song."

Keith has all the amps on, a couple extra chairs set up, and the garage door closed. As soon as Edie and Cherise see Treat behind me, they sit down.

"We're only doing one song," I say. "Then it's got to be a closed studio session so we can work on new stuff."

Cherise folds her hands in her lap real polite and Edie looks me over, and you know she's thinking this whole thing is artificial—a garage studio, a band with no drummer, and three guys who don't know what they're doing. Any second the whole thing could blow up in our faces. But as me and Keith put on our guitars, she smiles at us both, like maybe she's even a little excited.

Treat picks up the megaphone and turns to the electronic drums sitting on a box. "Solitary Man," he whispers and hits *start* on the drums. After the *tap-tap-tap*, me and Keith blast waves of distorted sound at Edie and Cherise. Treat starts singing at the exact right time, but instead of jumping out in front of us like usual, he's back by the boxes, facing the car cover with our logo on it. He sings the whole song this way. I can't look up for more than a glance without missing a string, but it goes pretty good. Edie's bobbing her head as the last twangs drain out of the amps and Cherise is a statue, staring at Treat's back as he finishes singing with three fake coughs, "Huh-huh-huh." Edie claps nice and loud and a millisecond later so does Cherise.

"You guys are really good," Edie says. "Right, Cherise?"

Treat sets down the bullhorn and moves the boxes a little, like maybe the acoustics were off because they were angled wrong.

"We really were good?" Keith says.

"Yes." Edie stands up. "Even Reece."

"Gee, thanks."

Cherise stands up. "Treat too."

Treat turns around then and looks at Cherise. "You like punk?"

She nods real serious like she's always liked punk.

"Who do you like?" he says.

"The Sex Pistols."

"Yeah?" Treat steps over to her. "And who else?"

It's so quiet all you can hear is the hiss of the amps. Cherise looks at Edie, pushes some hair behind her ear, and says, "Dik-Nixon."

Treat goes all grins, the Mohawk bobbing up and down. "Bitchin'."

As we walk the girls out of the studio, Edie gets this goofy smile and tells Keith she'll call him later when he gets back from San Diego.

"San Diego?" he says. "Oh, right. The SDSU gig."

Treat's bouncing all over the place after they leave, punching boxes, talking a hundred miles an hour about how we should work all night the way real bands do. "That's when the great stuff happens. When you're exhausted and pissed at each other and the sun's coming up. The air's different then. It's quieter and all the songs that haven't been written yet are easier to hear."

We get to work on a new song and get it down pretty good before Mrs. Dumovitch sticks her head out and asks who's staying for dinner.

"Everyone," Treat says.

"Okay," she says. "Then it's taquitos."

Treat turns around like a little kid who just found out he's having ice cream and cake for dinner. "You know what you should do, Reece? You should write a new song during dinner and then we can play it after."

"That's a lot of pressure," I say.

"You can do it," Keith says. "Your lyrics are so cool."

I take off the guitar. "Thanks, but I have to go home for dinner."

Treat grabs the guitar from me and sets it on its stand. "Have to?"

"Well, it's Friday. I'm just not supposed to eat meat unless it's fish."

Treat's looking at me like he's waiting for the punch line.

"It's a Catholic thing," Keith says. "They're weird about fish."

Treat nods like he totally gets it now. "But you can eat other stuff, right?"

"Yeah. Non-meat stuff."

"Then you can stay," Treat says. "My mom's making tofu taquitos."

"What the hell's tofu?" Keith says.

"I don't know. But it's not meat." Treat picks up the guitar and hands it to me. "Come on, we've probably got half an hour until it's ready."

∎

If you came walking into Treat's house at dinner, at first you'd think the Dumovitches were normal. There's bowls of food spread across this long, dark table and everyone sits down real polite and pleasant. But there aren't any plates, just these wicker trays with paper plates in the middle so we can compost them after we eat. And there aren't any chairs. They've got two long benches and everyone sits where they want because Mr. Dumovitch says there's no head at their table; everyone sits down as equals. Everyone except me. Treat puts a pencil and notepad in one spot and gives me a little shove: "You're there."

The taquitos are flaky and brown and stacked like a pyramid. The vegetables glisten with some sauce and there's at least three kinds in there I've never seen before. Still, it all looks and smells better than everything my mom has cooked ever. Even the glass pitcher of water looks good the way droplets are pinstriping their way down to the checkered towel Mrs. Dumovitch has wrapped around it like a skirt.

Mr. Dumovitch has us all join hands and tells us we should each say what we're thankful for. He starts by saying he's thankful for fall and his family. Treat's little sister, Jewell, says stuffed animals. Treat says, "The goddamned First Amendment," and Mr. D says Treat made his point in a clever way but he didn't need to show off in front of his friends. Mrs. D says she's thankful for me and Keith because we're such good friends to Treat. Keith says he's thankful for his dad, which probably looks sweet to Mr. and Mrs. D, but what he really means is money. I should say Neil Diamond, since he's probably cowriting the song I'm about to miraculously come up with. But Mr. and Mrs. D might know who that is, so without thinking, I say, "Uncle Ryan."

"Uncle Ryan?" Treat says.

"Treat!" Mrs. D says. "We don't question what people are thankful for."

"Sorry," Treat says. "I'm sure he's real cool. You should bring him over some time."

"Thanks," I say. "He's not around here."

"When's he coming to visit?" Keith says. "You talk about the guy all the time."

"He can't," I say, and the bottoms of my eyes start dancing. The corners of my mouth are reaching up to join them, so I take a drink of water, only my mouth isn't working right and I slurp in half a gulp and spill the rest.

"Why?" Keith says.

I can't talk or look at Keith. I'm dabbing the water on the table with my napkin and now writing a song doesn't seem so bad. It's been too quiet for too long.

"Because he can't," Treat says. "That's why."

"How do you know?"

"I just do," Treat says.

"Let's all dig in," Mr. D says, soft like he's introducing the next song at your little sister's recital.

My eyes and mouth slow down a little as the sounds of people eating start to rise, and I look up to see Treat is looking at me, but not all weird or angry or anything, just kind of waiting for me. Then he nods like we've agreed to something, you know, and it's pretty clear he'll keep a secret even if he doesn't know exactly what the secret is.

Mrs. D gets this excited tone in her voice and says she wants to know about everything we've been up to: school, the band, who the girls were, and why there's a pad and pencil at the table.

Treat says, "Good; good; friends; and Reece is working on a new song."

I look at Mrs. D. "I don't have to if you think it's rude."

"No," Mr. D says through a mouthful of taquito. "You keep working, Reece. Art is food for the soul." Mrs. D nods.

I can't think of any decent Neil Diamond songs while everyone else is eating and talking. I'm writing down anything that might get me going, the anarchy *A* with the circle around it, "God save the queen," "God save the children," "God bless Amerika," and "God has left the building." It's a bunch of nothing, but I keep going so it'll at least look like something's happening.

After dinner, Mrs. D gives us fig bars for dessert and we go back to the Two-Car Studio. Treat's munching away but I wait until Keith takes a bite of his. "What's it taste like?"

He looks at it. "It doesn't taste like a Fig Newton."

"It's a fig bar," Treat says.

Keith shrugs. "I thought that meant it was a big Fig Newton."

"Do they play country music in Soviet Georgia?"

"I don't know what that means," Keith says. He holds the fig bar out to Treat. "But whatever this is, I don't want it."

Treat snatches it from Keith like a manager taking the ball from a pitcher who just blew a two-run lead. He stuffs the whole thing in his mouth and asks me about the new song.

"There isn't one." I toss the pad onto a folding chair.

Treat picks it up and looks everything over. He taps one of my doodles. "What's this? The 'Terrorize Your Neighbor Tour'?"

"Nothing."

"It's like a concert poster." Treat holds it up for Keith to see and adds, "'Coming Soon to a Backyard Near You.'" He nods and looks at me. "This is what we'll do. A backyard party. Right here."

"Like Ted Three?" Keith says.

"No," Treat says. "Not like anything else. It can't be a secret. DikNixon is coming to your block. What could be scarier than that?"

"No one showing up," I say.

"Everybody will show up," Treat says. "Petrakis will bring his 'boys'—"

"And you can invite Astrid," Keith says. "If she comes, everyone will."

If I had stupid friends, I could say something like *I don't see how one person can make such a difference.* But everybody knows that if the captain of varsity cheer says she's going to your party, everyone who matters goes to your party. "Why do *I* have to invite her?"

Keith is pacing and grinning. "You talk to her all the time. You told me you said hi to her today and she smiled at you."

Treat slaps me on the shoulder. "It has to be you."

"It's not that easy."

Mr. D comes out to the studio, apologizing because he has to grab one of the boxes from our sound wall and take it inside.

Treat holds up the notepad. "We're having a party."

Instead of picking up the box, Mr. D lets his hands rest on it and looks at Treat. "Here? What kind of a party?"

Treat throws his hands out real wide. "A huge party in the backyard."

"People from your classes?"

"People from the whole school," Keith says.

Mr. D nods. "Uh-huh. And how can three freshmen throw a party and have the whole school actually show up?"

"The band," Treat says. "They'll come to hear our band."

Mr. D looks up at the rafters, really going over it in his mind, undoing and redoing his ponytail. "I really want this to happen for you, son." His face is all concentration, like he's trying to get the ponytail just right. "But I don't see it working out that easy."

Treat throws his arms up this time. "Jesus, Lyle. You're such a fascist."

"I didn't say no, Treat. I just want to make sure it works."

"It'll work."

"Your dad might be right," I say.

"You know what, guys?" Mr. D smacks one of the boxes like, *Here it is:* "Free beer. If you've got beer, it's a party. Even people who don't like beer, people who have never even drank beer, will come because they know if there's beer, there's a party. All those seniors will know that, and they'll come. And once you get the seniors, it's a chain reaction."

"We can put it on the flyer," Keith says.

"No, you don't," Mr. D says. "You tell people there's going to be free beer. But you don't write it down."

"Can we do that?" I say.

"I'll take care of it," Mr. D says. "I'll buy enough so everybody gets one."

Keith's smiling and even Treat's starting to. But not me. "No. I mean, can't you get in trouble for that?"

Mr. D picks up a box and shakes his head. "Oh, not if it's non-alcoholic."

"Won't people know it's fake?"

Mr. D walks to the door of the house and opens it. "Only if they can read German."

"I thought you drank real beer," Treat says.

"I used to," Mr. D says, stepping into the house. "Not anymore." He nods a *See ya later* and the door closes.

Instead of going back to work on our music, we make a flyer. We put the DikNixon logo across the top with a picture of Treat pasted below. It looks real fierce the way his Mohawk stands as tall as the band name. At the bottom, we paste on letters we've ripped out of Mr. Dumovitch's *Rolling Stone* magazines: *Terrorize Your Neighbor Tour. Saturday, Nov 6, 8 P.M.* At the very bottom, Treat puts his address and a map, and we give it to Mr. D to make copies for us.

It's almost ten at night by the time we're done with the flyer, and Keith's ready to go home, probably so he can call Edie and tell her everything.

"We really need to practice more," I say and Keith groans. "We've only got two weeks."

Treat nods. "Every spare second."

"Wait," Keith says. "What about Halloween? It's next week."

Treat picks up the bass and pushes it at Keith. "What are you, five? You're not going trick-or-treating."

Keith looks at me. "I just meant parties and stuff."

"We're getting ready for a better party," I say. "Our own party."

Keith sighs and puts the strap over his head, mumbling something about still being here at midnight.

Treat picks up the bullhorn. "You can call your girlfriend tomorrow."

"He doesn't have a girlfriend." I look at Keith. "Do you?"

"No," Keith says. "But Edie's our publicity person. We should tell her."

"Tomorrow," Treat says. "It's not like she's more important than Astrid."

"What?" I say. "We've got beer now. That'll suck in the best people."

Treat looks relaxed and understanding. "Look, Reece, we still need her. Even if she says no, she's going to find out you're in a band. Then you won't be the little boy next door. You'll be the guy next door. The guy in a band."

Keith's nodding. "I wish Astrid knew my name. I'm just the cute friend of the guy next door who's in the cool band."

My head's trying to go along with all this great stuff that happens *after,* but my stomach is already churning. Now I have to be the nobody freshman who says, *Happy Monday—here's a flyer for my band's gig.* "Fine," I say, "as long as we keep practicing. I don't want people saying they were let down by DikNixon."

Happy Monday

Saturday morning my dad's working an early shift and my mom's got Colleen with her at Brendan's football game. I get the sewing kit out of the upstairs hall closet and sit down right there on the floor. I've seen my mom thread a needle tons of times with my baseball uniforms in her lap, and that part goes smooth. The problem is getting the needle through a patch and then through the jacket. Pushing hard only makes the back end of the needle stab my thumb, the front end just standing there, the GBH patch repelling it like a shield.

Two bent needles and a throbbing thumb later, Colleen comes tromping up the stairs and stops, her red hair in pigtails on top of her head, making her look like a little alien. "What are you doing, Reece?"

"You guys are back?"

She nods. "Mom says you need to get Brendan's mouth thing for me."

"His mouthpiece?" I say, and she nods. "It's in the bathroom." She runs past me down the hall.

"Reece?" My mom's in the hallway now. Her hair is pulled back and braided the way she always does on the weekend or when she's cleaning house. You know, all business but kind of relaxed too. "What's the matter?"

There's no way to hide the jacket, or even the patch. "Nothing."

She looks at the GBH patch and waits.

"GBH is a band," I say and stand up. "Guitar, Bass, and Harmony."

She takes the patch and rubs it with her thumb. "These are hard to sew. I'll do it tonight."

"That's okay. Just tell me what the trick is."

Colleen comes out of the bathroom with the mouthpiece and stands next to me. "How about this?" my mom says. "I'll let Brendan go to the pizza party after the game with his team, and we'll come back here and have a sewing lesson."

Colleen's whole head turns into a smile. "Hooray!" she yells, and what can I say? How do you tell your little sister not to be happy and your mom *no thanks* for being nice?

■

As soon as she gets back, my mom sets everything up in the living room. Me and Colleen are on the couch with a couple pieces of practice cloth. My mom's on the easy chair with my jacket and the GBH and TSOL patches. I knew the pope and JFK would be watching over us from the dining room, so I stashed the Dead Kennedys patch in my room before my mom got back. I'll do that one later, on my own.

All the Saturday noise of people mowing their lawns or work-ing on their cars gets hushed out as me and Colleen each sew a piece of red cloth onto a piece of white cloth. We're real serious, paying total attention to everything Mom says. It's amazing how a tiny little string loops through a piece of cloth, over to the other, then back again, getting stronger at each loop until it's holding the two pieces together so tight they're pretty much one.

Mom holds up my jacket. "I'm about done with Guitar, Bass, and . . . ?"

"Harmony."

"Harmony." She nods. "Do you want to try True Sounds of—"

"Liberty," I say, and she smiles. "Sure."

Mom starts unhooking the TSOL patch from the shoulder. "Where did you get all these safety pins?"

"They're not yours. Treat gave them to me."

"But why do you need so many?"

There's like twenty for each patch because it looks more punk that way, but she's not getting me to say that. "Emergen-cies," I say.

"Emergencies," she says like she should have known. "I see."

My dad comes rattling through the front door just then, stone-faced until he sees all the cloth and thread. "What's this?"

"A little sewing lesson," Mom says.

He walks over and kisses her on the cheek; then he picks up the Packy jacket like he's never seen it before. He stares at the TSOL patch with its Statue of Liberty head and it's like some-body asked him the square root of 1776.

"True Sounds of Liberty," Mom says.

"True Sons of Liberty?" he says.

I want to sound tough, be punk rock and defiant, except there's a needle and a spool of thread in my lap. "Sounds," I say.

"Look at mine," Colleen says, holding up her cloth, the threads loose and way too far apart.

"Oh, that's good, Colleen," Mom says. "Isn't it, Pat?"

He nods the way he does when Brendan gets a 71 on a math test and brings it home like a dog with a dead squirrel. "That's lovely, sweetheart." He looks back at me. "Where's your Yankees jacket?"

I tell him upstairs but he keeps looking at me until I say, "It's fine."

Mom stands up. "Are you hungry, Pat?"

He keeps his eyes on the jacket. "What's with all the safety pins?"

"For emergencies," Mom says all matter-of-fact. She pulls the jacket from him, tossing it to me on her way to the kitchen. "Come on. I'll fry you up some tomatoes before I get lunch started."

∎

On the way to the stairs after Algebra on Monday, Edie says she's already bragged to five people about our show in San Diego and how we got out of there before the cops could arrest us. Just thinking how the rumor will be bouncing around at the speed of light—van Doren and Petrakis and Astrid all connecting us to DikNixon—makes me want to give Edie a big hug, my arms wrapping around her, my breath blowing across the back of her neck because her hair is short and there'd be nothing between her skin and my mouth.

I'm staring, saying nothing, just enjoying the niceness, when Edie's head goes a little sideways and her eyes narrow a little. "What?" she says, like she knows what I'm thinking.

"Nothing, except thanks, you know, for seeing us play Friday." I lean in close and whisper, "How many songs did we play?"

Her eyes go big and round and she whispers back, "Five." Then she puts on this fake voice. "Oh, and thanks again for letting us hitch a ride with you to San Diego. I don't know if we could have gotten there otherwise."

We laugh and Edie says she and Cherise will help us pass out party flyers.

"How do you know about the party?"

She says Keith told her, then looks me up and down, sort of squinting. "Is that okay?"

We get to the stairs and stop. "Yeah," I say without looking at her. "There's nothing to be mad about."

Edie laughs. "'Mad' means 'crazy.' But I'm glad you're not crazy."

I laugh. "Well, I'd be mad to be angry. Keith's your friend too."

"Good." She pulls a note out of her folder and hands it to me. "Then can you give this to him? Cherise and I are going to eat in the cafeteria today so we can keep talking you guys up."

"Sure. Thanks."

"Don't read it."

I put it in my pocket and pop my hand up like a magician who's just made a scarf disappear.

"Good," she says. She backs up a few steps to the stream of

people headed up the stairs, slips in with a turn, and just like that, disappears.

∎

Before English, Treat is crouched down in front of Mrs. Reisdorf's desk scribbling >*I*< on the front with a pencil. It's no bigger than a radio station bumper sticker, but it's the teacher's desk. Mrs. Reisdorf isn't in the room and everyone floating in looks at Treat for a second, then sits down like they don't see a thing. It's weird, you know, how a guy that big can be doing something this obvious and thirty people are looking around at each other or talking in pairs and doing everything they can not to see him.

Treat stands up when he's done and gives it a good look. "Hey, Reece," he says without looking back at me. "Is it dark enough?"

"Yeah, it's fine."

"Is it straight?"

I glance at the doorway for Mrs. Reisdorf. "Are you mad?"

Treat laughs and walks to his seat. "Could've gone bigger, huh?"

"You could've got caught."

The Mohawk shakes me off. "We've got a sub."

"It doesn't matter who catches you."

"He asked me where the bathroom was, and I said by the staircase."

"But there's one right here in the breezeway."

He looks at me, like, *Do I need to explain this?*

"Oh," I say and relax a little. "Did he say where Mrs. Reisdorf is?"

"Divorce court," Penny Martin says. She's in the desk in front of Treat and turns sideways. "Her husband's totally gay. Everybody knows."

It's weird how you never think of your teachers existing outside of school. How they have real lives and all. Even when me and Keith saw Mr. Krueger in the staff parking lot getting into this little MG convertible, I never thought about him actually pulling up next to me at a stoplight or cruising around on a Friday night with his wife next to him.

I try to imagine what Mrs. Reisdorf looked like when she first got married, before her eyes were red and puffy like they are a lot of the time now and instead of her hair being short and flat, maybe in a beehive or flipping around like Jackie Kennedy's. "Why would a gay guy get married in the first place?" I say.

"He probably didn't know he was gay," Penny says. "Happens all the time. He's in total denial and she just thinks he doesn't touch her because he's a gentleman."

"What about their honeymoon?" Treat says. "She'd know then."

"He probably faked it," Penny says.

I give that a "ha" and look at Treat. "Guys can't fake it."

Treat leans back in his seat. "People fake stuff all the time. Especially if they think it's what they're supposed to do."

Our sub comes rushing in, saying sorry he's late, and we start a read-around. Since I'm in a middle row, I've got a few pages before my turn, which makes it hard to follow along and not think about Mrs. Reisdorf being in love with some guy who hardly notices her. At least, not in the right ways.

After class, Treat reminds me to ask Astrid to the party, but instead of looking for her on the way to Spanish, I'm still thinking about Mrs. Reisdorf. What happens when she's not Mrs. Reisdorf anymore? I mean, not what do we call her, but who does she become when she's not the person she thought she was? It tickles my brain until I see Astrid, her white stockings clinging tight to her legs and disappearing into her Catholic school-girl skirt. She squints at me a little; then this half smile creeps out and she says, "Happy Monday."

My cheeks pull at my mouth, trying to stretch it to a smile, but I'm fighting it, keeping it tight and closed so I don't look stupid or say something stupid. She keeps staring and my hand shoots up on its own and it's all I can do to stop myself from waving like a kid seeing Mickey Mouse for the first time. I do this little pulse, forward and back, like the pope or something, like I'm blessing her somehow, and keep walking.

It's so dumb, so not what I'd wanted to do, that I'm too embarrassed to mention it until after lunch, after PE, when it's just me and Keith in the locker room.

"She talked to you first?" He grabs my wrist and stops me from stuffing my gym clothes into the locker. "She's not supposed to do that."

"Yeah, but the hand thing—"

"That's nothing. You didn't say anything, right?"

I snap my lock shut. "No. Nothing."

Keith shuts his locker. "You played it perfect."

"Doing nothing doesn't work," I say. "I've already done plenty of that."

"Nothing can be something." Keith pulls a note out of his back pocket, unfolds it, and puts it on the bench between us. "Look."

"You want me to read this?"

Keith shakes his head. "You're not supposed to, but if I drop it and don't realize for a minute—" He starts down the row of lockers to the bathroom. "I'll be right back. I'm going to check my hair."

Even without reading the note, you can tell a girl wrote it. It's in blue ink and swirly and neat, though a lot shorter than you might expect:

> *Keith,*
>
> *Even if Reece doesn't ask Astrid to the party, you guys still have to play. Cherise thinks that if she drinks a beer and Treat is real happy like he was after you guys played Friday, she'll be able to talk to him.*
>
> *Your friend,*
>
> *Edie*
>
> *P.S. Find out what Treat is going to wear because Cherise wants to try and wear something like it.*

I pick the note up and look harder at *Your friend*.

A second later, Keith comes around the corner of the lockers. "See?"

"Cherise likes Treat?"

Keith takes the note, folds it up, and stuffs it in his back pocket. "Yep. He pretty much ignores her and acts weird and she thinks he's a fox. Makes about as much sense as algebra."

Normally, we're at the door by now, waiting for the bell to ring, but today we keep standing there. "What about you? Doesn't Edie like you?"

"What's it look like?" Keith says.

"Sorry."

"It's okay. I bet you if I'd been like Treat, she'd like me." He picks up his backpack. "That's why Astrid talked to you. How many guys *don't* notice Astrid? You're like Fonzie."

The bell rings and we walk out onto the quad, people zooming by everywhere, and it's like me and Keith are invisible because we can talk about anything and no one is going to notice us.

"There's one other possibility," Keith says. "Maybe Astrid knows you're in DikNixon and just thinks she should be nice to you."

"Gee, thanks," I say.

"It's not a bad thing," he says. "And as soon as she sees us play, she'll be all Twinkie for you."

I'm trying to figure out if Keith knows something cool that I don't or if he's made this up on the spot. "Artificial colors and ingredients?"

Keith shakes his head. "Soft on the outside. Creamy on the inside." He grins and heads off to sixth period.

It's weird. Keith's pretty happy for a guy who keeps getting notes from the girl he likes that pretty much ignore him to talk about his friend and his band that isn't exactly real. I guess I'd have to be mad not to feel good about everything too, even if all the artificial colors and ingredients are starting to make me nervous.

Terrorize Your Neighbor

The thing no one ever tells you about California is that even though it gets to at least seventy degrees every day in the fall, the mornings don't always start out that way. A lot of times it's cloudy and gray, and even though you know you'll be dying of heatstroke by lunchtime, you need a jacket to get through the morning. That, and if I'm going to ask Astrid to come see Dik-Nixon, I need to do it in my Packy jacket now that the patches are sewn on. After I got the Dead Kennedys sewn on by myself and gave it a good look, I knew I wouldn't want to explain it to my dad, or even my mom. So I've been smuggling my Packy jacket in and out of the house by stuffing it in my backpack, which works fine until you've got a mess of homework and your mom sees you holding books while your jacket's peeking out of your backpack and *Why aren't you wearing your jacket? And why don't you wear the new one?* That's when parents start asking even more questions, or looking for patterns, or coming up with their own theories, and none of that is good. So after practice yesterday, Treat said I could leave my jacket in the Two-Car Studio from now on and he'd bring it to school for me.

Tuesday morning my mom's at the front door yelling at Brendan and Colleen to get it in gear. Her freckles are covered for the day, her hair up and tight. She's jingling her keys in one hand and has my Yankees jacket in the other.

"Here," she says.

I take it like she's handing me something to throw away. "Come on, Mom; it's California. It's not like it's *really* cold."

She opens the front door and the cold air rushes in like I'm in the ice-cream aisle at the A&P. "The weatherman said it's going to stay cold all day."

If my dad were home, I'd just put the jacket on, but he's been gone since before the sun came up. "I can't wear it."

"Can't?" She looks at the jacket, then me, as she folds her arms. "What's wrong with it?"

I fold my arms to hide the goose bumps. "Nothing. It's just, people here hate the Yankees. They'll make fun of me."

She stares at me, then lets out a big burst of air like she's blowing out birthday candles. "I don't have time to deal with this now. Where's your jacket with the patches?"

"I left it at a friend's house."

"Left it?" she says like it's a hundred-dollar bill. "At Keith's?"

I stare outside, wondering if a little lie is okay. The jacket really is at a friend's house; does it matter which one? And suddenly, Treat's out on the sidewalk in front of my house, looking around like he's lost a ball in the bushes.

"Never mind," I say and step out the door with the jacket.

"Put it on," she says as I'm pulling the front door closed behind me.

Treat's hands are plunged into the pockets of his ripped-up jeans. He's wearing his sleeveless Levi's jacket with a lumberjack shirt underneath, checkered and bleached, and his army satchel is bulging at his side.

I cut diagonal across the front lawn and head down the sidewalk so he'll follow.

"Hang on," he says. "I brought you something."

I wave him up but don't stop walking until I'm at the corner, across from Keith's house. Treat's just about caught up, only a few feet behind me. Over his shoulder, back at my house, Brendan is walking across the lawn. He's looking down at his feet and stepping in the footprints my feet left in the dewy grass.

"Come on," I say, because if Keith isn't ready, we can go inside until Brendan walks by and my mom leaves with Colleen in the car. Only, Keith comes slamming out his front door just as we get across the street.

"Hey, Treat," he says like it's no big deal, like we always walk to school with him.

"Let's go," I say and start walking up the sidewalk.

"Hang on," Treat says and digs into his satchel. He pulls out my jacket, crumpled down to the size of a football. He takes a good look at my Yankees jacket. "You're *not* wearing that to school."

Keith laughs. "Cool jacket, Slugger." He's wearing his Mickey Mouse Mohawk T-shirt over a black, long-sleeve T, and with some new crosses added to Mickey's ears, it's looking really punk.

Treat unfolds the Packy jacket and it comes to life. The Dead Kennedys and TSOL patches scream out from the shoulders, and the red of the GBH patch looks bright and serious in the morning gray. I slip it on and it feels good to be standing there, the three of us looking kind of different yet fitting together. Like a band should.

"Reece?"

Brendan steps up next to me on the sidewalk, his eyes huge and on Treat.

"Is this your bro?" Treat says.

"Yeah."

Brendan hasn't looked this scared since the Saturday he confessed about the trash can fire.

"What do you want?" I say and zip up my jacket.

Brendan's eyes move from Treat's real Mohawk to the Mickey Mouse Mohawk and then to my patches. "I don't want anything."

"Great. See ya."

"Okay," he says and walks away real fast.

"Bright kid," Treat says.

I push the Yankees jacket at Keith. "Can you put this in your house? I'll get it after school."

"Sure," he says and takes off to do it.

Treat looks back down my cul-de-sac.

"Astrid's already gone," I say. "She gets a ride with her friends."

"You have to ask her today. Three people congratulated me yesterday for our gig in San Diego."

"I'll try."

"Try?" He looks at the gray sky like there's something there, then back at me. "People know we're DikNixon. We've got less than two weeks until the party, and socialites like Miss Astrid have to make plans well in advance."

"It's not like it's easy to ask."

"You think carving our logo into desks all over campus is easy?"

Keith comes running back and we start walking. Treat puts a finger to my chest. "You've got to do more than try."

"Do. Or do not," Keith says. "There is no try."

"Yoda?" Treat says and gives Keith the stink eye. He puts an arm around my neck and squeezes a little. "Remember, this is bigger than all of us. If Astrid doesn't come, no cheerleaders come. No football players, no upperclassmen . . ."

"Not even the geeks will come," Keith says. "Except for me."

■

No one in first period actually asks if me and Keith are in Dik-Nixon. But it's like half the class watches me sit down. And halfway through class, when I look over at Keith to see if he's as bored as I am, I catch someone beside Keith watching him like something could happen at any second.

It's the same in Algebra. Edie sees it too. She passes me a note with a cartoon drawing of me surrounded by bug-eyed people. The little bubble by my face actually says something this time too: *I'm not Dick Nixon, but I play him in a band.*

In English, Penny Martin asks if it's true, that I'm in Treat's band, and Treat says it is. "Wow," she says. "Who knew you were cool?"

Van Doren hasn't been to the lockers all day and I'm glad. If he asks me anything, I know my answers will sound like I'm covering something up, because I am. We're not really a band with all this experience. And as soon as van Doren knows there's a cover-up, it's probably over for DikNixon.

I miss Astrid all day too, but I know how that happens. It's hard to see anybody on the way to English, or Spanish, or on the way to lunch when you're looking at your feet the whole time, and really, those are the only times I usually see her.

During practice in the Two-Car Studio, Mr. Dumovitch comes out with a box full of flyers. The cutout letters and huge picture of Treat look even fiercer with the little lines and blurriness the copier made. It looks like a ransom note, except across the top it says DIKNIXON / TERRORIZE YOUR NEIGHBOR TOUR.

Treat hands a bunch to Keith. "Give these to Edie and Cherise tomorrow, and make sure they tell people about the free beer." He hands me just one flyer. "You don't even have to talk to Astrid now; just say, 'This is my band. There's going to be free beer.'"

"That's talking," Keith says.

Treat keeps looking at me. "You know what I mean. The flyer will do the talking."

On the way home, Keith's going on and on about how great this is, how it's all fitting together like Legos. I'm imagining Astrid at her locker, folding the flyer into a paper airplane and sailing it into the back of my head as I'm walking away. Then real life hits me: Tomorrow is trash day. I can hand Astrid a flyer in the morning before school, before anyone else is around. Even if she smiles and drops it right into the can, at least no one else will see.

■

The quiet wakes me up. I'm sitting straight up in bed, light pouring through my window, but my alarm isn't blaring. I can't think what day it is. It feels too early to be Saturday, and if it was Sunday my mom would already be getting after me to get ready for church. Then the whir and bang of the trash truck echoes into my room and my stomach squeezes with tickle pain. The alarm clock is blinking *12:00, 12:00, 12:00* and I throw on the dirty clothes draped over my chair, grab the flyer, and run downstairs.

The truck is next door and only the trash cans people put out last night are on the curb; everybody else is going to miss it. Even Astrid. I pull my cans out onto the driveway and then go for hers. The driver stops the truck between our houses, and while his partner's dragging my cans to the truck, he jumps out to help me with Astrid's. He's got a red bandana like a headband and the rest of his black hair is braided into a thick rope going down his back. And even though his jumpsuit is baggy, like maybe he's skinny, he carries a trash can in each hand while I drag one. His arms are brown and veiny and covered in tattoos, barbed wire wrapped up with a rosary and a bloody Jesus head with the crown of thorns. When we get to the truck, he dumps both his cans and slides one into the other before pulling mine from me. He dumps it real fast, slides it into the others, then puts out his gloved hand to me. "You throwing that out too?"

The flyer is crinkly in my hand. "No."

The driver takes a good look at it and nods. "That's a pretty scary dude," he says, sliding the trash cans over to me.

"He's cool."

"Oh yeah," he says as he's walking around the front of the truck to get back in. "Guys like that, they already had their trouble."

Astrid comes walking out onto her driveway, baggy sweatpants and a giant Go-Go's T-shirt sagging from her shoulders. It's kind of funny because all the girls on the shirt have their hair in towels and cream all over their faces and you can tell they're probably pretty but this isn't them at their best. And here's Astrid, her hair messy and eyes squinty and she might as well have on face cream and a towel too. It makes her sort of real.

"Reece?" she says, her arms folded and goose bumps all across them. "Did you pull out our trash cans?"

"Yeah," I say, nice and slow. "There wasn't time to get you—"

"You're so sweet," she says and touches my arm. Her eyes go to the flyer and she tugs it from my hand soft and slow. "What's this?"

My body is so warm even though it's cold outside and kind of relaxed because all the excitement is over. For the first time ever, talking to Astrid feels normal. "Oh. That's for you."

While she reads it, she keeps one arm folded across her chest, her hand tucked into her armpit. "Do *you* know DikNixon?"

"I'm in DikNixon. Me and some other guys."

Her mouth opens and she looks up. "That's you?"

"Yeah. I write the songs."

"Wow." She smiles and it's so big it has to be real. "That's *very* cool."

I'm nodding and have to actually think *Stop nodding* to make myself stop, but it doesn't go on too long and I say, "You should come to the gig. There's going to be free beer."

She studies the flyer for a second more. "Maybe. It depends on what my friends are doing Saturday." She looks up and gives me this uneven, almost dirty grin that takes out my knees like a game-saving tackle. "You're DikNixon," she says and folds up the flyer. "Okay."

"Yeah," I say, trying to keep from smiling. "And if you can't make it, we'll have other shows."

"Okay," she says and backs away.

"Okay," I say, wondering now if I've just undone what I've done. Then I notice my dad's truck still in the driveway. "Happy Wednesday," I say and take off running.

■

When he looks at his watch on the nightstand, my dad says, "Damn," and heads straight to the bathroom. My mom says to get Brendan and Colleen going while she writes their late notes for school.

With everyone running around fast and a little frantic, I leave my hair sticking up in every direction, throw on some clothes quick, grab my backpack, and get out the front door without a jacket.

It feels colder now that I'm not dragging around trash cans, my face getting tight and tingly in the air, so I'm happy to see Treat walking foot over foot on top of the wall between my yard and Astrid's. His arms are out sideways, his face concentrating. He thuds down on our driveway, glances up, then yells past me, "Morning, Mr. Houghton!"

My dad is almost to his truck, keys in hand, and staring past me. "Morning." He gets a really good look at Treat before unlocking the door and climbing in. He looks at me, says, "See you tonight, Reece," and closes the door.

Treat steps up next to me. "This is kind of late for your dad, isn't it?"

My dad backs out of the driveway, his head turned away and eyes on the street. He doesn't have any reason to look back now, but as soon as the truck's pointing in the right direction, he takes one more peek before driving off.

"We had a blackout," I say. "Didn't you?"

Treat pulls my jacket out of his satchel and hands it to me. "Nope. We must be on a different grid."

Keith's been up for about five minutes when we get there, so we sit in his room while he scrambles to get ready, yelling from the bathroom that maybe he should just have his mom call him in sick since he doesn't have time to shower.

"Are you kidding me?" Treat says, lying back on Keith's unmade bed. "Look at Reece. His hair looks bitchin' today. Maybe a little Echo and the Bunnymen, but kind of Joe Strummer too."

Keith sticks his head in the room and looks me over. "Okay, two minutes."

I tell Treat about what happened with Astrid, how I was so panicked about the trash cans that I was kind of relaxed when I gave her the flyer, which seemed good at first, but then she said the thing about only trying to make it and hadn't totally promised.

"She'll come," Treat says. "She knows it's a big spotlight now and she needs to be in it."

Keith comes back in the room, one whole side of his head soaking wet. "I told you," he says. "The less you care, the more they like you."

"Just like Cherise," I say, and want it back as soon as it's out of my mouth.

"Cherise?" Treat sits up.

Keith's eyes bulge for an instant as he grabs his backpack off the floor. "Come on, we're gonna be late."

Treat grabs Keith's backpack, stopping him right where he is. "We're already late, Turbo. What's this about Cherise?"

"You idiot," Keith says to me.

Treat lets go of the backpack. "Does Cherise have a crush on one of you guys?"

Keith slips on his backpack. "She has a crush on you."

"Me?" Treat says. He stands up the way a cowboy in a Clint Eastwood movie does when he knows he's about to get shot, kind of slow and stunned and looking around like he doesn't recognize anything around him.

Keith heads to the stairs. "Don't tell Edie you know. It's been a secret."

"Been?" Treat says as he gets to the top of the stairs. "For how long?"

Keith's at the bottom now, so Treat stops and waits for me. "How long have you known?"

"I *just* found out," I say and fly past Treat.

The whole way to school, Treat grills Keith for more answers, completely forgetting that Astrid may come to the party, that all the best people might be coming to hear us play.

As we set foot on campus, Treat makes us swear to keep secret what is already supposed to be kept secret, shakes his head, then takes off for his locker.

"He's mad," Keith says.

"And angry," I say, and we both laugh. "I'd be so stupid happy if *anyone* liked me."

Keith pets my arm. "I like you."

"Yeah. But that only makes me feel stupid. And gay."

Keith rubs his chin. "Gay means happy, right?"

"Yeah," I say.

"Well, I'm just so gay about the fact that I can make you feel gay." I'm busting up, so Keith isn't about to stop: "We should wish everyone to have a gay day today. And gay birthdays, and a Gay New Year, and a gay old time, and . . ."

Judas with Pom-poms

Treat's so angry with me and Keith that he won't talk to us at lunch the rest of the week except to say something about new songs he's heard by bands we've never heard of, or what time to be at the Two-Car Studio for practice. At practice, he'll only talk about the songs we're working on. It's still fun, though. Between songs, while Treat fiddles with the drum machine or changes a lyric, me and Keith study our periodic table flash cards or joke around a little. Then Treat says to focus, which we do, and we get going again.

We're getting pretty good. Our songs sound like songs most of the time now, and by Saturday afternoon, a week before the party, Treat holds his hands up in the middle of a song that's going pretty good and we stop. It's quiet for a second, just the hum of the amps, and then he says, "I'm giving you both a pardon." He doesn't say for what, but it's got to be the whole Cherise cover-up. Keith looks at me like maybe he's going to start explaining what happened but I shake him off and say, "Thanks. Let's get back to the music." Treat nods, says, "Walk Like a Man," then hits *start* on the drum machine and we're back at it.

We don't practice on Sunday, though. Treat says it's so we'll be fresh for Monday and not so he can stay home to give out candy while his parents take Jewell trick-or-treating. Keith comes over to my house to jump out of the bushes and scare kids while I work the door, and it's pretty fun until my parents come back with Brendan and Colleen. Keith has to go home then, so it just feels like a normal Sunday night after that. At least, as normal as things have been in California.

We're back to practicing Monday after school, and again Tuesday, and by Wednesday night I'm feeling pretty good about DikNixon and write a letter to Uncle Ryan. I tell him all about what happened last week with Astrid and the trash guy. I even draw the barbed-wire Jesus tattoo for him in the middle of the page. I tell him how good DikNixon is sounding, how it's just in time with the party in a few days, and I give him the set list we're thinking about using. Then I tell him how Keith and Edie and Cherise have been passing out flyers all week to freshmen and sophomores, and how Treat says we'll hit the upperclassmen tomorrow. Astrid's had a week to get them all talking about Dik-Nixon, so Treat thinks one last push will have them all in a frenzy for the party. I finish the letter by drawing the >I< logo at the bottom, tell Uncle Ryan I wish he could be here to see the band even though I know he can't, and then go to bed with the glow of Astrid's room as my night-light.

■

Thursday morning my mom's at the front door, the Yankees jacket in her hand. When I take it without a fight, she opens the front door and tells me to have a good day.

Treat thuds down from the wall and meets me at the sidewalk. His satchel is bulging with my Packy jacket stuffed inside. When I go to reach for it, he looks past me and snaps his hand to his forehead like a salute, "Good morning, Mrs. Houghton."

The front door is still open, my mom fiddling around with the lock like maybe there's something wrong with it, which there isn't. She stands up and folds her arms over her work blouse. "Good morning." She touches the lock again, gives it a *humph*, and shuts the door.

"Nice lady," Treat says.

"She's okay, for a spy."

On the way to school, Treat gives me and Keith each a fresh stack of flyers for the upperclassmen. He won't pass any out himself because he says Mr. Marshall is just looking for an excuse to bust him again. I believe him and try not to think about how me and Keith will have to take the fall if we get caught.

When we get to campus, Treat reminds us, "Just be smart about it." Then he takes off for his locker. Keith takes off too, saying he's going to go give some flyers to Edie before Mr. Krueger's class.

I'm stuffing the flyers in my locker when van Doren comes walking up with a few other guys. He's laughing and saying how maybe they should go up to Santa Monica Saturday night and party at his cousin's place. I'm a tenth of a second from getting out of there, my General Science book in my hand, when van Doren's calculus book smashes down on top of it, knocking it out of my hand and both books flopping open on the ground. Van Doren's hand drops down next to my face and he says all casual, "Do you mind getting that?"

He turns around to his buddies and keeps talking. "His parents are out of town for the weekend . . ."

As I grab van Doren's book, I pull a DikNixon flyer out of my locker, fold it in half, and tuck it into the calculus book with all the other papers.

"Here." I hold up the book and van Doren puts his hand back, nowhere near it. I stand up and look right at him. "Right here."

Van Doren turns and his eyes go a little round as he gives me a half smile and takes the book. "Thank you, Mr. President."

When I see van Doren later in the morning, he's talking to Astrid after third period. He's got the flyer in his hand and looks like he might actually say something to me. Then Astrid says, "Happy Thursday," and van Doren looks at her, kind of surprised.

At lunch, me and Keith walk to the edge of the Senior Circle and get Petrakis to come over. As soon as he sees Treat on the flyer, he says to give him the rest of the stack. "We'll make this party go off, little dudes."

Petrakis slips back into the circle and right away he's showing people the flyer. Treat's watching from the Bog and when he asks how it went, Keith says, "Legos."

Treat looks at me, so I translate: "Everything's fitting together perfectly."

■

Edie's at my locker after school, her arms folded and foot tapping. "Where have you been?" she says and doesn't wait for an answer. "Look what somebody did."

She hands me a flyer, only it's on yellow paper now and *DikNixon* is gone. It says *Ted*, and Treat's address is covered over with a new one. It's almost my house, just off by two numbers.

Keith and Treat come walking up with yellow Ted flyers. "She screwed us," Keith says.

"Who?" Edie says.

"Astrid." Keith flicks the address at the bottom. "This is her house."

Treat shakes the Mohawk at me. "Fucking Judas with pompoms."

"Maybe it's the house on the other side," I say, because how could Astrid do this? She said "Happy Thursday" to me.

Edie looks at me like I said the earth is flat.

Treat crumples the flyer in his hand. "We should rip the fucking ribbons out of her hair and choke her with them."

Keith crumples the flyer in his hand. "I hope she chokes on her pom-poms."

"That doesn't make any sense," I say. "Besides, how do we know Astrid's even connected to this? Are we going to dust it for fingerprints?"

Everyone glares at me. Treat snatches the flyer and holds it an inch from my nose. "It's her address, Reece. Connect the dots."

"It doesn't mean *she* did it." I look at Treat. "Maybe it's a conspiracy."

"Are you serious?" Edie says. "She does stuff like this all the time."

"Like *this*?"

"Devious stuff." Edie looks around, then lets her voice go a little lower. We close in to hear and she says, "Not obvious things, but secret things so she can still look sweet in public when she's really not."

"How do *you* know?"

"People talk. You think you guys are my only friends?"

Treat steps back. "Emergency band meeting at three thirty."

"Let's do it right now," Keith says.

"No," Treat says. "At three thirty. After I rake leaves."

Keith folds his arms. "Okay. But then we come up with a plan that gets right in Astrid's face and says, 'You know what, you bitch? You're a ... a ... you're a bitch.'"

"Yeah, something like that," Treat says, "but something that's actually good."

Treat and Edie get going. Keith waits for me to get my stuff, and when I open my locker, one of those yellow flyers falls out. It's folded in half so someone could slide it in, and there's a note on the back in swirly, perfect, girl writing:

> *Dear Reece,*
>
> *I'm so sorry about the mix-up. I totally forgot about the party I'm throwing on Saturday. It was kind of a last-minute thing and I hadn't made flyers yet. So, my friend Lori changed your flyer and Xeroxed them during fourth period work-study so that my party won't compete with yours. She shouldn't have done that,*

*and I'm sorry, but now you can change your party for
the next weekend and everybody can go to both parties.*

*Plus, you have to come to my party too. You
can bring your band, except you can't play. It got too
loud last time. But I really want you to come, okay?
You're the best neighbor ever and if I could have
anyone in the world living next door I'd pick you
every time. So come to my party and give me a new
flyer for your party with a new date on it and I'll
tell all my friends.*

> *Your friend, neighbor,
> and trash buddy,*
>
> *Astrid*

Keith reads it after me. "She did do it."

"On accident."

"There are no accidents," Keith says just like Mr. Krueger does when he's talking about discoveries and experiments. "Just happy mistakes."

"Okay. So, a happy mistake."

"Maybe," Keith says. "But I'm not happy. Are you?"

I'm thinking, *Kind of,* because I finally got a note from a girl and it's Astrid. It hits me big then; she knows which locker is mine. She came over, stood right here, and slid the note through the door. She even spelled my name right. "We can make this work for us. You know, more time to practice and promote the band."

Keith leans against the lockers and looks out at the quad. "I guess. But I hate it when people play with my Legos."

"Liar. You're dying to let somebody play with your Legos."

Keith grins and we start walking. "You're right. I've been playing with myself way too much."

■

Treat's got the Bug out on the driveway with the car cover actually on it. Keith's guitar and amp are sitting next to it and Treat's inside the Two-Car Studio, folding up chairs.

"What are you doing?" Keith says.

Treat folds his arms. "Nobody's going to have DikNixon to kick around anymore. I won't let that happen."

My heart feels like it just swallowed itself and I pull out the flyer with Astrid's note on the back. "Here." I hold it out. "Astrid apologized."

Treat steps around me and starts rolling up the carpet. "Does she say it was all an accident?"

"Yeah."

"And that she didn't mean anything by it and she'll make it up to you?"

"Pretty much."

"And that she's a lying whore who only cares about herself?"

I step onto the carpet so Treat has to stop and look up at me. "She says she wants us to come to her party."

Keith steps onto the carpet next to me. "She says it twice."

Treat stands up and I hand him the note. He reads it and hands it back. "You know she's lying."

"Maybe she's not," I say.

"Look, she's lying. I know you like her, and I know you're probably the only freshman she's ever talked to, even counting when she was a freshman, but she's lying."

"She invited us. We'll know if there isn't really a party."

"There's going to be a party." Treat grabs a chair, unfolds it, and sits down. "The only thing she's sorry about is that this makes her look bad. There wasn't a Ted Three until today."

I unfold a chair and sit. "That doesn't mean we have to end the band." As I say it, I feel it, you know? We are a band. I know it now because it feels like we're losing something. "Come on, Treat."

Keith squats down between us. "It's not very punk rock to let some cheerleader break up your band."

Treat keeps quiet, his head down and eyes on the floor. "I'm not going to her party. No way."

"Okay," I say. "But we're still a band, aren't we?"

Keith slips the flyer out of my hand. "You know what we could do? We could change their flyer back to make it ours again, like 'Never mind Ted Three—here's DikNixon.'"

Treat looks up at the flyer. "Almost," he says and the Mohawk swings over toward me. "We need it to be more of a *fuck you* than that."

I laugh. "A *fuck you* flyer?"

"Who doesn't like to get fucked?" Keith says and we look at him. "I mean, hypothetically."

Treat's grinning now. "Hypothetically fucked?"

Keith is serious. "When you think about it, *fuck you* is a compliment. If a good-looking girl said, 'Fuck you,' to me, I'd say, 'Okay, when?'"

"That's not what it means," Treat says.

"I know," Keith says. "It's just hypothetical."

"Fuck you," Treat says.

Keith stands up. "No, thanks. I like girls."

Treat busts out laughing and tells me to go get the guitar and amp off the driveway. We put the carpet and chairs back in the right places and then we bring the car cover back in. Me and Treat stuff the top corners up high under boxes while Keith holds it.

The cover unfurls in front of us and Treats says, "Ready to jam?"

Keith is nodding and I know now, for sure, this is going to happen. DikNixon is back. Again.

Ted Airlines

On Saturday night, me and Keith tell my mom we're going to the library. I put on my Yankees jacket, stuff the periodic table cards in my back pocket, and grab my backpack, only there isn't a single book in there, just my Packy jacket and our new flyers. We actually go to the library and quiz each other for about half an hour; then we go to Keith's to drop off our backpacks and get ready for the party. About nine, we sneak down my cul-de-sac on the opposite side of the street to get to Astrid's. Her driveway is filled with cars, three wide and three deep, spilling out into the street, where even more cars are curled around the bend. It really is Ted Three.

Me and Keith knock at the front door and stand there for five minutes before Keith just opens it. Music blares from the living room stereo, but the room is totally empty. We walk through to the kitchen and it's senior city around the kitchen table: Sergio Ortiz (still with his clothes on), Ted, a couple guys from Filibuster, and Kylie Smith sitting on Petrakis's lap. They're playing quarters and drinking beer from plastic cups, except for Kylie, who has a wine cooler.

"Hey, little dudes," Petrakis says. "What'cha got there?"

Keith holds out the stack of flyers and Petrakis grabs half of them. Kylie leans into his chest and they read one together. The new flyer is a big picture of Treat's head and it looks like he's got a cigarette hanging out of his mouth, only it's not a cigarette. If you look close, it's actually a picture of a white United Airlines jet with the wings missing and the plane smoked down to ashes so it only reads *ted*. That's the *fuck you* part of the flyer.

Kylie points the plane out to Petrakis and he says, "Oooooh"; then she hands flyers around the table.

"There's still going to be free beer," I say.

Ted's looking at the plane. "Why does it say that, Ted Airlines?"

Sergio hands a couple flyers to the guys from Filibuster. "Check it out," he says, excited. "Ted's got his own airline."

"That kicks ass," one of the other guys says.

Ted looks around and sees everyone looking at the flyers and nodding. "Totally," Ted says. "This will be epic."

Petrakis points at the glass sliding door to the backyard. "The keg's out there, little dudes."

■

The patio's swarming with people, but it's easy to spot Astrid by the keg. Her hair's up on one side, tight with pink flower pins that match her lacy socks. She's got a giant hoop earring on that side and just a little diamond on the other. She's huddled with two other girls, one I don't think I've ever seen before at school and the other is Lori, the girl who changed our first flyer and made all the copies.

Lori is going on and on about a girl named Theresa and how she's upstairs right now and "thinking about actually calling him. Can you believe that?"

"I can't," Keith says, and all three girls look at him.

The girl we don't know grins. Lori rolls her eyes and turns back to Astrid. "What should we do?"

"You know how she gets," Astrid says.

Lori's hands fly out. "I know. He's probably coming anyway, so why—"

The third girl holds her hand up, stopping Lori. "Who are these little boys, Astrid?"

Astrid turns around. "This is my neighbor, Reece, and his friend."

"Keith," Keith says.

Lori looks like she couldn't care less, like she might say, *Yes, it's terribly boring to meet you.* "Anyway," she says.

Astrid gives Lori a *Be nice* glare. "Guys, this is Lori—"

We've always known who Lori is because she's a cheerleader, but Keith says, "The Xerox girl," and holds a new flyer out for her.

Lori takes the flyer and kind of bulges her eyes at Astrid for a second, like, *Did you really tell them it was me?*

Astrid doesn't react. She just keeps on going with the introductions. "And this is—"

"Sascha," the girl next to Lori says. And now that I have an excuse to really look at her, I know I've never seen her before. If there's a cute, brown-haired, green-eyed girl at your school who is only as tall as a freshman but has the body of a senior, and her name is weird, you remember her.

"Sascha?" Keith says.

She looks at Astrid. "Is my name not Sascha?"

Astrid waits a second, then nods along with a "Yes."

Sascha puts her hand out flat, palm down, to Keith. "Sascha."

I think she wants Keith to kiss it or something but he sticks out two fingers spread real wide and grabs Sascha's hand. "Scissors cuts paper."

She pulls her hand back and laughs and it makes the giant hoop in her left ear swing around a little. Then I see the little diamond in her right ear. *That's* who found Astrid's other earring. I nudge Keith but he's staring so hard at Sascha he just absorbs it like rain in the ocean.

Astrid says they need to get upstairs and Lori agrees. "Reece," she says, "can you do me a favor? If you see anyone coming out here to pee, can you tell me who?"

"Check," I say and can't believe *that* is what came out of my mouth.

"You're sweet," Astrid says and heads inside with Lori right behind her.

Sascha steps behind them, sticking out her left hand and letting a couple fingers glide across Keith's chest as she walks by, "See you later, Scissors." She looks at me and lightly tugs a flyer out of my hand. "Thank you, neighbor."

The door is barely shut before Keith's in my face. "Did you see that? Oh my God. What do I do?"

"How should I know? Did you hear me? 'Check.' I could have said, 'No problema,' or 'You got it.' But 'Check'? I'm such a nerd."

Keith gets a cup, fills it with beer, and gulps it halfway down. He fills a cup for me, fills his up again, and we hand out flyers to everyone on the porch before going back inside.

■

The kitchen is packed now, chairs pulled all around the table as people play quarters and other people stand behind them, cheering or awwww-ing every shot. Ted's digging through the refrigerator, getting ready to make his famous bacon quesadillas, and Sergio has his shirt all the way unbuttoned.

Behind me, some guy snaps his fingers. "Hey, Mr. President. A flyer."

It's van Doren. He's sitting on the kitchen counter, legs crisscrossed and a bottle of Gatorade between them. I give him one and then anyone in the kitchen who doesn't have one suddenly says, "Me too."

We get through the kitchen and back to the empty living room. We could leave now, but Keith says maybe we should get another beer. His is empty, but mine's still full. "Well, we should give away all the flyers before we leave," Keith says. He looks at the staircase. "Are you sure Sascha got one? Maybe I should go up there and check."

"If you want to," I say, but he doesn't. Instead, we sit down on the floor by the stereo and start going through the albums spread across the carpet. There's Adam and the Ants, Echo & the Bunnymen, and the Go-Go's, the bands cool girls like. And even though there's an Air Supply album, there's also some punk tapes: Adolescents, Agent Orange, and Black Flag.

Keith can't stop staring at the cover of the Cars album *Candy-O* because the cartoon girl lying on the car is pretty much naked.

"She's not real," I say.

Keith says, "I know. But if I was Fred from *Scooby-Doo* . . ." He taps the cartoon picture right in the crotch and his eyes get real big. "Forget Daphne."

The album that's been playing ends and there's a bunch of shouts from the kitchen for more music. It scares me, like I've been caught with a *Playboy* or something, so I play it off like I was just about to put on the Cars album anyway. As soon as the *hiss, click, click,* disappears into "Let's Go," we hear cheers in the kitchen and me and Keith become the unofficial deejays of the party. And even though Keith's spending most of the time looking for albums with more half-naked girls on the covers or on the sleeves, we're doing a good job of changing albums after every song and handing flyers to anyone who comes through the front door. We've got the next three songs picked out and are studying a new stack of albums when a pair of legs wrapped in tight pegged jeans appears right behind Keith. Sascha leans down and says, "Hey, Scissors, want to help me win a bet?"

Keith doesn't ask what the bet is. He just stands up, says, "Sure," and lets her lead him up the stairs without looking back.

I'm not sure if I should be happy or scared for Keith, but then Sergio sort of staggers into the living room, naked except for the shirt tied around his head. "She got any Buzzcocks? I need to dance, man. And piss."

He staggers off into the hallway. I start digging through the tapes, so afraid he'll come back that as soon as I see the Dickies, I throw that on and figure it's close enough.

There's a couple guys playing pool in the family room, and over in the corner is the bar me and my dad built. It looks really good with a little studio light shining down. The shelves are filled with all these blue and brown bottles that have ships and maps and swirls on their labels.

I squat down behind the bar to check out the mini-fridge Mr. Thompson put in. "I already checked," someone says. "No wine coolers." I stand up and there's a guy about my height right across the bar. He's got white-blond hair, pretty flat and plain, not at all punk, and an English Beat T-shirt. "Can you make drinks?"

"Sure," I say, because Uncle Ryan taught me how to make him rum and Cokes one Thanksgiving. "We got any ice?"

The guy's gone and back in a flash. He slides a bowl full of ice across the bar and hops onto a stool. "Set me up, barkeep."

Carey, who tells me it is a guy's name too, like Cary Grant, knows even fewer people at the party than me. I slide the rum and Coke over to him and he says he needs a coaster so he doesn't stain the bar. You'd think there'd be a few coasters but there aren't, so I pull a flash card out of my back pocket and toss it onto the bar.

Carey slides it under his drink. "What's this?"

It's Na. "Sodium," I say.

Carey takes a drink and nods. "I get it, because there's soda in the drink and it's kind of sweet." He finishes it off. "Sodi-mmmmm. What else you got?"

I toss out another card: Ne. "Neon."

He scans the bottles over the bar. "You'll need a tall, skinny glass, orange juice, annnnnnd, there, that, the lime vodka."

I mix the drink and set it on the card. "This one's on the house."

He laughs like it's the best joke ever, then drinks the whole thing in a gulp and tells me to toss another card out. We invent a bunch of drinks, putting vodka and ruby-red cranberry juice together for rubidium and Captain Morgan with a lot of different things, trying to make neptunium.

He asks why I'm not having any and I make up a story about my parents busting me last week and having to lay low awhile.

"I've been there. But I'm staying at Marc's tonight, so it's no biggy."

It takes me a second. "Marc van Doren?"

"Yeah," Carey says. "He's my cousin."

I make Carey a Krypton, which we figure should have just about everything in it, and he tells me more about van Doren than anyone at school must know, how recruiters really are calling him about track scholarships and how the one he wants most is UCLA.

You might think it's not punk rock to run track. Treat didn't think so until we saw van Doren at his locker one day right before practice. His shorts went down to his knees, his socks were black, and he had on a band T-shirt with the sleeves cut off: the Cramps. Carey says that van Doren always wears a band T-shirt under his uniform too. "Always the Misfits."

"That's the 'Misfit Mile'?"

"Yep," Carey says. He tells me van Doren took seventh at states last year, which is why schools have been recruiting him. "Seventh in California is like first in forty-nine other states."

When Ted and Sergio come over to the bar and ask me to make them a drink, Carey says, "Get a Krypton. Nobody makes them as good as this guy."

"Super," Sergio says and laughs.

Carey laughs too and gets up. "Must . . . get to . . . bathroom. Need to . . . release . . . Kryp-ton . . . from system."

Ted and Sergio hang out and ask me a bunch of questions about DikNixon. They promise to show up for the party. Ted says he'll make bacon quesadillas for everyone and other than Sergio being totally naked, they're pretty normal guys. I'm having so much fun I don't realize Carey's been gone awhile until I head to the kitchen for more ice.

In the living room, van Doren has Carey around the waist and leaning on his shoulder as they walk real slow toward the front door. "You do this?"

"He was fine a few minutes ago."

"Get the door."

I sprint past them and open the front door. As they step through, Carey loses his balance a little and lets go of van Doren, stumbling in slow motion until he crash-lands on the front lawn and splays out like it's a king-size bed.

Van Doren pushes me out the door. "I'll get his arms. You get his feet."

Carey's so limp and oozy he's hard to control, but we finally get him over to van Doren's Squareback Volkswagen and stuff him into the backseat. Van Doren says to wait by the car while he runs in the house. A minute later, he tosses kitchen towels to me and says, "If he yaks in my car, you're cleaning it up. Now, get in."

We take off, out of the cul-de-sac and onto Yorba Linda Boulevard. Van Doren is silent and the radio is off. We wind down Imperial Highway, through some hills, then onto a freeway. We go west on the 91 for a few minutes, past the 55, then the 57. The numbers don't mean anything to me until we merge onto the 5 north and I see *Los Angeles* on the sign. "Where are we going?"

"Santa Monica," van Doren says, barely louder than the rattle of the car.

The billboards fly by, Camel cigarettes, Continental Airlines, and Colt 45 malt liquor. The night sky is a color you can only get in Southern California, Day-Glo black. Carey sleeps in the back the whole time and van Doren stays silent. You might think he'd say something when the big buildings in downtown LA appear up ahead, but we go right past them and they disappear behind us the same way Manhattan does when you go deeper into New Jersey. If he wants to, van Doren can push me out of the car right now and that'll be it. I'll be lost in the middle of who knows where.

"Why didn't we just take Carey to your house?"

Van Doren waits, then without looking at me says, "My parents."

"What about his parents?"

Van Doren looks over his shoulder and changes lanes. He reads a sign, thinks about it, and says, "Not home."

■

It's really late when we get to Carey's house, way after two in the morning. Van Doren finds a spare key in a flowerpot, and I hold doors open while he drags Carey in and to his room. Van Doren puts some aspirin and a glass of water on Carey's dresser and a bucket next to his bed, and then we leave.

Back in the car, it feels good, like one of the missions me and Keith do. "He's gonna feel pretty confused when he wakes up in his own bed, huh?"

Van Doren starts the car and when we get to the end of Carey's street flips on the radio, loud. At the freeway, I lean back in my seat and rest my head on the window, the way you might go to sleep when your parents are driving and you know you aren't stopping for pretzels or sodas because all they really want is to get home.

Sunrise at Sunset

It's funny how you learn to sleep in the car when you're a kid. It's not like the hum of the wheels is a lullaby and the turnpike rocks you to sleep, but it works out that way. And just like that, exit ramps are your mom laying her hand on your chest real light and making small circles so you wake up soft and slow.

It seems like we've been driving for an hour and my eyes open automatically as we stop for the light at the bottom of the ramp. The thing is, the hills of Yorba Linda aren't spread out before me. There's rows of skyscrapers, not exactly New York, but tall enough to make you look out the car window sideways to see them. They're all skinny skyscrapers except for this wide rectangular one with a big yellow sign about thirty stories up: "Monty's?"

"Yeah," van Doren says. "If UCLA is recruiting you big-time, they take you to Monty's for a steak."

On the left, there are blocks of shorter buildings, two and three stories high, restaurants and record stores lit up even though they're closed. "Is this UCLA?"

"Westwood Village. We're going to Tommy's."

There are no signs around that say *Tommy's*. "Is Tommy another cousin?"

We're waiting to make the left into Westwood Village so van Doren turns his head to me and holds it there. "You from a different planet or something?"

"New Jersey."

He waits a second and gives me this Mona Lisa grin.

We turn and there's more restaurants plus little shops with every kind of clothes you could imagine in the windows: disco, punk, prep, even zoot suits. Van Doren pulls into a parking deck that still has some cars in it. We walk out to the sidewalk, cut through an empty gas station, and cross the street to this little yellow shack with a plain sign: TOMMY'S WORLD FAMOUS HAMBURGERS. It must be three or four in the morning and we're ten people back in line.

"You've really never had a Tommy burger?" van Doren says.

"No."

He thinks a second. "You ever go surfing at Trestles before school?"

"I don't know how to surf. It's not really a Jersey thing."

"All right," van Doren nods. "You ever see a sunrise at sunset?"

"Yeah, right."

"I'm serious," he says.

When we get to the front of the line, van Doren asks if I want onions on my burger. I say I don't have any money so he tells the guy in the window two Cokes, two fries, and two cheeseburgers with no onions.

At the next window, drinks and cardboard boxes appear in about a minute. Van Doren hands me mine and walks over to this little cinder-block wall next to a driveway. It's maybe two feet high and van Doren balances his drink on it, sits down, and starts eating. I do the same thing, and since he isn't talking, I finally ask if we're anywhere near Dodger Stadium. In the '78 World Series, me and my dad watched all three games from LA, including game six even though it was a school night. It was worth it to stay up past midnight and be tired at school the next day, though, because I got to tell all my friends I saw the Yankees win it all. We watched a little of the '81 World Series too, but it wasn't as much fun because the Yanks lost and all the stuff with Uncle Ryan had just happened.

Van Doren shakes his head and finishes off his food. Then he stands up without a word and starts walking up the street, in the opposite direction from where we've left the car. "Come on."

I'm a couple steps behind, my fries still on the wall, my Coke in one hand and half-eaten burger in the other, chili running down my arm. "Is this the sunrise thing?"

Van Doren doesn't answer and I'm already ten yards behind, trying to finish my burger and keep up.

The street rises into a hill, bends to the right, and gets darker as huge houses replace all the stores. A couple of the houses are crowded with people out on the balconies even though it's later than late.

A little farther up, the houses on the left turn into apartment buildings and the buildings on the right disappear into trees. Every once in a while a trail or sidewalk opens up in the trees, but you can't really see where they go. Van Doren keeps a steady pace before suddenly turning onto one of the trails. The last place in the world I want to go is off into some dark trees, but I follow along to the shuffle of van Doren's footsteps until the trail opens up onto a wide sidewalk. A bunch of office buildings are lit up in the distance, but van Doren's crossed over the sidewalk. There's a huge chain-link fence, twice as high as the ones at school, and van Doren goes up and over it like there's a prize on the other side. I'm hoping he'll say *Wait here,* or *Come on, I'll spot you,* or something. He doesn't. He just disappears into the dark, so I trash the rest of my food and start climbing.

You can't see it from the outside in the dark, but a few feet past the fence there's a running track. On the left are stands built into the side of the hill, stretching from the start to the finish line and rising to the trees at the top of the hill.

I catch up to van Doren at the edge of the track, right on the first turn. "This is bitchin'. What is this place?"

"Drake Stadium."

"Sir Francis Drake?" I joke.

Van Doren doesn't laugh or look at me. "UCLA," he says and steps onto the track, crossing over every lane until he stops at number one.

It's one of those fake tracks like you see in the Olympics. The lines are painted so perfect and glowing white a race could break out at any second. The track grips my feet at every step, pushing me forward like it wants me to run.

"This is so punk rock," I say. "You're gonna kick butt on this track."

He looks at me. "What?"

"When you go to college here."

"I don't think so." He shakes his head. "My indoor times are slow this fall."

"You win just about every race," I say. "Carey told me."

"That doesn't matter. I'm racing the clock this year."

Van Doren starts walking the turn and I go with him. It's quiet because the track doesn't crunch and scrape the way our dirt track at school does. We're in the middle of LA on a Saturday night, and even if it is something like four thirty in the morning, you'd think there'd be some noise from the parties we walked by or some cars. But there's nothing. Not even our feet. The track just absorbs everything.

We go a full lap in the quiet until van Doren stops on the front straightaway and says, "I don't know your name." He says it almost sad, like he lost his dog.

"It's Reece."

He's staring down at lane two like it's going to move or something. "That's not what I meant. You know my name, right?"

"Van Doren."

"What's my first name?"

"It's Marc."

He nods and lifts his head to the trees. "How do you know?"

"Everybody knows. You're a senior. You're in Filibuster. You run the Misfit Mile."

He's nodding along like I'm listing off his sins. "And I've got the locker above yours."

That makes me laugh a little. "Yeah. Hard to miss that."

Van Doren sits down on the track, pulls his knees up, and wraps his arms around them. "I had no idea what your name was."

"I'm sorry."

"You don't have to be sorry, you idiot."

Van Doren rests his head on his knees and doesn't talk for a few minutes. It's weird because I'm staring at him and it's okay; I know he isn't going to raise his head all of a sudden and ask me what I'm looking at. We stay there awhile until van Doren slides off his shoes and socks. He stuffs one sock in each shoe, stands up, throws them over into the darkness of the grass infield, and sprints down the straightaway. I walk after him a little ways, thinking he might stop at the finish line; only he runs past and leans into the turn.

My eyes have adjusted enough to make out his shape on the back straightaway, and the *tap-tap-tap* of his feet helps me follow along. He comes around the back turn and flies past me on the front straightaway, going on for a second lap. I get to the finish line and wait, and you might think he'd stop after the second lap, but he crosses the line and leans into the turn for a third lap, strong and steady, like he's Bruce Jenner or something.

On the fourth lap he's breathing in short, loud puffs. His feet slap down on the track in a heavy rhythm, and as he comes down the straightaway you can see his teeth in the darkness, then his face, scrunched and tight. It should be over now; that's sixteen hundred meters, a Misfit Mile. But he runs through the finish line again—fifth lap.

The short puffs and slaps are louder, and somewhere on the backstretch the rhythm goes erratic and silent for a moment before van Doren lets out a grunt like somebody's punched him.

I sprint across the infield to the sound and he's there in lane three, on his knees. "Are you okay?"

He stands up, shakes his legs out a bit, and takes off diagonally across the grass, back toward where we came in. "Your shoes!" I yell, but he doesn't stop. The fence rattles with him climbing over and I'm suddenly squinting in the dark of the infield, trying to find his shoes.

Van Doren is long gone by the time I get to the fence. I toss his shoes over to free my hands for the climb and a couple of my fingers get wet on the chain link. It isn't light like water, more slick between my fingers and then sticky, and it doesn't take a genius to know it's blood.

■

Van Doren's waiting for me in the car with the engine going, both hands wrapped in napkins and resting on the steering wheel. I get in and hold up his shoes and socks.

"Toss them in back."

"You okay?"

He stares straight ahead like we're already on the road. "Never better."

As we back out, van Doren cranks the wheel to turn, loosening his grip so it slides as the car straightens out, never once letting go of the napkins. We get to the parking deck exit and with his head turned to check for traffic, he says, "Listen. I made Astrid have the party tonight just to fuck with you." He makes the turn and keeps staring ahead like driving needs all his attention.

"*You* did that? Why?"

He lets out one of those long, loud sighs and says, "Because I can."

It sounds so mean my eyes tingle. Then my face goes heavy and my mouth pulls tight the way it does before everything goes loose and you cry.

"It's territorial," he says and glances at me. "But you came back tonight with that flyer." He leaves it there for a minute, the road straight, the lights green every block, but I'm not talking. I can't. "You guys really are for real," he finally says and glances at me one more time. "I totally respect that now."

My throat is tight, and if I say much of anything I'm afraid I'll sound like a three-year-old who lost his teddy bear. So I sort of whisper, "Can we go home?"

"No," van Doren says. "I promised Astrid I'd make this up to you."

"Astrid?" Just hearing she said something about me makes everything numb up except for the flutter in my stomach and maybe a tingle or two in other places.

Van Doren's shaking his head. "I lied to her too and said 'okay,' I'd make it up to you. But now I really do want to make it up to you." He looks at me sort of a long time, like the car's on autopilot, and even with the stupid cropped hair and the black T-shirt, his face is Uncle Ryan warm, you know, like he can make everything all right if I let him. "I'm going to show you something I've never showed anybody else, not even Carey: a sunrise at sunset."

We drive away from the freeway, leave the row of skyscrapers behind us. I get a good look at Monty's as we pass and ask van Doren if they have those waiters who fold your napkin for you every time you go to the bathroom. We went to a place like that for my mom's birthday once in Manhattan.

"I don't know," he says. "I've never been to Monty's."

We drive in quiet after that, switching streets a few times, block after block of two-story buildings with colored lights around doorways and framing windows. You'd think you were passing a hundred tiny discos the way these places are lit up, and then you see it's just a nail salon or a tailor, and it's not even open.

We turn onto Sunset Boulevard: giant billboards for movies and TV shows, lit up so bright the sky is blue right above them. Then it all comes together: It must be getting close to sunrise and we're on *Sunset*. A sunrise *at* Sunset Boulevard. It seems impossible it could be that easy. That stupid. Even when van Doren parks the car, puts on his shoes, and we walk up to the corner, I'm wondering if maybe the sunrise shines off a glass building, reflects onto the Hollywood sign, and you see the Virgin Mary, or maybe the MGM lion.

We stand on the corner, a few cars whishing by even this late, or this early, and it feels cold for the first time. "Where's the Chinese Theatre?" I say.

"We're nowhere near that."

"How about the stars in the sidewalks?"

"Nope." Van Doren points across the street to an old two-story building hugging the corner. It's got giant posters, each a full story high, running down its sides. The curved corner has a marquee, like a movie theater sign, with dates and names listed. "That's the Whisky right there."

"Is that place famous?"

"World famous," van Doren says. "Everybody's played there."

None of the names on the marquee sound famous to me: the Gun Club, Captain Beefheart, and the Stranglers, though the last one might be on *The Nixon Tapes*. I'd have to check. "Is it a punk place?"

"It's everything. The Doors played there."

"My Uncle Ryan used to love those guys."

Van Doren nods. "Before everyone goes off to college, we'll play here too."

"Filibuster? They asked you guys to play?"

"They don't have to ask you."

"But it's the Whisky," I say like I've known about it my whole life.

"Doesn't matter." Van Doren lets a couple cars go by, then says, "Some nights, anybody can play. You just have to buy a block of tickets and sell them."

"You pay them to play?"

"That's pretty much how it works everywhere. You can't wait around hoping to get discovered. You've got to put yourself out there."

He points to the hills behind the Whisky, has me look above all the dots of light in the hills to the top and over to a spot in the sky where the Day-Glo black is going more charcoal and the charcoal is getting scribbled with purple. It's so gradual, but it doesn't stop, and I could watch forever because crayons can't make colors like this. The purple gets lighter and lighter until reds and oranges slip in, the backdrop goes dark blue, and then, *bam,* the sun peeks over the hill like a lighthouse flipped on up there. A fraction of an earth turn later, it spreads over the whole ridge, the sky warming to the old familiar blue. The hill wakes up into that washed-out California brown I've seen since summer, and the dots of light begin turning into houses and apartment buildings.

Van Doren claps a hand on my shoulder. "Was it everything you expected?"

When you think about it, sunrises don't have much of a finish. They're like the day after Christmas or, worse, the week before Christmas when you're seven and you find a grocery bag full of presents in the basement with *From Santa* on all the tags.

"Where's the sunset part?"

"You know where it is," he says.

"No, I don't."

Van Doren gives me a little shove. "You've known all along."

"Okay. Then why did you still show me?"

"It's something this senior on the track team told me when I was a freshman." He flicks his head to get me to start walking to the car with him. "It's good to know how to figure a thing out and realize it's not that big a deal."

"So I ruin things for myself?"

He shakes his head. "So you don't waste your time operating under the delusions of it."

"That's depressing."

"I thought so too, at first," he says. "Then I figured out how to make it work for me."

.

We drive home with the radio on. We talk a little, normal stuff about how letterman jackets are lame and who the best teachers are to get for calculus. When we get to my house, van Doren doesn't ask me not to say anything about how he freaked out or that he isn't going to UCLA next year, but I'm not going to tell anyone. I mean, when I found out there wasn't a Santa Claus, it was still fun to keep it going for Brendan and Colleen.

Just before pulling away, van Doren tells me through the car window, "Sorry about the book thing."

It takes me a second. "At our lockers?"

"Yeah. Someone used to drop books on me too."

"Really?"

"Really. Pretty stupid, huh?"

I nod.

"Reece," he says. "I'll see ya Monday."

"Yeah," I say. "See ya Monday, Marc."

The Squareback putters out of my cul-de-sac and the sky is as bright as day as I'm coming through the front door. "Reece?" my dad says from the kitchen. He's wearing church clothes and putting away dishes from the night before. I stop in the doorway and he looks me over. "Are you just getting home?"

"Yeah," I say. "One of my friends had kind of a tough night."

He turns around and leans back against the counter. "A tough night?"

I start playing with the phone cord, not looking at my dad. "His cousin got sick so we had to drive him back home to LA."

My dad steps over to me and I stand up stiff. "You been drinking?"

"No."

He sniffs the air. "Where's your Yankees jacket?"

It doesn't make sense to me at first, why he's asking that. Then the picture of the Yankees jacket lying on Keith's bed comes to me. "Keith borrowed it."

"Uh-huh," he says and pinches the TSOL patch on the Packy jacket. "What do all these letters stand for again?"

"I already told you: *TSOL* stands for *True Sounds of Liberty.*"

My dad's head goes sideways as he looks up and down the sleeves of his old jacket. "Tell me the others."

I lie, telling him again *GBH* is *Guitar, Bass, and Harmony.*

"And this one?" He points at the ax for Dead Kennedys— the only one that looks as dangerous as its name.

"What does it matter?"

"You tell me. If they're just bands, you can tell me their names."

I let go of the phone cord, try to be totally relaxed the way van Doren would be. "They're the Dead Kennedys." I trace the letters on the patch. "See? The *D* and the *K* make an ax."

He goes back to the cabinet and starts putting dishes away again. "Get ready for church."

"We're going to early mass?"

"Just me and you. And put on something nice. I don't know who you've been running around with and why you've been dressing so strange—"

"Well, maybe you would know if you were around once in a while."

He slaps his hands down so hard on the counter I feel it in my chest. "Jesus. Go get ready for church."

My eyes well up with tears and I step back out of the kitchen. "No. I'm going later, with Mom."

"Reece!" my dad says like he's saying *Stop!*

The tears start rolling down my face. "I don't want to go *anywhere* with you, Packy." I step into the hallway, out of his sight, and sort of mumble, "You're the one who made Uncle Ryan go away. It's all your fault."

Packy steps heavy and fast out of the kitchen and towers over me. He's only hit me once in my whole life, when my mom was away at Grandpa Quinn's funeral and I'd played ball in the house and broke her favorite lamp. But I'm ready now, ready to get slapped in the face or hooked by the arm and dragged outside. So I look him full in the face. "It's not my fault you feel guilty for everything."

Packy looks at me the way he used to whenever something awful would come on the six o'clock news and he'd reach over and turn my head toward him. He'd keep his fingers up near my eyes just in case I tried to sneak a glimpse. I never did, though. I'd watch him turn his head a little, watch his eyes get squinty until they got a little bigger, and just as his mouth would open, he'd catch it and close everything up tight.

"Go to bed," he says, stepping past me to the front door.

And that's it. No lecture. No grounding. No church.

Air Force Three

Brendan wakes me up. He's wearing an old R2-D2 T-shirt that's too small. Everyone else is downstairs, back from mass long enough to already be changed out of their church clothes. There's still the smell of bacon from breakfast, but my mom doesn't ask if I've eaten or why I missed church or anything. I get some cereal and sit down with Brendan on the couch to watch some ski race with a bunch of guys named Ingemar and Franz.

Packy stays busy the whole day with who knows what out in the yard and the garage and then the side of the house. At dinner, he asks Brendan if he thinks the NFL strike will ever end and Colleen about her catechism. He lets them both go on and on and even asks questions. Nobody asks me anything, not even my mom, and when dinner is over I do the dishes by myself because it's my turn, then go back to my room.

In my letter to Uncle Ryan, I tell him about Ted Three, and Tommy's, and UCLA, and how Astrid was actually looking out for me the whole time. It feels good to relive everything until I get to the part about my dad. *Packy sucks,* I write. *Don't ask.* It jerks at my eyes a little, seeing that on the page, real and impossible to take back, but it gets my heart going too and there's no way I'm scribbling over it. *That's just how it adds up right now. I know you know what I'm talking about.*

I'm in bed before Astrid's light is out, thinking about her thinking about me. I imagine her saying how sorry she is and taking me by the hand and up the staircase to make it up to me. It's almost too much and as soon as her light goes out, the thought of her in bed sends me over the top and I get discreet.

■

Treat's in front of my house Monday morning and it doesn't matter who sees him now. I meet him with my hair already messed up and my Packy jacket on. "Nice," he says.

Keith's waiting for us outside. Even with his jacket on, you can see he's got a polo on underneath with the collar turned up.

"Somebody's been reading *The Preppy Handbook*," Treat says.

As soon as we're up the sidewalk a couple houses, Keith yanks down his collar. "Look!" He's got so many hickeys it looks like just his neck got into a fight.

"Sascha did that to you?"

Keith's all grins and head-nodding. "My mom's so pissed."

"Sascha?" Treat says.

"She goes to El Dorado," Keith says. He walks backward in

front of us, feeling the hickeys with his fingers. "Astrid knows her from cheerleading camp."

"So is that what the bet was? That she could give you a hickey?"

"No," Keith says. "The bet was whether or not she would kiss me."

Treat turns to me, his eyes squinty. I nod. "She's real."

"And hot," Keith says. "She said she was marking me so all the girls at Esperanza would know I belong to her."

"She pissed on you," Treat says.

Keith looks at his hand like maybe it'd be wet or something.

"No, man," Treats says. "It's solid. Did you mark her too?"

"I couldn't. She's got a boyfriend."

Treat stops. "So you're hers, but she's not yours?"

Keith nods, fast and happy. "Yeah."

Treat starts walking again. "I guess ignorance is bliss."

Keith falls back in line with us. "Yeah."

I laugh. "Do you know what *ignorance* means?"

"It means I went to Ted Three, made out with a girl, and I'm blissful."

Treat puts an arm around Keith and gives him a big squeeze. He doesn't look happy or sad or even mad that he missed everything. He just shakes his head and says, "Better you than me."

I don't know what this means, why Treat doesn't like football games, or how he can not care all that much about dances or parties. I guess it's punk rock, although I don't see why you can't be punk rock and still have fun.

"It was good for the band," I say, and me and Keith give him the lowdown on how Ted Three went, how people like Petrakis and Ted had taken the new flyers and said they were coming to our party.

Treat says we have to keep the momentum going, spreading the word all week at school, working on songs all week after school, and making it to the football game on Friday for the last push. "We're going to eat lunch behind the tennis courts this week so we can stay focused and not get distracted by your little girlfriends."

"Sounds like we're avoiding them," I say.

"One of them, at least," Keith says, and me and him laugh.

"See?" Treat says. "You guys are already losing focus."

In Algebra, I give Edie some new flyers and say Treat has lunch detention all week and me and Keith are going to sit with him to work out some song lyrics.

At my locker, van Doren puts his hand down and says, "Five." It takes me a minute to dig the flyers out, and the fifth one sticks with another one. Van Doren's hand stays there the whole time, relaxed while he's arranging things in his locker with the other hand. As soon as he has the flyers he slams his locker shut and bops me on the head with a folder. "Timing," he says. "Everything comes down to timing, Reece."

■

Wednesday in English, Treat shows me the stack of DikNixon flyers he folded into paper airplanes during second period. He keeps them hidden in his satchel until class lets out, then he walks to the rail near the stairs and flicks them from the satchel and over the side real quick, and it's Air Force One, and Two, and Three, and Twenty-Five bringing DikNixon to the people down below.

In his fourth-period World History, where Treat sits in the front of a row because Mrs. Wirth makes people sit alphabetically, he slips some flyers in with the stack of handouts on Egyptian irrigation and watercraft. And every day at lunch, he's been rolling flyers up and sticking them in the chain-link fence by the tennis courts. They're all gone by the next day, and he does it again.

We keep working hard in the Two-Car Studio, staying late and Mrs. Dumovitch bringing us weird things to eat and drink with ginseng and bee pollen and anything else she can think of that gives you energy and keeps you focused. I don't eat dinner at home Monday, Tuesday, or Wednesday, and when my mom asks I say there's a big test coming up and I'll be at the library, or Treat's. She lets it go every time with, "If you say so. Just be home by ten."

By Thursday evening, we've got nine songs down and play our whole set through. And even though we mess up a bunch, Treat says to take rest of the night off so we don't burn out. That, and he has to go to some new sushi restaurant with his parents.

It smells like spaghetti when I get home, but my mom's upstairs giving Colleen a bath and Packy's on the end of the couch, his hand under the lamp and Brendan kneeling in front of him with the needle and tweezers.

"Ah." He yanks his hand back. "Go light until you feel the metal."

"It all feels like metal," Brendan says.

Without looking at me, Packy says, "There's leftovers in the fridge."

"Okay," I say, and then to Brendan, "You got this?" He shakes his head no.

"He'll get it," Packy says. "You go eat."

I'm guessing Packy was home in time for dinner since he always says pasta only tastes good the first time and my mom won't make it if he's going to be late. I heat it up in a frying pan and sit in the kitchen by myself to eat. I hear the living room clear out and don't even finish my plate because Packy's right, it does taste awful if you don't eat it on time.

■

After school Friday, Treat has a bunch of thick wood planks leaned against the boxes in the Two-Car Studio. We've been planning to put planks over the Jacuzzi so the deck won't have a hole in it and can work like a real stage. "I'm going to stay and help Lyle get the stage ready tonight," he says."

We can do all that stuff tomorrow," I say. "It'd be better if you came to the football game tonight."

Treat pulls planks down one by one and sets them on the floor like he's counting them. "You guys can handle it. I want to get started on this stuff tonight."

"In the dark?" Keith says.

"Yeah, I'm going to do stuff in the dark. Are you an idiot?"

"That's what I mean," Keith says.

"Then what are you going to do?" I say.

Treat nudges a plank with his boot. "Other stuff. Important stuff."

Keith's giving it some thought, his face sort of scrunched up. "You could probably set up the lights."

"Where are the lights?" I say.

Treat looks around real fast. "I think they're in my dad's car."

"Dad?" I say. "Did you get in trouble?"

Keith steps closer to me and Treat. "Did you? We're still playing, right?"

"You guys still want to play, don't you?"

"Yeah," Keith says.

"Then we're playing. Nobody's quitting." Treat opens the garage door. "It'll be bitchin'. Totally punk rock." He waves me and Keith out. "Now, go get ready for the game. Make some paper airplanes."

"Got any messages for Cherise?" Keith says and makes a kissing sound.

Treat holds out his fist. "No, but I've got one for you to give to the paramedics."

"That's okay," Keith says.

"Okay," Treat says. "See you guys tomorrow."

■

Edie and Cherise meet us outside the football stadium and we give them some flyers. Cherise's face is total attention until Keith says that Treat's not coming; then she's waving to friends and looking bored as we tell them what we're going to do.

Me and Keith walk along the bottom of the bleachers with

our flyers, our hair messed up perfect, and our second-best punk shirts (we're saving the best for the show). Astrid is maybe ten feet away on the field, looking up into the stands like she sees everyone all at once, but I bet she sees me too. Maybe not exactly like I want her to, but how many guys has she made a point of looking out for? That's got to mean something.

We start going around to groups of people and reminding them about the party and the free beer. For people who don't know about the party, we use the Ted Fischel theory: say you're trying to keep it low profile and nobody says anything out loud, but everybody finds out. Some freshmen and sophomores go up to Edie and Cherise and get flyers from them. Some juniors and seniors wave me and Keith over and say, "You guys throwing the party with the free beer?"

"And the band," Keith adds each time.

When we run out of flyers, some people write the address on their arms, and Keith tells them if they carve it in with a razor it won't smear.

■

We're at Del Taco after the game, Edie and Cherise sitting across the table from us. Edie knows we ditched them all week and she wants to know why.

"Doesn't matter," Keith says. "We're here now, aren't we?"

"Does this have something to do with your hickey?" she says.

Keith smiles and touches his neck.

Edie looks at my neck and I pull at my jacket so the collar opens wide. "Not me."

Cherise giggles, but Edie just squints at me. "You wish you had one," she says and squeezes a bunch of hot sauce all over my half-eaten burrito.

"Hey, you owe me a burrito."

"Here," Edie says and pushes her burrito over to me.

The burrito's barely got two bites out of it. "I can't take that."

"Yeah," Keith says. "He'll get cooties."

Cherise giggles again. "He might like her cooties."

"Just take it," Edie says. "Since you guys are giving us a ride home."

"We are?" Keith says, but it's not like he'll say no. It always looks good when people see you getting into a car with girls, even if they aren't cheerleaders.

When Mr. Curtis pulls up in the parking lot, Keith opens the back door like a valet. Cherise climbs in and slides across behind the driver's seat and Edie follows her, sliding to the middle. Keith takes a step like he's getting in and I grab him. "What are you doing?"

Keith turns and whispers, "You can have shotgun."

"You have to take shotgun," I whisper back. "It's *your* dad."

He looks down at the empty seat and then steps out of the way. "Duh," he says nice and loud. "I'm just getting the door for everybody."

We aren't out of the parking lot and Keith's turning half around in the front seat and saying, "Tomorrow is going to be so great."

Mr. Curtis sticks his arm right into Keith's shoulder. "Sit back, Keith. I'm trying to make this turn."

"You're not even looking this way."

"I'm not saying I am. But if I suddenly needed to—"

"Fine," Keith says and sits back.

Mr. Curtis yells, "Hold on, everybody!" like he's Peter Pan; then the tires chirp and the seat goes heavy on my back. We make a sharp right and the weight of me rolls left and there's no way to stop the side of my body from sliding into Edie. I go as tight as I can—my stomach and legs and arms—but I'm pressing so hard against her I feel everything from her shoulder down to her knee. At least, I think I do. There's the squish; then something's making the side of my body feel different, like I'm leaning against an electric fence, except one that doesn't hurt.

Cherise giggles because Edie's squashed into her too. Edie starts laughing, then I do, and then Keith turns around and yells, "Slam pit!"

It's half a block before Edie says, "Excuse you." I'm still pressed up against her and she presses her thigh deeper into mine a little.

I slide over an inch. "Sorry."

"No, you're not." She quick-smiles as she scooches half an inch away from Cherise and closer to me.

My eyes drift down to my lap, taking in Edie's and a little of Cherise's too. We all have on jeans but none of them look quite the same. It's like one of those maps in your geography book where the legend has ten shades of blue to show the differ- ent parts of Australia—Victoria in light blue, Queensland in sky blue, the Northern Territory in navy. Cherise's jeans are deep blue and pretty tight, and since she likes Treat, that makes her Indian Territory. Or maybe the Forbidden Zone. Or better yet, the Twilight Zone, since she's so spacey and weird but you still like her. Edie's jeans are a faded blue but smoother and tighter than Cherise's. She's so cool and ready to do anything. The Fun Zone. No, Adventureland. That's more than just fun.

My jeans are loose, full of holes, and so faded they're almost white. Frontierland. New Frontierland? Maybe Tomorrowland since things are getting better every day, especially after tomorrow when Astrid sees me with the band.

We stop at a red light and Mr. Curtis says, "You guys make sure you stay buckled in." He's looking at us in the rearview mirror, sort of serious. The light turns green and we roll forward, gentle and smooth. "You might not think seat belts are important. A lot of people don't. But a lot of people out there drive a little crazy." He swerves into the left lane real fast. Cherise pushes up against Edie and Edie up against me, and we all laugh, even Mr. Curtis.

"Sorry," Edie says as she scooches away from me.

"No, you're not," I say and give her the same quick-smile she gave me.

For the rest of the ride every turn is sharp and fast, every lane change a jerk left or right. It's a roller coaster, everybody *wooing* and *aahing*. When Cherise points out her house we go just past it and Mr. Curtis says, "Hands up." He stops hard without making the tires slide. We bend forward together, still laughing, and just as we start to relax, Mr. Curtis jams the car in reverse and hits the gas. My hands dip with the force of going backward, and when we stop all of a sudden, my left hand slaps onto Edie's thigh. You might think the scratch of Edie's jeans wouldn't be all warm-glow electric fence like Astrid's silk panties, and it's not. It massages the palm of my hand and there's no imagining what her thigh might feel like; this *is* what it feels like—tight and maybe not warm through the material but perfectly curving into my palm and pulsing, like every atom in my hand is swirling around and trying to find something to bond with in those jeans.

It's going to be like Velcro prying my hand away from Edie, but it'll be weird if I don't. I raise my hand and grab the back of Keith's seat. I don't actually need to grab Keith's seat, so I'm leaning a little forward now, with one hand stretched out like somehow that's relaxing to me, which it isn't, and I'm feeling weird because I know it looks weird, and if I'm acting and looking weird, I must be weird, which, I guess, is better than looking like a perv.

Cherise laughs as she gets out, saying, "Thanks," and "See you guys tomorrow." Edie unbuckles and slides over into Cherise's seat, and I take my hand back.

The rest of the ride, Edie is, "Turn here," "Not this street but the next," and "You'll see a yellow Honda in the driveway."

"Oh," Mr. Curtis says. "Those are great cars."

"It's my brother's," Edie says. "He got it for college."

Mr. Curtis brings the car to a smooth stop. "He'll save so much on gas it'll pay for itself in four years."

Edie thanks Mr. Curtis for the ride and thunks the door shut. She walks in front of the car to get to her driveway and waves, sort of at Keith, or maybe all of us, as we pull away.

I'm staring out the window the rest of the ride home, my

hand tingling. This is my first thigh. And if Edie's thigh feels that good, Astrid's must be, what, the Promised Land? I try imagining Astrid's thighs. They're brown and smooth and disappearing into her cheerleading skirt. Then the skirt becomes blue jeans, only not hers, Edie's. Then it's Edie wearing her white shirt and puka shells and grinning at me like she knows what I'm doing. Even though it's all in my head, you'd think it would embarrass me, but somehow, I guess since it's Edie, it makes me laugh. I'm thinking, *You're Adventureland, not Fantasyland.* Edie rolls her eyes and grins and instead of getting the heart attack and jelly knees Astrid gives me, these nice warm waves roll out of my chest and down my arms and legs.

■

The TV is on as I come through the front door. "Reece," my mom says. "Can you come here?"

My parents are on the couch and Packy flips off the TV with the remote. "Who won the game?" he says. When I hesitate, because I have no idea, Packy says real calm, "Have you been drinking?" I shake my head, partly because the answer is no, and partly because there's more words than I can say. Why does he keep asking that every weekend? What's he thinking?

"What about your friends?" Packy says. "Who drove?"

"Mr. Curtis drove," I say and slide my hands into my jacket pockets. "I think he was high on angel dust, but he hadn't been drinking."

"That's not funny," Packy says.

"Reece," my mom says. Her hair is down, pilled robe on,

freckles out. "Is everything okay?" Her hands are folded in her lap, resting over the top of something. It's hard to make it out in the dark of the living room; then the DikNixon logo filters through.

"Why do you have my notebook?"

"We found it," Packy says and holds up *The Nixon Tapes.* "With this."

"Found?"

"Well," my mom says, "with the way you're dressing now and your friend with the Indian haircut—"

"It's a Mohawk."

"Okay," she says and looks down at the >I< logo. "The clothes and the haircuts. It's a lot. But this . . ." She grips the notebook and looks at Packy again.

"My band?" I say.

"Band?" Packy says and looks at my mom. He holds up a hand like he's stopping something. "Okay, that's fine. We're glad you're making friends—"

"It's the letters," my mom says. She holds the notebook up and lets it flop open to anywhere, pages and pages of writing, doodles, and band logos.

My breath goes short, like when the ball's in the air and you know it's coming to you. Everybody's watching, but it just floats up there and won't come down. You've got plenty of time to think about what will happen if you miss it, if you've misjudged and it gets away from you. My voice pushes out some sound just above a whisper that doesn't sound like me: "You read my letters?"

My mom pats the pillows beside her. "Come sit down."

"No," I say, my voice back. "Did you read everything?"

Packy stands up, rubbing his eyes with the heel of his hand like maybe there's just some sleep in there and not tears. "Son, Uncle Ryan is dead."

"It's okay," my mom says. "We all miss him."

I don't know what they know—the band, Astrid, the things I've said about Packy, all of it, most of it. They know enough. Or they think they do. "So then, what?" I say, pushing my hands deeper into my pockets. "You think I'm out getting drunk and trying to kill myself?"

My mom shakes her head. "There's just so many letters to someone who, someone who isn't . . ."

"I'm not crazy," I say. "I know Uncle Ryan's dead. And you know what? I know he was drunk and walked in front of that car." The tears should be streaking down my face now but they're not. "I used to think it was my fault because of the keys, you know? If he'd had his keys he wouldn't have been walking home."

"Sweetie," my mom says and pats the pillows beside her again.

"We've told you," Packy says. "None of it was your fault."

"I know," I say and step over and take the notebook from my mom. I hold it up and fan out the pages like I'm trying to get a lost dollar to fall out. "And I haven't told Uncle Ryan that I know whose fault it really was. But I heard everything that night."

"Reece," my mom says. "It's more complicated than that."

I put my eyes on Packy. "We moved here because you guys felt guilty for making Uncle Ryan go home."

Packy folds his arms, looks at my mom, and steps over to me. "Your uncle Ryan," he starts, then takes a breath and starts again: "We loved Uncle Ryan. You don't know how hard . . . how many times your Aunt Mary called in the middle of the night or your uncle Ryan just showed up and . . ." And he stops again. "Oh, Reece, if we could go back—"

"But you can't." I hold the notebook up like it's proof of something. "And you go and make everything worse. You make us leave everyone we know. You're never around. You snoop through my stuff." I glance at my mom, you know, to make sure she knows she's part of this too, then back at Packy. My hands are shaking, my face is tingling, and now I'm talking loud, just short of a yell. "California can't make everything okay, Packy. It's still your fault Uncle Ryan died. It's always going to be your fault."

I want it back as soon as it's out of my mouth, even before Packy's slap explodes across my face and he yells, "Stop! You will stop that right now."

My hand goes to my cheek, my fingers barely touching the hot spot, the sting echoing strong, then less so, then strong again and settling into some rhythm while I stare at the floor.

"Reece," Packy says soft. His hand cups my shoulder, right on the TSOL patch, and I shake him off without looking up.

I put my hand out in the air in front of me. "Give me my tape." The hard plastic slides onto my palm and I head for the stairs, listening for Packy's footsteps behind me. But they don't come.

In my room, I kick my shoes onto the floor and slam my jacket onto the bed. I lie down and bury my face in the jacket, trying to smell Del Taco or maybe the Two-Car Studio. Maybe Edie. But I get none of that and soon I'm bawling like a baby, holding the jacket tighter around my face to muffle the sounds until my head is hot and aches and there's nothing left to do but fall asleep.

Deck/Stage

The smell of coffee surrounds me, invisible and awful. My stomach creaks from hungry-empty to nervous-empty. Packy's downstairs getting ready for a Saturday shift. Sometimes, on weekends, he wakes me up to say good-bye. Not today. As soon as the thud of the front door reaches my room I'm eyes open, clothes on, out the back door, and over the wall into the park.

The ground sucks my shoes in, wet and soft. In the low morning sun, the dew across the soccer fields glares like new snow. At the corner of one field, the grass is thin and worn away so the white out-of-bounds line is painted right onto the dirt. It reminds me of our old front lawn in Jersey. We'd go out and play in the first snow, me and Brendan and my dad too if Uncle Ryan came by, trampling it down so fast the green and brown would come through right away. It wouldn't feel cold at first like you might think, not with all that running around and snowball throwing. But when the wind got blowing good, you felt it because the cold doesn't care what you're doing or what you're wearing; it finds a way inside you.

I plunge my hands into my jacket pockets, start walking diagonally across the field. It feels good because in California even a little jacket can protect you from everything.

Looking back from the middle of the field, I've painted a dark green stripe everywhere my feet have pushed down the blades of grass, flattening them and spreading out the water. I head diagonally to another corner and stop, making an arrow in the grass, the *D* for the >I< logo.

Running around the outside of the field to the opposite end, I walk diagonally from one corner to the center, then back to the other corner to make the other arrow, the *K*. Then I run around the outside of the field one more time to get back to the center, where I can walk straight across the middle to make the *I*.

As I'm backing away across the next field, the lines get clearer and clearer until the >I< logo appears. My Converse are soaked to my socks, but it's perfect. If soccer season was over, it would stay there all morning until the temperature rose and evaporated the dew. DikNixon released into the air instead of getting trampled.

∎

Treat's little sister is already up watching cartoons and she lets me in. Treat meets me in the living room, the Mohawk fluffed out like a cat. We sit quiet, watching the shows, and on commercials Jewell tells us about the slumber party she's going to tonight because of our party. Mrs. D gets up and makes real oatmeal with almonds, brown sugar, and honey, and it fills my stomach like someone's hugging me from inside.

Keith's pretty angry when he shows up around nine thirty because he went to my house and when my mom couldn't find me she wanted to know why I wasn't with him and where were we going so early anyway? "I told her I must have got mixed up and was supposed to meet you at the library, but she didn't look like she believed that."

Out in the Two-Car Studio, Treat shows us how he sanded the boards last night so there wouldn't be any splinters. He also hammered them together in two long sets to put across the Jacuzzi, except there's no cross boards for support and the nail heads are sticking up everywhere.

"We can't stand on this," I say.

"That's good wood," he says.

"It's not the wood." I squat down to show Treat. "What if we catch a cord on this nail or if the slats come apart in the middle of a song?"

"You got a better idea?"

"Well, for starters we can pull out these nails, get a drill, center little dimples in the wood where the nails go so they're sunk, fill in the rest of each hole with wood putty, and then sand it over so it's nice and smooth."

Keith squats down next to me. "That's just for starters?"

Treat has Lyle find us everything we need. Then I show Keith and Treat how to pull nails without ruining the boards or the nails, how to bore the dimples with the drill, and how to steady the boards so they won't rattle and cause the nail to go in crooked. We add crossbeams for support and lean the boards on the Jacuzzi deck while the putty dries.

We need to drain the Jacuzzi, but Treat says we should have a confessional first, for good karma, so me and Keith borrow some shorts from him. Mine come down past my knees and Keith's are to his shins, but Treat's squinty eyed and serious. "Okay," he says once we're all in. "Who's got one?"

Everything from last night comes back into my head—popular people at the game letting us talk to them like we're in their universe, Edie's thighs, my parents snooping through my stuff, Packy slapping me. I don't say a thing.

Keith isn't talking either, and after looking back and forth at us, Treat says, "Here's what we can do. We'll each ask the other one a question we want to know and your answer is your confessional."

"What if it's a question we don't want to answer?" Keith says.

"You have to," Treat says. "Or we won't be in balance."

I look at Keith. "What if we lie?"

Treat shakes his head. "That'll mess everyone up. So even if you don't care about yourself, you shouldn't do that to your brothers."

"Brothers?" Keith says.

Treat looks up at the beams over us where he duct-taped three utility lights, one for each one of us tonight. "We're not a band if we don't think of each other like brothers."

Keith giggles. "Okay."

Treat splashes a line of water into Keith's face. "If you don't knock it off, I'll be Cain and you'll be Abel."

Keith nods, his eyes shut, and his nose and chin drip water.

"I thought you were an atheist," I say and a stream of water hits my face.

"I thought you hated doing projects with your dad."

"I do."

Treat nods. "Well, you sure know a lot about home construction, Slugger."

Keith laughs and I shoot a stream of water at him, then ask Treat, "Do you like algebra?"

"It's all right."

"You've got, like, a ninety-five in there, right?"

Treat pulls both arms up out of the water, resting them on the sides of the Jacuzzi. "Okay, I get it. You learn stuff even if you don't care."

"Not me," Keith says. "I hate algebra and I've only got, like, a seventy-five in there."

Treat shakes his head. "Who cares who likes what. We're violating the sanctity of the confessional." We settle down, and when there's just the hum of the jets Treat says, "Okay, Keith, what's your question for me?"

Keith looks at Treat. "Have you ever beat anybody up?"

"Not on purpose," Treat says, totally straight-faced.

"What does *that* mean?"

"I used to lose control a little. That's all."

Keith asks if I'm nervous about the party, and just hearing him say it makes my stomach tighten up. "A little. I mean, I know it'll be okay because we'll all be up there—"

"Like brothers," Treat says.

"Yeah, like brothers. I don't think I could do it otherwise."

I ask Keith if he's nervous and he says not yet but maybe later.

"How 'bout you, Treat?"

He's tight-lipped, watching the bubbles and then shaking his head. He looks up at Keith, down at the bubbles, then up at Keith again.

"What?" Keith says.

"How long has Cherise liked me?"

Keith shakes his head. "I don't know."

"Then how long have you been passing notes about me?"

"That's two questions to the same person," Keith says.

"You didn't give me an answer to the first one."

Keith looks up, eyes squinty and thinking. "About three or four weeks, I guess."

Treat looks down at the bubbles like he's calculating his next move. Then he asks me the atomic bomb of questions, the kind where no answer is safe no matter which side of it you're on: "Do you think Cherise is a babe?"

Treat's massive, squared body is leaning forward a little, his Mohawk oozing to one side in the steam. I try to imagine Cherise sitting there next to him, a bikini on her skinny body that shows how nothing really changes from her hips to her shoulders. A rectangle with her springy hair shooting out in every direction so even a ponytail can't hold it. Square and rectangle. "I think you guys would look good together. You know, you mix just right."

Treat looks me over, then nods like he just got the A he was expecting. He motions me and Keith to the middle of the Jacuzzi, where we lock arms, making a triangle. Treat holds us in place awhile before finally saying, "Okay, I think we're in balance."

We drain the Jacuzzi and fit the boards in place over the top. Mrs. D brings out asparagus wraps, which look like brown burritos except they're cold and taste like grass, but we're so hungry we wolf them down and ask for more.

After lunch, we nail the car cover along the back of the deck and Mr. D digs up one more utility light for us to tape up and aim right at the logo. We get the guitars and amps out there and plug everything into an extension cord Mr. D has snaked along the fence, through the garden and rosebushes, and over to the deck.

Back on the patio, we set out coolers and Mr. D brings out the beer. The bottles are brown with some kind of fierce-looking lion on the label, his head and body turned sideways and *Löwenbräu* written in giant blue letters beneath him.

"That's real beer," I say. "Isn't it?"

"This is their nonalcoholic brew," Mr. D says.

Keith looks closer at the label. "It won't get us drunk?"

Mr. D shows us the little red ribbon at the bottom of the bottle where it says *Alkoholfrei*. "Not even a little."

"Will people know?"

Mr. D says if we're worried we can scratch that part off real easy. Then he shows us where it says *Imported from Germany* on the back. "Just tell everyone it's an import. They'll get drunk on that." He tells Treat he's printed up signs with little skulls on them for every door in the house except the bathroom by the kitchen. "That's the only reason anyone should be in the house." He says he'll be dropping Jewell off at her slumber party around six, and then around eight he and Mrs. D will be back from dinner and will go into their room to hang out the rest of the night. "You won't know we're here unless you need us."

Mr. D opens the glass sliding door and pats the wall inside. "The switch for the lights is right here, Treat. Not the one for the patio light. The one underneath that."

"I know, Lyle."

"Okay," he says, and we hear the click of the switch flipping on. We look across half a soccer field of empty grass leading back to the Jacuzzi deck. Even though it's, like, three o'clock in the afternoon, there's a pale little egg of light on the *K* part of the >I< logo. We walk closer to get a better look, and halfway there we see three more eggs of light hitting the deck, one right next to Keith's amp, half on the deck and half on the wood slats over the Jacuzzi. Another is almost in the middle of the slats, not too far off, and since Treat will be singing through the bullhorn anyway, he can move into that spot real easy. The last egg, where I'll be standing, is on the right, or the left if you're Astrid looking up from the yard.

The deck is gone. It's a stage now, and it makes me wonder how van Doren does it, you know, standing in front of a bunch of people on a patio, or at a bowling alley, or someplace really real like the Whisky. My stomach goes tight and squeezes up to my heart.

Solve for Why

Me, Keith, and Treat are standing on the back patio looking out at an empty backyard. Treat reminds us that only dorks show up to parties on time. "We got a can't-miss formula. Free beer and a band. Totally punk rock."

The words are barely out of his mouth when a couple guys who lettered in Academic Decathlon come walking in through the side gate.

"Great," Keith says. "Dorks."

Treat snaps his chin up like he made those guys appear. He grabs a couple fake beers from one of the coolers, walks across the grass, and slips one to each of them. They're all thanks and head bobs because neither one of them has probably ever had a guy that looks like Treat actually be nice to him.

"See?" Treat says when he gets back to the patio.

"That's two people," I say.

"Yeah," Keith says. "That just makes this a Math Club party."

Treat folds his arms. He's wearing his black Buzzcocks T-shirt, the one with the sleeves cut off so it matches his sleeve-less Levi's jacket. "Come here," he says, and waves me and Keith over to a little red cooler hidden behind the big ones. He digs down below the Löwenbräu on top and pulls out bottles of Coors. "This is the real stuff." He clicks the caps off one at a time and hands them out. "It'll help us relax."

"Awesome," Keith says and takes a big drink from one like it's a soda. He pops the bottle out of his mouth and coughs with his whole body, and some beer foams out of his lips and crackles down onto the cement.

"You okay?"

Keith sucks in a deep breath and wipes his mouth with his sleeve. "Fizzy," he says, his voice hissing like he has a cold.

"You don't suck it," I say and pull the bottle up to my mouth. "Tilt it back and let the beer come to you." This is how Uncle Ryan showed me one summer at Seaside Heights. I've only done it with birch beer, though, so when the real stuff hits my throat, it's bitter and the back corners of my mouth squeeze like they're trying to stop it from getting to my throat.

I only mean to show Keith how it's done and that's all, but Treat clinks my bottle, then Keith's, and we all take a good draw. This time the beer washes around and then attacks the insides of my cheeks. I swallow and a breeze swirls around inside my skull. My mouth tugs at itself again and there's still a taste in there, kind of dry and slowly going away. Almost good.

Treat takes another good swig and opens the glass sliding door to the house. "I'm going to tell Lyle people are starting to show up."

They are. It's mostly freshmen and sophomores forming into small circles out in the grass, standing and looking over at the coolers. When one guy breaks free and comes over to the patio, Keith says, "Grab a beer." The guy looks relieved and waves up his group. A few more people break off, get a beer, and head back to re-form their circle. Pretty soon, everyone's getting chattier and goofier and breaking off old groups and re-forming new ones around the yard.

I'm nearly to the bottom of my beer when two girls wearing ripped-up jeans and T-shirts come walking around the side of the house to the patio. One of them has this black leather jacket, kind of Fonzie but with buckles and silver studs. The other girl has short black hair spiked up and flaring out.

Keith's digging out a couple beers for them and I say, "Do you know who that is?" because it's Cherise and Edie. Cherise is the one looking tough with that jacket and thick black eyeliner. Edie's eyeliner is in these long thin lines that make her eyes look sharp and less relaxed than usual. Up close, she's got purple streaks in her hair, like fireworks arching up into the sky right before they explode. Her striped shirt is supertight, and her jeans have two massive slits in them, one by each thigh.

I hand Edie a beer. "Where'd you get those?"

She pushes a leg out, the slit parting like a curtain to show lots of skin. "I made them." She takes a sip of her fake beer, wrinkling her nose a little as she pulls it away. "Are you guys nervous?"

Keith takes a swig of his beer and it looks smooth now the way he lets it come to him. "I'm a little nervous."

Not until my bottle is an inch from my lips do I realize how light it is, that I must have finished it off on the last drink. "Me too," I say and tip the bottle back anyway.

Cherise is looking out into the yard. "Where's Treat?"

"He's around," Keith says. "Probably making changes to the set list."

Cherise and Edie nod, real serious. The way Keith says "set list," it's like we really are a real band. Treat's Mohawk is as big as ever, and even though Keith's wearing a plain white T-shirt, he's written *Muck the Fan* on it big in black marker, and it looks good with his collared long-sleeve shirt unbuttoned over it. I've got Treat's black Minor Threat shirt underneath my Packy jacket, which makes everything okay the way it covers the fact that this shirt is way too big for me. And even without Mohawks, me and Keith have our hair messed up and stiff with hair spray Keith stole from his mom.

Cherise tugs at Edie's shirt and Edie gives her an *All right, already* look. "We're going to go walk around a little," Edie says.

The yard is changing by the second. You can't see all the way to the deck/stage anymore. Every few feet is a clump of people and this chatty murmur hovering over everything. I don't even realize Petrakis is talking to us until Keith taps me. He's got a six-pack of Pabst in one hand and shakes our hands with the other. It's actually a normal handshake, not like he's trying to prove he can bench-press a Pontiac. "Good party, little dudes. Where's the beer?"

"In your hand," Keith says.

He laughs and I point to the coolers. "Right there."

Petrakis half turns his body, like a door opening, and a

couple football players walk by and start fishing around in the coolers.

"You gonna spit on people?" Petrakis says. "Like van Doren does?"

"You know it," Keith says and clinks his beer bottle to Petrakis's cans.

"How 'bout you?" he says to me.

"I might just throw up on them."

Petrakis clinks my empty beer bottle. "Kick ass." He looks out into the yard and tells Keith he wants him to meet some of the guys from the team. It's been a good season and they think Keith really is a good-luck charm.

The yard is full now, the groups grown together into a single mass of people. I don't recognize anybody, and that's what gets my stomach tightening again. My eyes go to the grass, trying to focus on the most basic thing I can see, a single blade catching some light from the back of the house. For a minute, my head rises above the murmur, blocks out the sounds of people laughing and asking their friends when they think DikNixon will get there. It's just chatter and blur until the clacking of wood gets me looking over at the side fence. There's a guy in midair, one hand on the fence and feet flying over sideways. He thumps to the ground and three more guys pop up and over right behind him. Everybody along that side of the yard looks and you don't need much light to know that a guy in combat boots with cropped hair and three friends behind him like bodyguards has to be van Doren and the rest of Filibuster.

Van Doren looks out at the yard while a couple of the

Filibuster guys come over and grab four beers. They bring him one and he barely tilts his head at all, instead lifting the bottle, letting the beer come to him, then dropping his hand so the bottle slides through until the last second when he catches it with two fingers around the lip. It dangles there the way you'd hold a lantern or something, like he's forgotten he even has it until the next sip.

Keith comes back then, a new beer in hand. "How's he do that?"

"I don't know. My uncle Ryan never had a move like that."

Van Doren looks right at me. His eyes move just a bit to the side, to Keith, then back to me. He doesn't blink or look away either. He walks through the middle of his own group and over to us.

"Good crowd," he says.

It's a great crowd. Bigger than Ted Two or Three. Maybe as big as them combined. So I nod, but Keith doesn't. He looks down at his beer, the cap still on, studying the label like it'll say *Vintage 1925* and he can talk about what a good year that was. "It's not bad."

Van Doren looks at Keith without moving his head. "Not bad? I'd have been shitting bricks if this many people showed up the first time we played."

Keith looks up. "I'd be shitting bricks too, but it's not our first gig."

"Then you know better than to wait too long to play," van Doren says, his eyes back on me. "So you don't lose the crowd."

Me and Keith nod and van Doren steps back and looks us over. "Okay, then, boys, break a face."

As soon as he turns around I say, "We better play soon or he might."

"We can wait a little longer," Keith says. "Make them really want us."

I just want to get it over with now. It's like one of those huge tests you've been dreading all day and keep thinking: *Three hours from now I'll be taking it,* then *two hours,* then *forty-five minutes.* The closer it gets, the less chance for the teacher to go home sick or the Soviets to attack and save you. "Where's Treat?"

"Somewhere," Keith says. He swishes the beer around in his bottle and flicks his head like something is over my shoulder. "Guess who."

Over by Mrs. Dumovitch's rosebushes is a circle of girls away from everyone else. It's dark over there except for the garden lights along the ground and the light shimmering through the bottles they're holding. Wine coolers. I can't tell one silhouette from the other at first; then the shape of Astrid's hair appears. It's parted down the middle tonight with the Farrah Fawcett feathers on each side. It couldn't be less punk rock, but it's so perfect.

One of the girls, Sascha, comes walking over to the patio. She's wearing these dark blue jeans that are about as tight as security at the Kremlin. Keith grabs a beer for her, tucking his own beer into his armpit, using both hands to dry the new bottle off with the bottom of his shirt.

She clinks the bottle with one of the rings on her fingers and doesn't take it. "I'm fine," she says. With Keith holding a beer in each hand now, it's like Sascha's got him handcuffed. She pushes open Keith's collar and inspects his neck. "Looks like I'm going to have to freshen up your marks tonight."

Keith nods and tries not to smile too big. "Maybe I should mark you too."

Sascha puts a hand on the back of his neck and pulls him closer. It looks real sexy the way her head tilts sideways and her mouth opens just a little right as she starts kissing him. She pulls away and pushes him back a little. "Better. Much softer that time."

"Thanks."

"If you play good," she says loud enough for me to hear, "you can mark me somewhere no one can see." You might think she'd smile with that, leave it open in case she wants it to be a joke, but it's not. Her face is serious, her eyes locking Keith up until she walks away.

Keith sips a beer and holds it there until Sascha's turned completely around. He pulls the bottle from his lips and it's the wrong one, the one with bottle cap still on it.

"Smooth," I say.

"She is," Keith says and turns to me. "We need to play *right now*."

"Okay. Where's Treat?"

Even in a yard full of people and just patchy light, it should be easy to spot a Mohawk sticking up. But we don't see him.

"He's got to be in the house," Keith says and looks out at the deck/stage. "You go check and I'll stall."

"How?"

Keith steps over to the coolers to pop open the bottle he got for Sascha and a second new bottle, which he gives to me. "Flip on the utility lights when you see me up there; I'll do a sound check." He nods once, looking more excited than nervous, and heads into the crowd.

I step inside the glass sliding door and close it, the house as quiet as a confessional. Nobody is even looking at the deck/stage when Keith hops onto it without using the steps. I flip the switch and the deck/stage lights up, even brighter now that it's night and so dark back there. Everyone in the yard turns around. There's a muffled cheer that dies down as Keith steps into an orb of light. Behind him, the DikNixon logo glows in white light and Keith picks up the bullhorn: "Check, check, check. Fuck, fuck, fuck. Check-check. Fuck-fuck." Every time he says "fuck" a few people cheer, then a few more after the next one, and even more after the one after that until everyone is getting into it. "Check. Fuck. Check, fuck," he says faster and faster. "Check, fuck, check-fuck, checkfuck, checkfuck, checkfuck." Everyone's cheering and Keith waits until they quiet just a little before yelling, "Fuck Czechoslovakia!" The yard explodes in a roar. Van Doren and the guys from Filibuster are at the front edge of the deck/stage, holding up their beers, saluting Keith as he waves and sets the bullhorn down.

Mr. Krueger always tells us it's important to be thorough so you don't have to go back and check what you've already checked. So I look for Treat in the bathroom, the kitchen, the hallway, and his own room. In a corner of the dark Two-Car Studio there's this guy and girl making out, arms and hair twisted up and fused together so you can't see who's who or where one person ends and the other begins. "Treat?" The guy's head peeps out at me. No Mohawk. "Sorry," I say.

Now I'm nervous. I mean, it's easy to lose a person in a crowded backyard, but not the lead singer of the band that's about to play, and not at his own house.

I'm down to two rooms, Jewell's and Mr. and Mrs. D's. The last thing you want to do is go into a guy's parents' room, so I step into Jewell's room, running my hand along the wall for the light switch.

"Don't," says a low voice.

My eyes haven't adjusted to the dark, but I can feel the voice coming from the beanbag chair by the window. And there, with just the glow of streetlights coming through, is the silhouette of Treat's Mohawk.

"Treat. We're ready to start."

His voice comes through the dark just louder than a whisper. "I'm not."

"Come on, everyone's waiting for us. Didn't you hear the sound check?"

The Mohawk drops a little and his face is so dark there's no telling what he's up to. "Let them wait."

"Come on, Treat. Astrid's here and everything, just like you said."

Nothing.

"Cherise is here too. Have you seen her? She looks so cool."

"What the hell do I care?"

"I don't know. Just, come on."

Treat takes a deep breath and lets it out with his words: "I can't."

"What do you mean, you can't?"

He doesn't say anything and I start rubbing my hand along the wall again. My thumb finds the switch, and *bam,* the lights are on.

Treat is slung across the beanbag chair, his arms out to each side, his feet on the ground and knees up almost as high as his head. He's surrounded by stuffed animals, elephants and cartoon dogs, some of them falling over and resting on his arms like they crawled up to him. He squints at the light and right there on the floor by his boots is a lunar surface of barf.

"Are you sick? How many beers have you had?"

The Mohawk fans out sideways and Treat talks to the floor. "Go away."

An ache shoots from my heart and through to my fingers and toes. "Everybody's here, Treat. Everybody. They're waiting for us."

He throws Goofy at me but misses. "Get the fuck out of here, Reece."

It's not real. It's that dream where your locker won't open and the bell's ringing and you're spinning the dial and the combo won't come. Your heart's rattling in your chest and then you're running and it's the wrong classroom, and the wrong classroom again, until finally it's the right one. You hit your desk and the teacher doesn't say a thing but there's a test waiting for you that's worth 150 percent of your complete high school career. Only then, at that very moment, do you remember that, yes, there was a test coming and, no, you haven't studied for it. It's all your fault. You're not ready, not even a little bit, but you pick up your pencil anyway and, *poof,* wake up.

Only, I'm not waking up. The murmur from the backyard

seeps into the house. The bathroom door shuts with a soft click and a girl giggles because she's not in there alone. It's all happening. Now. None of this seems real. Not when Treat yells, "Go! Get out of here!" Not when I'm walking through the hallway and toward the glass sliding door.

From the back patio, the deck/stage glows like sunrise. Everybody in the yard is a silhouette, staring at the stage, watching Keith pretend to tune his guitar.

I slip through a forest of people. When I get to the top of the three steps on the side of the deck/stage, a few people start chanting, "Nix-on, Nix-on." More people notice and the chant grows nice and steady.

Keith grins and says, "What's *Cf*?" He sets down the bass, takes a sip of beer.

His words don't make sense. "I don't know, Keith."

"Californium," he says. "The element that keeps the state warm all year-round. Atomic number seventy-two."

I don't laugh and Keith looks back at the steps. "Where's Treat?"

I step around him, set down the beer I haven't taken a single drink of, and pick up the bullhorn. It's heavy in my hand and when I step into the orb of light, everything goes quiet. I'm the center of the universe, and with the utility lights, I can't see anyone past the first couple feet. But this is almost how it was supposed to be: Astrid out there in the darkness with her cheerleading friends, Ted and Sergio and Petrakis ready to start a slam pit. And van Doren's below me for once, right there at the edge of the deck/stage and waiting to see what comes down on *his* head. Only, it feels more like I'm standing up in class about to recite the periodic table. If I get it perfect, nobody will care. If I get it wrong, I'll look stupid-times-everybody, squared.

"Check, check," I say, and a couple people yell back, "Fuck, fuck," and then everyone laughs. The voice coming through the bullhorn is not the me I know. "We just got some bad news," I say and let the weight of the bullhorn make it sag. It's quieter now. Everyone listening. Nobody joking. The guys next to van Doren look like I'm about to tell them disco is back and they have to play it.

"We just found out," I say and it sounds like me again until I pull the bullhorn closer. "We just found out we're not going to be able to play."

Everyone groans and somebody yells out, "Bullshit!"

Keith looks at me, like, *What the hell?* and I need something better than *Our lead singer is yakking in his little sister's bedroom.* "The police said they'd shut the party down if we played."

Everyone groans again, and van Doren says, "Fuck the pigs, man."

I let the bullhorn drop and it's me again. "Yeah. F them."

"No." Van Doren shakes his head. He leans forward, one hand on the deck/stage, the other cupped around his mouth. Without making a sound, he mouths one word at a time: *Fuck. The. Pigs.*

It's like I'm staring at him for five minutes before it hits me. Then the bullhorn is at my lips and I hear the other me say, "Fuck the pigs."

"Yeah!" someone yells and everyone cheers.

"Fuck. The. Pigs."

Everyone cheers again and van Doren says, "Go with it."

"Fuck the fucking pigs!" I yell, and the cheers bounce back at me right away. I have the crowd. Everyone is waiting like the next thing out of my mouth is proof, not hypothesis. "The pigs can't handle DikNixon," I say. Everyone cheers. "DikNixon is above the law." Everyone screams. "You know why the pigs are scared of DikNixon?"

Van Doren turns to the crowd and raises his hands as he shouts out, "Why?"

"Because DikNixon *is* punk rock."

Through the roar van Doren starts the chant, "Nix-on! Nix-on!"

Keith steps out next to me, his bass in his left hand, his other hand out like the pope on his balcony. The people at the front of the deck/stage slap the boards with their hands to the beat of "Nix-on, Nix-on." Me and Keith lock arms. I hold up my other hand too, the bullhorn reaching up high, and we take it in, the whole backyard chanting, "Nix-on, Nix-on. Nix-on, Nix-on."

I pull Keith down with me into a bow, rise back again and say, "Fuck you very much. Good night!" I fling the bullhorn down, letting it bounce off the planks, and shove Keith to the side.

As I'm leaping off the stage, van Doren hops up. He's got the bullhorn and he's keeping the chant going, "Nix-on, Nix-on." A path opens for me through the middle of the yard. People reach out, shaking my hands, grabbing my shoulders, slapping my back the whole way to the glass sliding door. I get into the house alone, and I don't know if I'm going to walk straight down the hallway to tell Treat we saved DikNixon or if I'm going to slip into the bathroom and wipe off whatever is making my face feel like it could bust out laughing and crying at the same time right now.

The bathroom door swings open and out steps Astrid. She's wearing Dr. Martens lace-up boots with black tights that have a cheetah pattern if you look real close. It all disappears into an oversize sweatshirt, and even if it doesn't quite go together with her hair, it all looks good, like she's one of the Go-Go's. Her eyes find me but it takes a second before they open up kind of wide and she says, "Reece?" She looks past me to the backyard, where the chanting is dying down. "Is it over?"

I can't believe she's missed it. The first time ever I've looked sort of cool in front of everyone who matters and she's looking at me like she just heard we landed on the moon. "You didn't hear any of that?" I say. She shakes her head.

Van Doren is still at the bullhorn. It's muffled through the door, but the word *Filibuster* comes through and everyone cheers. Then it goes quiet and Astrid gives me the school nurse smile, the closemouthed one that says it's all going to be okay. She puts a hand on my shoulder and looks at me, a little unsteady. "Listen, there's something I should tell you. I don't think people should ever lie, especially if other people could get hurt." Her hand slips from my shoulder and she takes my right hand in both of hers. "That's a rule for me. There shouldn't ever be a reason to break it."

Her eyes are more relaxed than I've ever seen, and even though I'm expecting her to say something more, she doesn't. She blinks too long, a tiny nap, and I guess that means I'm supposed to say something about lies. Then the list of my lies rolls out in my head—the real reason we aren't playing, why we tried to be a band in the first place, our gig in San Diego, our gig in LA, and me the fake songwriter—which is fine until me in the bathroom with her panties makes the list. A surge of sick goes through me. My face heats up, and I start talking fast: "Remember how I told you I write the songs?" Astrid doesn't nod or anything, but I don't stop. "I had a little help . . ."

The glass sliding door rattles and swishes open. Astrid lets go of my hand as Sascha steps through and over to us, the door wide-open behind her. Astrid turns back to me and I finish, "From Neil Diamond."

Sascha leans into her. "Neil? Is that the guy I kissed?"

Astrid thinks about it a second, then smiles and says, "Kar-en! Neil Diamond? The singer?"

"Karen?" I say.

Sascha/Karen puts her hand on my chest and pushes me back a step. "You know Neil Diamond? My mom's gonna shit when I tell her."

I start explaining, but Astrid puts her hand in the middle of my chest and pets me. "Okay. It's okay." She turns to Sascha/Karen. "What?"

Sascha/Karen shrugs. "I think this party's *finito*."

Astrid nods. "Okay." She breathes in, thinks, and says, "Del Taco, then that party by the Orange Circle." Sascha/Karen nods and Astrid says, "Go tell everyone. I'll be out in a sec."

"Okay, chick." Sascha/Karen weaves her way back to the door. "I'm gonna go mark that little band boy one more time before we go."

Astrid smiles and it's off a little, kind of crooked. "Sometimes Karen takes little vacations from her boyfriend and scams on other guys."

"That's who Sascha is?" I say, and Astrid nods. She's still giving me that relaxed stare. "Is that what you're talking about? The lying stuff?"

Astrid stares at me, her eyes moving back and forth at each of mine. "I think so. Yes." Her eyes get big for a second; then she takes another breath and says, "Definitely. Don't let your friend take Karen too seriously."

"I think Keith's just happy somebody kissed him."

Astrid nods, her eyes close too long again, and I know now where I've seen that. Uncle Ryan would do it when he was drunk. Astrid gives my jacket a tug by the zipper and it pulls tight around me for a second, like a hug. She leans forward and kisses my cheek. I can't take a breath in or let one out. This is it! Sort of. It's a little wetter, I think, than it should be. It's soft, but somehow too soft. Loose. I mean, it's not like a ton of girls I'm not related to have kissed me on the cheek before, but this feels sloppy and too long for a cheek kiss.

Astrid pulls back and says, "Stay sweet, trash buddy."

"I will," I say, because what do you say to that? I'm waiting for a tingle from the kiss to spread across my whole face. It doesn't. It's more like a good-bye kiss your mom gives you when she's going to the store. Astrid is out the door, not looking back, and I want to say, *Hang on, I need you to help me win a bet*. I don't. I just watch her walk across the patio, pull Sascha/Karen away from Keith, and head for the gate.

The yard's still full and more people slap me on the back as me and Keith go back to the deck/stage to start unplugging things. I'm winding up cords when Cherise and Edie come up. Cherise is panicked, asking if we know which police station they took Treat to.

"He got arrested?" Keith says.

"Yeah," I say. "When you were doing the sound check." Cherise is totally buying this. "It's okay. He's back now."

Cherise puts her hands over her mouth the way Miss America does her happy cry. I tell her that Treat's inside, pretty sick over the whole thing, but if she doesn't mind a little barf he'd probably like to see her. She nods and Keith says he can walk her into the house and show her which room is Jewell's.

Once Cherise and Keith are out of sight, Edie sits down on the steps and says, "What were you talking to your girlfriend about?"

"Cherise?" I crouch down to put Keith's bass in its case.

"Astrid."

"She's not my girlfriend."

"You'd be her boyfriend if she let you." When I don't say anything, Edie shakes her head. "You don't even know her."

"I know her."

"Do you know she calls the police on her own parties to break them up?"

"That's stupid. No one would call the cops on their own party."

Edie stands up on the second step, taller than me now. "Are you playing dumb, or are you really just dumb? She calls the police so her parties won't go too late and she can pretend it's not her fault."

That sounds like it would work, you know? Like it could be true. Like I just did something exactly like that.

"You're such a fraud, Reece."

"Me?" I want to tell her all about the real Treat, or van Doren at the Whisky, or my parents ever since the night Uncle Ryan died. But Edie's looking at me like I'm so ugly and sad she can't figure out if I'm even human.

"The band conveniently doesn't play," she says, "and you get to act like a hero. And you pass all those notes and pretend you never read them. Or even care."

"I care," I say, but I'm not sure what I'm saying I care about.

A few people around us are looking over and whispering. Keith's coming back from the house and stops when he gets close to the deck/stage. He looks at Edie, then me, then turns around and disappears into the crowd.

"If you cared about anyone but yourself," Edie says, "you wouldn't be kissing the girl who tried to ruin your party."

"She kissed me."

"You let her. What's the difference?" Edie stares at me and waits, like maybe I'm hiding something behind my back. "Well?"

Edie's been with us the whole way. The fake San Diego gig was her idea. If I'm a fraud, what's she? "I don't understand why you're mad at me."

"Of course you don't," she says. "You never have the answers." She goes down the steps and into the yard. "See you in math class, *friend*." She slips past a couple people, then shoves through a group that's in her way.

This shouldn't matter, you know, not with all the good stuff that's happened with Astrid, but my stomach goes from spinning to falling. It's like watching the string break and your kite fly away—you're stunned for maybe a second, maybe less, but that's all it takes. If you didn't go after it right away, you're not going to get it back now, so you don't even run.

Keith comes up to the steps a few minutes later, smiling. He says the guys in Filibuster want us to play a party with them in a couple weeks. "We're for real," he says. "Our fourth gig and it's with Filibuster."

"Fourth?"

Keith nods. He's doing what Mr. Tomita always warns us not to do, mix up the known with the unknown. *Then you do not solve for* x, he says and bounces on his toes. *You have to go back and solve for* why. Why *did I do that?* Why *won't the answer come out right?*

When Keith heads back to talk to the guys from Filibuster, I go through the house and into the Two-Car Studio. I look around without turning on the light, the chairs and carpet and boxes, there but not there in the dark. Then I rip off my jacket and throw it out into the nothingness. I don't know why exactly. It's like it can't come home with me or something even though my parents know all about it now and what it all means and there's no taking any of that stuff back. But I leave without it anyway..

·

Walking home, I try not to think about Treat, or the band, or anything. You'd think having all those people cheer for you and a girl like Astrid Thompson kiss you would be the greatest thing ever. But Edie won't get out of my head, how great she looked, how mad she was. Angry too. And why is that all for me? Keith and Treat are frauds too.

I have a beer in me so I'm careful to stick to the sidewalks all the way through Treat's neighborhood. And even though there aren't that many cars around, I walk to the corner and wait for the WALK sign at Yorba Linda Boulevard before crossing. My eyes are wide-open the whole way, but all I can really see is that disgusted look on Edie's face.

My arms are chicken-skin cold and hurting a little by the time I get to the soccer fields. The dew is collecting again, the dampness hovering just above the grass, and my toes stiffen up and get achy inside my Converse. The fields glow in the park lights. They're smoothed over again like they haven't been trampled on all day. Like nothing's happened at all. Or maybe it's just that after everything that did happen all day, nothing has really changed.

102175—Orange County Jail

Colleen's voice is outside my door, this little chant, "Mom-mom-mom-mom? Is Reece going to church with us?"

"I'll be ready in two seconds!" I yell out, the covers still on me.

"We'll be in the car," my mom says from just outside the door, her voice calm but loud enough for me to hear.

My hair is accidentally punk rock, sticking up everywhere and stiff even after I've splashed water on it. My shirt is melting paisleys and untucked. But as I'm walking across the lawn, my mom's standing next to the open car door with one of those close-mouthed smiles.

Only Colleen talks to me on the ride. Do I want to see her watercolor that she brought home from school? She was going to show me yesterday because she thinks it's pretty only she hasn't hardly seen me and did I know it won third place and maybe should've been first but Holly Dirkson dropped a cup of blue and some of it splashed up and got on the barn which was supposed to be just red except for the horse's head but now has some blue on it too, right there, and do I like it?

I do.

After church, Packy makes a big breakfast and Brendan wants to know if I knew that since the NFL is still on strike they're going to show Super Bowl III on TV today and that's the one with Joe Namath and the Jets and do I want to watch the game with him even though we already know who wins?

I do.

I spend the whole day with Brendan and Colleen, watching reruns of football, sewing tiny blankets for the dollhouse, making PB&Js for lunch. My mom keeps busy with laundry and stuff. Packy stays out in the yard and the garage, only coming in to get a drink or to ask how the game is going since Brendan looks so worried even though he knows the Jets win.

At dinner, Brendan pretty much retells the entire Super Bowl but says he didn't really like it because there was so much running and defense that it was kind of boring.

I'm focusing on getting four peas on my fork instead of just three, so I don't look up when I say, "It was a different time." Uncle Ryan used to say that about baseball when Packy would complain that all the new players were too flashy or weren't loyal to their teams like the old days. I always liked that Uncle Ryan said that because it made it okay for me to like the new players without having to say there was anything wrong with the old guys.

"Reece is right," Packy says, which isn't a surprise. Of course he likes the old way. But then he says, "But I like the way they play now better too. It's more fun to watch."

In my room, I catch up on a whole weekend's worth of homework. Between English and algebra, I pull out my notebook and flip to a new page to tell Uncle Ryan about last night. Only, the words won't come.

My mom does the knock-as-you-enter move where it seems like she's being polite but really she's trying to catch me doing something I shouldn't. She's got her nightgown on and her hair down, and even though she puts her hand on my shoulder and says, "Hi, sweetie," her eyes go right past my algebra book to the open Uncle Ryan notebook. "I'm glad you made it to church today."

"Why wouldn't I?"

"Well," she says. "You had a late night."

"It wasn't that late," I say.

"Your father said it was after ten."

I came home to a dark house, sort of shocked Packy wasn't waiting at the stairs like a border guard. "How would *he* know?"

My mom sits on the bed. "He wouldn't go to sleep until he heard you come in."

I turn around in my chair to face her. "Did he think I wasn't coming home or something?"

"No. He loves you. We all love you."

So this is it, you know. This is what they say right before adding, *And that's why we're sending you to St. Spartacus Military School* or *So we think you'll be better off helping your great uncle Gomer pick cotton this summer in Louisiana.* "Am I in trouble for something?"

"Should you be?" She grins, a real one that sends lines through the constellation of freckles on her cheeks.

Maybe, I think.

She looks at the notebook again. "I just wanted to tell you I'm sorry. I never realized just how much you loved Uncle Ryan."

I guess I didn't realize it either. Not until I started writing the letters.

Her arms are crossed, not in the angry way, though. She asks if it's okay to ask me something. I nod, and she says, "When did you start writing to Uncle Ryan?"

"Not until here," I say. "After we moved."

"So, almost a year after . . ." she says and doesn't have to finish the sentence. We both know what she's talking about. "Reece, we've all been unhappy here."

I want to agree with her. I'm tired of arguing with Packy. Tired of being wrong, or having to explain the things I do or hide them so I don't have to explain. But I'm actually starting to like it here. I like my school. My teachers. I'm glad the secret element californium means I won't be shoveling the driveway this winter even if it does get colder than I would have guessed. I like Keith, and Cherise, and even van Doren. I like Edie more than I knew. And up until last night, I liked Treat. "I'm happy here," I say. "I like everything about this place except . . ." and I don't finish because I don't want to have to say it.

"Except what?" she says, her head tilting a little.

"Well, Brendan and Colleen seem happy. And you even said your job here is better than the one in Jersey." She closes her eyes with a slow nod. I look at my pillows for the last part. "But since

Uncle Ryan died and we came here, the Yankees could win the World Series and Dad would tell me to stop cheering so loud because he has work in the morning."

She looks at the floor, then back at me, her face steady, and I can tell now that she doesn't think I've gone cuckoo for Cocoa Puffs with the letters and all. "Your father is still sad about Uncle Ryan," she says. "But he loves you very much."

"He has a hard time showing it."

"I know. He's never been good with words, but he does love you, Reece. I don't doubt it for a second." She leans forward and takes my hand in hers. "You shouldn't either."

I know she wants me to say I know and I love him too. And even though I probably do, I just squeeze her hand, slip mine from hers, and say, "Okay. I need to get back to my homework."

My mom waits a second, then stands up, kisses me on top of the head, and says not to stay up too late.

■

I've been rehearsing in my head what I'll say to Treat on the way to school Monday. In one version, I call him a dickweed for screwing over me and Keith like that. In another, I ask if he forgot what Dr. Andy said about talking straight and what's that all about anyway? There's also a version where I just say I hope he's feeling better and that we should work on some new songs this week.

He's taking forever to come over the wall, and I'm freezing without my jacket. When Keith appears behind me, I know we're running late and have to go. "Dickweed," I say, and Keith, for once, totally gets it. "Treat?" he says.

Near my locker, van Doren's talking to one of the other guys from Filibuster. He doesn't look at me, but as soon as I'm hunching down and putting my books away he steps over. His locker door clicks, some books shuffle around, then something brushes my head and floats past. It's a sheet of orange paper that lands about a foot from me. Without looking up, I grab the sheet and hold it back up for van Doren.

"That's for you," he says.

It's a flyer for Filibuster, Saturday night with four other bands at the Wonder Bowl banquet room.

"Check it out," he says. "You guys might want to play there sometime."

He slams his locker and the other guy says, "Good job Saturday, bud."

"Reece," van Doren says as they step away. "That guy's name is Reece."

■

On the way to Mr. Krueger's class some sophomore tells me how great DikNixon is and asks if I know when Treat's getting out of jail. By the time first period's over and I'm walking to Algebra, the rumors have split a million ways: The cops broke up our show before it started, while we played, after we played; nobody got arrested, everybody got arrested, only Treat got arrested; they tried to arrest Treat and he got away by hitting a cop, by stealing a car, by hitting a cop with a car. I'm nodding and shrugging at the questions and backslaps. People I don't know, people who I don't think were even at the party, are saying how awesome DikNixon is or asking about Treat. Sometimes both. I'm almost late to class, and seeing Edie there, already settled into her seat, gives my stomach a shot of Astrid-quality nervous.

"Hey," I say. She barely gets a quiet "Hey" back before two people lean over and ask me if what they've heard is true. Who knows what they've heard, so I say they should ask Treat when he gets back to school. And that seals it. Confirming Treat hasn't made it to school makes everything else true.

The bell rings and Mr. Tomita has so much to tell us he's smiling and bouncing and he hopes we had a great weekend and got to play and play because now is the time to work. And since it is the time to work, Edie works. She doesn't tap me on the shoulder or whisper one thing to me the whole time.

We walk together after class, neither of us talking. It's different now. Her hair is new, a calmer version of the spikes she wore at the party, but that's not it. Her shampoo, or lotion, or whatever it is that makes me know it's Edie even with my eyes closed, is clouding my head, familiar, but since when did I know that I knew it? And has she always glided through each step as we're walking? Have I always waddled along next to her like an astronaut trying not to trip over a moon rock? I'm counting the silence in steps—ten, eleven, twelve—until we're at the stairs. "Sorry," I say.

"For what?"

"Saturday. Everything at the party."

Edie hugs her book and folder. "Never happened."

"Never happened?"

"Yeah," she says and slugs me in the shoulder, a good one,

enough to be there a minute later but not so much she's starting a fight. "Isn't that what buddies do?" She smiles quick, all lines, no lips or teeth. "See you in math class," she says and trouts up the stairs, fast, without bumping anyone.

Buddies. It spreads through my ears to my cheeks and down to my throat, where it sticks. I carry it with me to English, and it doesn't matter that Treat's not there; I want to keep thinking about Edie even if it makes me ache.

Penny Martin asks if what she heard about Saturday is true. I nod and keep nodding to each thing she says because it doesn't matter what you say once the rumors get going.

When we get time to journal, I'm all set to write Edie a note except Mrs. Reisdorf comes down the aisle and asks me to step outside. She asks how Treat is and if I'll see him after school. It's not to give him the assignment, though; she wants me to tell him not to worry about anything he misses. "The important thing is that he's okay."

"Okay," I say.

When I get to Spanish, I realize I forgot to look for Astrid on the way. Halfway through class, I don't even know if we've gotten new vocabulary words and I'm not sure where we are in *Don Quixote.* Or where he is. I just want to get to the Bog. I'm going to ask Edie to meet me after school for help with algebra. And she knows she can; she always gets the right answer.

As quickly as I get to the Bog, Keith is already there, alone. I'm trying not to look around for Edie and it's impossible to tell if she's running late or if the clocks are melting and time is messed up. Keith is done with his sandwich and on to his potato chips and how did that happen so fast? And has everybody in school stopped by to ask us about Saturday? Everyone except Edie.

At the bell, Keith says we've got to go to Treat's right after school. "DikNixon is going to rule as long as we can keep our story straight."

"Yeah," I say. "That and if our lead singer can actually make it to the gigs."

•

The Two-Car Studio is shut, so me and Keith knock at the front door awhile. Nothing. We go through the side gate to get to Treat's window and Keith sees him out at the deck/stage. The lights and boards are all gone, the water back in the Jacuzzi. Treat's in there, the bubbles and steam going and his Mohawk soaking wet and clinging to his head sideways like a bald guy trying to hide it.

Keith pops right up to the deck/stage. "Cherise and Edie were asking about you."

Treat sits up a little higher in the water. "Yeah?"

I come up the stairs. "When did you talk to them?"

"Before lunch." Keith looks back at Treat. "Cherise said she'd call you."

Treat stares down at the water to hide his grin. Keith tells him about all the rumors and Treat listens, calm and quiet. At the end of each rumor he looks back and forth between us and says, "What else?"

When he finishes the last one, Keith asks, "What do you think we should do?"

Treat looks at me. "What do you think, Reece?"

I shrug. "Pick one and go with it."

"Maybe," Treat says and leaves it hanging out there in the steam for a minute. "First, a Jacuzzi confessional."

He doesn't mean us, though. He starts talking to the water, about how sometimes people aren't themselves and how hippies are such junkies and there are even hippie doctors now because what did we think, that Berkeley just let people in because they were good at sit-ins? Some of those people really were smart, and a few of them actually made it through and became doctors. He rambles off a bunch of names we don't know, his voice calm and steady like he's reading the Old Testament: This doctor referred that doctor and that doctor referred this one and he had seven associates and their names were this and this and the other. "And just because you get a little depressed they think taking pills will make it all better," he says and looks up at us. "Would you take pills from a guy named Dr. Andy?"

Keith thinks about it and doesn't shake his head until he sees me doing it.

"Exactly," Treat says. "That's why I stopped."

"So you *were* on drugs," Keith says.

Treat looks right at Keith but his face is blank, almost sleepy. "I wasn't wasted. Sometimes I just don't care about anything."

"Even us?"

"Anything." He looks back at the water. "I just want everything off me."

Treat promises it will be different now. He's getting a new prescription since his parents found out and he'll take it every day. He'll care. And DikNixon will make history. "It's out there in the steam now," he says. "It has to happen."

I want to believe him. I know stuff happens to people and they can't always be who they were or who they think they're supposed to be. But knowing that doesn't mean I'm okay with it. It's more like what Mr. Krueger says about black holes: We can't wish them away, so we'd better learn as much as we can about where they are and how they work so we don't get sucked in.

■

Tuesday morning I'm waiting out front of my house again, still with no jacket. Keith finally yells to me to come on and I look at the wall for one more second. Still no Treat.

Before Algebra, a guy is passing around our flyer from the party, except this one is autographed: *Dumovitch, T. 102175—Orange County Jail.* Edie smiles when she hands it to me and that makes the whole thing almost okay, even funny.

On the way to the stairs she asks if I've got Dylan Long in any of my classes.

"Why?" I joke. "You need me to give him a note for you?"

Edie grins. "Maybe." She says they're in United Nations Club together and do I think she should even bother trying to talk to him since he's a senior? As her buddy, what do I think is the best thing to do?

I want to say, *Nothing.* "Well, you know I'm an expert when it comes to getting upperclassmen to notice you." She nods. "Meet me at the library after school and I'll trade you my top secret info for some algebra help."

"I can't. We've got a pizza party fund-raiser." Edie digs a flyer out of her folder and hands it to me. "You should come."

"Maybe," I say. "I think we have band practice."

Edie understands, and she leaves wearing the grin that showed up with the mention of Dylan Long.

In English, Treat's so busy signing autographs he only has time to tell me practice is canceled; he's got some appearances to make. "Appearances?" I say, but he goes back to signing notebook paper and lunch bags without answering.

After class, Treat tells me he's doing good promotional stuff for the band but me and Keith don't need to come.

"Maybe we want to come."

Treat stops walking. "Look, they just want me this time."

"Who are *they*?" I say, but he won't answer. "Do they think DikNixon is just you?"

"Maybe. But it doesn't matter." He gives me a good, friend shove. "No one's getting sacrificed here. I'll straighten them out."

"Sure," I say. "Sock it to 'em."

■

Me and Keith spend the whole afternoon at the public library doing homework and quizzing each other. When Keith's out of notebook paper to fold into airplanes and toss at junior high kids, I give him the pizza party flyer so he can do one more.

I'm home after dark, the house pretty quiet and smelling like meat loaf. My mom and Packy are watching TV, Colleen's playing in her room, and Brendan's on his bed, a *Sports Illustrated* lying over his homework.

With my homework already done, I'm at my desk thinking a letter to Uncle Ryan. Even if Dylan Long is nice to Edie, he'll never take her seriously. It's not like she can drive up and see him at college next year. And if she gets a ride there, he can't even take her to an R-rated movie. So it can't work. The numbers don't add up. But I don't write any of that down. It's not like Uncle Ryan can do anything about any of that.

■

Wednesday morning at the wall: no Treat.

"The border guards keep getting him," Keith says when he gets down the sidewalk to me.

I turn around and we start walking to school. "You think he's quitting the band?"

"I don't know," Keith says. "He sort of is the band. If he quits, we're screwed."

Keith's serious, not even a little grin or stupid joke after, and that makes me think his *I don't know* is really an *I think so too*. But at least Keith's sort of got Sascha/Karen. I'm right where I started. Or maybe even farther behind. Astrid definitely knows who I am now, and I don't think it matters at all.

So I'm sort of desperate to talk to Treat by the time I get to English.

He's in the middle of a story and flicks his head to me as I walk in the room. The Mohawk is freshly bleached, as tall as ever, and he has some new orange streaks in it. It'd be nice to hear how the promotional stuff went so I can know DikNixon still matters, and so I can stop thinking about the stupid United Nations Club pizza party and how great it was, and how much money they raised, and how Dylan Long asked Edie to stay late with him to help count the money. There was more to that story and Edie was ready to tell it until I said I probably had a quiz coming third period and needed to get in an extra couple minutes of studying, which is true even if I couldn't have cared less right then if Don Quixote made it home.

■

At lunch, the Bog fills with people who want Treat to tell them more about the cops and jail and the party, and he spends the whole time talking to everybody except me and Keith.

Right before the bell, right after I ask Treat about the promotional stuff and he says it fell through, he says he's got too much going on again today for band practice.

"What the hell?" I say. "Are we a band or not?"

"Hell, yeah, we are," Treat says. He looks right at me and it's hard to say he's lying. "We'll practice tomorrow."

"Really?" Keith says.

The bell rings. "Totally," Treat says.

He starts to take off toward the cafeteria but I grab his arm. "Why aren't you at the wall in the morning?"

"I will be," Treat says and shrugs free. "I gotta go now."

He fast-walks through the crowd of people heading out for their lockers and fifth period. Like I said, it's hard to lose a guy with a bleached Mohawk in a crowd. Especially if he wants to be noticed. Treat steps up on a planter and when Cherise comes out of the cafeteria he throws out his arms and bows to her.

Everyone over there laughs and Cherise smiles; then he hops down and they walk off in the direction of her locker.

And now I see the pattern: no Treat at the wall in the morning, no talking to him in English, no talking to him at lunch, no band practice. Ever. He is Dik-*Fucking*-Nixon now. I'm Vice Idiot Nobody. Keith is Secretary of Stand There and Stay Quiet.

Twenty-four hours later, my hypothesis is playing out perfectly: no Treat at the wall, no real conversation in English, and now he's a no-show in the Bog. "Did he say anything to you?" I ask the Secretary of Stand There and Stay Quiet.

Keith talks through a mouthful of sandwich. "I haven't seen him today."

I haven't touched my food. "Should we go over to his house after school?"

"He won't be there," Keith says.

He says it so confident I figure he must know something. "Did you hear that from Edie or Cherise?"

Keith shakes his head. "I haven't seen them today either. I can just tell." He takes another bite, calm, and shrugs, like, *That's that*.

Me and Keith hang out at the library again after school. We get all our homework done and he shows me the note he's working on for Sascha/Karen. It's eight pages so far with what he's done every day this week, pictures, lists of places they can meet to kiss so her boyfriend won't find out, and the lyrics to a punk rock love song that go, "Missing kissing / got a mission for kissing / you, you, you / Frenching and necking / scarring my neck again / for you, you, you."

"How are you going to get it to her?" I say.

He slides it over to me. "You, you, you."

I pull my hands away like it's radioactive. "I don't know where she lives."

"Yeah," Keith says. "But Astrid does and—"

"Nope." I shake my head. "I'm done playing pony express for people. You're on your own, cowboy."

Keith takes the note back. "I'll find a way. Like Romeo did. Our forbidden love will triumph."

I haven't read *Romeo and Juliet* yet—we're supposed to read it and see a production sometime in the spring—but I'm pretty sure it doesn't go the way Keith thinks it goes, though I don't say anything.

■

Nothing changes on Friday except that Treat doesn't even look at me in English. After class, he says he's in a hurry and we'll talk at lunch, which would be fine if he actually showed up at lunch. So me and Keith wait for him at his locker after school. He walks up with Cherise, all smiles and both her arms wrapped around one of his biceps. "Hey," he says, "I'm glad I caught you guys so you can be the first to know." He looks at Cherise, who squeezes into him a little tighter, and then back at us. "I'm resigning from DikNixon."

It punches me right in the heart even though I knew it was coming.

Keith looks at me, then Treat. "There's no DikNixon without you."

"Sorry," he says. "No band should play past its prime. Why do you think the Beatles broke up?"

"Yoko Ono," I say.

Keith gives me a *Who?* look, but I shake him off.

"Yeah, well," Treat says, "if the Beatles never break up we never get 'Imagine' or 'Band on the Run.'"

Keith says he's never even heard of those bands, then looks at me, like, *Right?* I shake him off again.

I want to ask Treat who he thinks is going to cover for him the next time he messes up. Does he know it'll take him down? Then I think, *Good, be your own worst enemy.* Which isn't nice, I know, so instead I say, "What if we just put it on hold awhile?"

Treat shakes his head, the Mohawk making the *no* look huge. "It's got to be a clean break. I'm moving on to other things."

My arms flail out, Jesus-like. "Come on, at least think about it."

"I already did," Treat says, kind of quiet, like he's afraid he'll scare Cherise. "It's over for DikNixon. There's no coming back this time."

Keith steps forward, his finger right at Treat's face. "You said we had to care about each other like we were brothers, and that even if we didn't care about ourselves on something, we couldn't do that to our brothers."

You might think Treat would swat his finger away, but he just stares at the ground.

Cherise looks at all three of us, and she looks just as sad as Treat. "You guys can still be friends. You don't have to be in a band together to be friends."

"I know," I say. "But a band is something different. It means more."

"Brothers," Keith says, nodding at Cherise, and I want to say, *Don't talk anymore. You'll ruin what you already said.*

Treat finally looks up, says, "Sorry. I gotta go," and leaves so fast Cherise has to fast-walk to catch up.

Keith starts saying what a jackass Treat is, what a dickhead move that was, how we should call him Been-a-Dick Arnold now. He's right about all of that, and I'm angry too, but mostly now it feels like it did when Uncle Ryan died, where your face is heavy and stopped up so you can't laugh or cry or hardly breathe. Everything just aches.

■

Keith's dad drops us off at Wonder Bowl Friday night, saying he had no idea kids still liked bowling and to call when we're ready to come home. There's a sign outside the banquet room with four bands on it, including Filibuster. After the first band, people come up and ask us if Treat really left DikNixon because he got a solo record deal or if it was because of his probation. Nobody asks what we're going to do now without Treat.

Van Doren gets there after the second band plays and tells us why the bands he missed suck and why the next one is worth getting in the slam pit for. Then he points out which guys to stay away from in the pit because they just want to hit people. "Assassins," he says.

The next band is good, and me and Keith are huffing and sweaty when van Doren calls us over to the side of the stage. He tells Keith that Filibuster needs a roadie tonight, which means he'll be running guitars and picks and strings out to the guys as they need them. "And you're going to introduce us, Reece." When I ask what he wants me to say, he says, "The truth."

From the stage, you can see how long and skinny the banquet room is. It's crammed full of people, but I'm not nervous. I step up to the microphone, a real one, and even though I'm not sure what I'm about to say, it just comes out: "This is what you've been waiting for, you sick bastards." There's a cheer, not too big, but it gives me a beat to think, and everything comes together: "Get ready for the band your dad likes best, because it scares the pants off your mom . . . Filibuster!"

Van Doren's next to me right as the words leave my mouth. He wraps his arm around my neck for a second, a weird little hug, then shoves me into the pit as the music explodes.

Filibuster plays a great set, people thrashing everywhere the whole time, Keith keeping up with breaking strings and shouts for *The blue guitar! The brown guitar! No, not for me, for him*, and *Good job, dude*.

Afterward, we help the guys load up their stuff; then van Doren drives us to a Denny's restaurant and we all eat breakfast at one in the morning. We sit around the table, the six of us drinking off the two coffees we ordered, everybody talking about the gig and bands and school and college and whatever else. When it gets quiet, Keith starts talking about how his mom wants him to garage sale all his *Star Wars* action figures and I'm sure that's it—van Doren will never hang out with us again. But one of the guys in Filibuster says Keith will probably make some serious bank if he has some vehicles too. Keith says he has the *Millennium Falcon* and the Death Star and van Doren looks at him like he's mad. "You can't sell that stuff yet. Tell your mom to put it all in Ziplocs, and in about five years some freak will give you enough money for all that stuff to pay for college."

Van Doren is serious, and everyone agrees, and now I know Edie was right when she said it sucks to be cool. I mean, talking about *Star Wars* toys or debating whether or not the two girls in the B-52's are cuter than all four of the Go-Go's is a million miles away from cool. Just like gas station shirts and the sixteen-hundred-meter race. But whatever all this is, it's real, and it's nice, and it makes me feel like I matter.

[Encore]

Since fall, I've been depending on californium to keep the state pretty warm just like Keith said it would. And it has. I got through Thanksgiving and Christmas with long-sleeve shirts over the new band T-shirts I've been getting at gigs and record stores. My mom says she doesn't see how a couple of shirts can keep me warm enough, especially since I'm always ripping holes in them on purpose, but there's no way I'm going over to Treat's house to get my Packy jacket, and it's not like he ever does anything more than say, "Hey," to me in English, and I say, "What's up," and he says, "A preposition," and we laugh, but that's it.

On rainy days my mom's at the door with my Yankees jacket, which I wear as far as Keith's house before stuffing it into my backpack, but I can't complain. It's only cold in the morning. Even on days when our front lawn is crunchy with frost, I can shove my hands into my ripped jeans and squeeze myself warm all the way to school.

It's a late winter morning like that, cold but not exactly freezing, when we get into the heat of Mr. Krueger's classroom and everyone's quiet. Keith's in the middle of a story about Sascha/Karen deciding if she's going to break up with her boyfriend for spring break so she can ditch school some days and go to the beach with him.

"That doesn't make sense," I say. "If she has a different spring break, why would she need to do that?"

Keith doesn't answer. He's staring at the front corner of the room, which does look different somehow. Mr. Krueger isn't sitting behind his desk like he usually does until seven seconds before the bell rings, but that's not it. "Oh my God," Keith says, and then I see it too. The periodic table chart is covered in butcher paper. Mr. Krueger is at the podium, a stack of papers in his hands. This is it.

Right after Christmas, Mr. Krueger told us we needed to get the holidays out of our heads. The periodic table test was coming soon now and we needed to know, in case we didn't already, that life doesn't take a vacation. "The elements keep doing what they do whether you got what you wanted for Christmas or not. Whether your team won or lost. Whether you got a date for the big dance or stayed home." He tapped the chart. "Life goes on, people. So you have to as well."

It was good that he reminded us. Me and Keith had stopped studying even a little bit on the weekends. Sometimes we had Filibuster gigs. Sometimes there were parties van Doren told us about. And there were two times Sascha/Karen broke up with her boyfriend for the weekend so Keith could come over to her house to practice things she said any girl would want Keith to be good at and her boyfriend wouldn't do. On those weekends I'd go to some G-rated movie with my family, maybe a recital or some little show Colleen was in, and let Packy give me a lesson on making brunch if he didn't have to be up too early for his overtime Saturday shift.

So me and Keith started going to the public library again most days right after school to get our homework done and get ready for the test. You might not think Keith would still want to do that, but if all his homework is done when he gets home, his mom lets him talk if Sascha/Karen calls, which isn't all that often, but when she does call, it's these two-hour conversations where Keith mostly just listens.

When Mr. Krueger hands out the test seven seconds before the bell rings, it's just like he promised: a blank periodic table and that's it. "Show me what you know," he says.

The thing about a big test is even if you know it's coming, you don't actually know how it's going to go or what exactly you'll do until you're doing it. I number all the boxes first, 1 to 103. It's easy. The top left one is 1, top right is 2, then back to the left for 3 and on like that until you get to 57. Somehow, 57 is magical and starts the lanthanide series, the separate table at the bottom of the sheet. The first row there goes 57 through 71; then you run out of room and have to pop back up to the regular table for 72.

I fill in the easy stuff next—hydrogen and helium, ones like that. The periodic table on my desk is looking like the real one now even if a lot of things are still missing. There are people around me whose pencils aren't scratching and clicking anymore, but I knew I'd get to this moment where the easy stuff was done and I'd have to let things get a little weird, trust that my instincts will get it right.

I can remember 19 on the chart is *K* because in baseball scoring you make a *K* when a guy strikes out and the record for strikeouts in a game is 19. And if 19 is *K,* 18 is *Ar* so it can spell out *ArK.* And Noah needed a forest of trees to build his ark and a famous forest is the Argonne, and so 18 is argon. It's right; I know it is. Then I remember to go back and write *potassium* under the *K* and that reminds me there's a lot of potassium in bananas and so 20 is calcium because I like to put bananas in my cereal before the milk.

I'm getting all the answers like that, the ones that make sense to me in ways our textbook never tells us. I even get californium right because of Keith, then berkelium because you always put the city right before the state.

It probably sounds crazy to anyone listening when me and Keith are talking about it later in the Bog. You might even think we liked it the way we're interrupting each other to tell different things we each did on the test the way guys talk about making a great catch or getting some girl to kiss them. Then Keith says he guesses we don't have to go to the library every day anymore and I say, "Yeah, thank God for that," and we both get quiet.

■

In my journal later, I write about how it's weird to think I'm going to miss studying at the library every day. I know what it is, though. Everything's changed. A couple times a week, Astrid gives me a wave or says, "Happy Wednesday," which is nice and makes me look good in front of other freshmen, but it's not like she's waiting at my locker after school or abandoning the Senior Circle to have lunch with me in the Bog.

It's weird not having Treat around either. Keith's still mad about it, and I mean crazy angry. "He stabbed us in the back like Caesar did to whoever he did that to," Keith says, and I say, "You mean Brutus," because we just read that in my English class too. Keith looks confused but he nods, and I know he's talking about betrayal. It's just, I feel more sad about it now than betrayed because Treat isn't a bad guy. Not really.

One time in English, right after Winter Formal, Treat passed around pictures from the dance, saying how lame it was but he had to go because he'd been voted Freshman Ice Prince or something. And there he was next to Cherise in his black boots, black pants, and black T-shirt, one of those joke ones that's just a picture of a tuxedo, no real jacket or tie. It made me smile and feel kind of happy for him. There was another picture with the whole winter court, including Astrid, which you might think would make me jealous, but that feeling didn't come until I flipped to the couples picture with Treat and Cherise squeezed next to Edie and Dylan.

Worst of all, me and Edie are just math buddies now. It's been that way all winter and into spring. She won't even walk to the staircase with me after class. There's always a poster that needs to be put up for a UN Club meeting or flyers to get at Dylan's locker, or something else super important. It doesn't stop me from wanting to walk with her, and talk to her, and look at her, but at some point back in January I figured the least I could do, as her buddy, was stop making her come up with excuses. So I started bolting for the door every day as soon as the bell rang, even before Edie had time to gather her stuff and stand up.

■

It's a Friday in spring, just after baseball season has started, that I wait for Edie just outside the door after Algebra. She looks surprised when I step up next to her. She's headed for the stairs, so she can't make an excuse this time.

I hold up a note I've folded into a tiny square. "I need you to deliver this to someone for me."

She takes the note without looking at me, flipping it over since there's no name on the front.

"It's for you," I say and she nods, serious-faced, and keeps walking. "Me and Keith used to do this thing with Treat where we'd put stuff out into the air to make it honest and true. I guess I was doing that in these letters I'd been writing to my uncle even if I'd never actually—"

"Okay," she says and slides the note down into a front pocket of her jeans. "I'll deliver it to myself after school, when I have time to read it."

I take a breath. "Okay."

We're at the bottom of the stairs, stopped, and I'm out of things to say.

Edie nods. "Now is the time to go," she says, grins just a little, and steps away without looking back.

The thing about Astrid ever being my girlfriend was that it was all hypothesis, like how Mr. Krueger says cold fusion is hypothesis: "Even though it's possible, if we're honest about it we know it's not going to happen anytime soon, if it ever happens at all." But the stuff with Edie, it was theorem. Everything I needed to solve it was right there the whole time. So that's kind of what the note says. As Edie's math buddy, I wrote, she needs to know Dylan Long isn't the right guy for her. Not that he's a bad person, but if she's x, he's $x + 3$ (because he's three years older and is going away for college next year), and that can't be solved. *He'll be living far away and busy with hard classes and maybe his fraternity or Frisbee golf or whatever else college guys do,* I wrote. *So what you need to do is solve for y. Why you should go out with someone from your own class. Why you should go out with someone who has been friends with you since day one. Why you should go out with me.*

∎

Saturday morning, with Packy already off for his overtime shift, I make brunch for everyone. And just after, just as I'm washing the dishes and Brendan's drying, the phone rings.

I'm all soapy hands so Brendan gets it. "Hello," he says, stays quiet for a minute, then covers the phone and looks right at me with a dumb smile on his face. "It's a girl, and she asked for you."

This shock of nerves runs through me so fast and so hard I feel it swirl down my arms and into my bubbly hands. I rinse off real fast and say, "Is it Edie?" as I grab a dish towel. I'm saying it more for myself than Brendan, but he uncovers the phone and says, "Is this Edie?"

I put my hand out for the phone, giving Brendan the *You just dropped an easy fly ball* look, but he nods real calm, like he's gotten the out anyway, and hands the phone over. "Yep. It's Edie."

"Was that your brother?" she says.

"Yeah, for about five more minutes until I kill him."

She laughs and so I do too, and then we both breathe a couple times.

"I read the note," she finally says, and the whole world outside the phone line stops. Now it's just my ear, Edie's mouth, and whatever she might say next, which is, "It's good."

I start wrapping my wrist in the phone cord. "Thanks."

"It really got me thinking about a lot of stuff."

My cheeks tingle with how nice she sounds, with what she might mean by *stuff.* Then my mom's head pokes into the kitchen from the hallway. "Brendan! If you want me to drop you off at Kyle's, let's get a move on."

Brendan tosses his dish towel on the counter as he walks toward my mom. "Reece is talking to a girl."

"The car," my mom says like she didn't hear a word Brendan said, but Colleen's behind her asking if I'm talking to a girl from her class.

"Hold on a second," I say into the phone.

My mom turns to watch Brendan and Colleen, I guess to make sure they're heading for the front door; then she turns back to me. "Lock up if you go out anywhere with . . . ," she says, her eyebrows up, her face frozen.

"Edie. You know . . . ," I say, all casual, raising my eyebrows too because my mom really doesn't know.

My mom smiles. "Oh yes, Edie," she says nice and loud. "Be home for dinner." She blows me a kiss and is gone.

"Sorry," I say.

"That's okay," Edie says.

"You know, Filibuster's playing tonight—"

"I can't," she says. "That sounds really fun, but I've got a date." The world goes quiet again, library-on-a-Friday-night quiet, but Edie breaks it quick this time. "Aren't you going to ask me what I'm doing on my date?"

"Do I want to know?"

"Solving for y," she says, and I can just see her standing in her kitchen, that grin she gives only to me.

I laugh and Edie does too. "Okay."

"Okay," she says soft and smooth.

"Now is the time to go?" I say.

"Now is the time to go," she says, soft and final, and we hang up. I'm so happy I don't care there's still a mess of dishes and they're all mine. I hit it hard and happy, wash-rinse-dry-return. My head is going to all kinds of happy places—first I'm just walking Edie to the stairs after class and holding her hand; then we're sneaking in a quick kiss at the bottom of the staircase before she heads off for her next class; then we're sitting side by side on a planter in the Bog, her thigh pressed up against mine, maybe her hand on the back of my neck, sort of tickling it.

The front door whines open and I almost drop a plate. I didn't hear anything until just now, just as someone is stepping into the house. Packy comes around the corner. "Good," he says. "You're here." I nod because where else would I be? "Where is everybody?" Packy says, and I tell him. "Good," he says again. He looks me up and down. I'm wearing shorts and a black TSOL T-shirt.

"What are you doing home?" I say.

"Put on some shoes," Packy says. "We're going somewhere."

∎

In the truck, Packy won't say where we're going. We get on the 91 freeway, then the 57 south, so not LA. I'm guessing that if he's about to drop me off at Salt Mining Camp or Saint Bend-over's Torture Academy for Boys, he'd look grim or be talking about when he and Mom would come back to visit me. We're not talking, though, and I don't even turn on the radio. Half the time I'm wondering where we're going, and the other half my mind is on that date with Edie and Dylan, trying to solve it so y comes out the right way.

Finally, I say, "Will we be home by dinner?"

"I think so."

"*We* will?" I say. "Both of us?"

Packy looks around like who else do I think is in the truck? "Don't worry about dinner."

"I'm not worried. It's just, there's a gig tonight and I prom-ised van Doren I'd be there."

"The kid with the *crap* haircut?"

"*Crop.*"

Packy smiles. "I know. I'm just busting your chops."

We exit the freeway into traffic that leads us into this huge parking lot, an ocean of asphalt with Anaheim Stadium rising in the middle of it like an island. Cars and vans and trucks and buses are everywhere, and people are funneling in from all directions like the stadium has its own gravitational field.

"We're going to a ball game?"

Packy looks me over. "Yeah. You still like baseball, don't you?"

Out the side of my eye I can see him keeping his head turned toward me, driving slow in the stadium traffic and glancing forward to spot-check. I keep my eyes on the stadium. "I guess so."

The Angels are playing Seattle: an okay team versus an awful one. Inside the stadium, there are plenty of guys my own age hanging out, though none of them are with their parents.

We get in line for hot dogs and the guy right in front of us has his arm wrapped around this girl beside him, his hand inside the back pocket of her shorts. She's leaning into him hard, and I don't know how the guy is going to get through nine innings without exploding. Packy's trying to ignore it by talking to me like I'm five, saying I can have anything I want—hot dog, pop, even Cracker Jacks. It's awful.

·

When the game starts, I try getting into it, but I couldn't care less about either of these teams. It might help if the Angels fans would get excited about their team, or razz the other team, but they're just polite about everything—clapping at the good stuff, groaning at the stuff that almost goes right or goes a little wrong, and being quiet the rest of the time.

"It's not the Bronx," I say.

"No," Packy says. "It's a nice stadium, though. Clean. Safe."

He's right. The plastic of the seats isn't faded and scratched. Even the concrete looks like you could go five-second rule if you dropped your peanuts. But it's still not the Bronx. "It's a boring stadium. They don't have any plaques. They don't have a short porch in right or a deep gap in left center. They don't even know how to razz a guy when he comes to the plate."

Packy smiles, which makes no sense. "You're right."

We spend most of the game just sitting there, staring at the field and every once in a while saying, "Nice play, huh?" "Yeah. Nice play." Then this guy Lenny Randle comes to the plate and somebody yells, "You're a bum, Randle!"

It's what Uncle Ryan would have said, especially since Randle used to be a Yankee and he was terrible, but Packy is the one who said it. Some of the Angels fans look back and up at us, but since Randle's playing for Seattle they aren't angry, just confused anyone would yell at some guy who isn't even hitting .200.

"I've seen backstops hit the ball farther than you," Packy yells out, one of Uncle Ryan's favorites, and the people right next to us laugh.

We spend the rest of the game razzing Seattle players with Uncle Ryan's best digs. And we try to come up with good nicknames for the Angels players: Ron "I Wish I Were Reggie" Jackson, Reggie "I'm Glad I'm Not Ron" Jackson, and Bobby "the Grich Who Stole Second." They aren't the best, but it's like Uncle Ryan is there with us so it's more about having fun than getting it exactly right.

After the game, we're coming off the last stadium ramp to the parking lot and Packy asks if I want to go find where the players come out. I can see what he's doing, what Uncle Ryan would have done, and it's nice. I'd be tempted, too, if it was the Yankees. "We should go. Mom's probably making dinner right now."

"Are you sure?" Packy stops walking just outside the main gate. He jiggles the keys in his pocket. "It's up to you."

It really isn't that late, and it doesn't take a rocket scientist to know it'd just be easier to do what he wants than to argue the whole way home, maybe even get grounded for the night. But I can't help it. "I don't want to break my promise to van Doren," I say, which is true.

"Sure." Packy takes a couple steps into the parking lot. I'm slow to move, trying to read him and make sure this isn't a test. "Come on, Methuselah."

I catch up. "Methuselah?"

While we're sitting in the parking lot traffic, Packy gets this grin and asks if he ever told me about the time Uncle Ryan hung out with some of the Yankees.

"No." I look him over. "Is this a true story?"

Packy nods and says Uncle Ryan used to offer to buy beer and pizza for any player who wanted to meet him after the game at Rocco's in Bayonne. One time, a pitcher named Mike Torrez took him up on the offer and brought a couple other Yankees with him.

Packy's smiling as he tells it, and I can just see Uncle Ryan there, pushing the mugs across the red-checkered tablecloth because he always liked to be the guy who gave you something good.

Uncle Ryan never talked about that day, Packy says, because he'd already had too much to drink at the game and fell asleep at the table right after the players got there. I laugh and so does Packy, and we do again when he gets to the part about the players paying the bill, putting Uncle Ryan in a cab, and paying for that, too. "He had no idea what happened until the next time he went to Rocco's and the owner told him everything."

Packy keeps smiling, the best smile I've seen on him since I can't remember when.

I smile too, and when he looks over at me I say, "Tell me another Uncle Ryan story, Dad."

My dad rubs his chin. "Okay. Do you know about the time he got kicked out of Studio 54?"

I don't even know what Studio 54 really is, but I don't care. "Tell me," I say, and that's how we get home: story after story, Dad looking somewhere over and beyond all the cars on the freeway, feeling his way up the hill to Yorba Linda and that sign that reads LAND OF GRACIOUS LIVING.

■

Saturday night, I'm still wearing the TSOL shirt, and now I've got on some Dickies work pants van Doren gave me since he's moving on to plaid, and Dad's old Converse. Filibuster's playing a great set, the pit's swirling, Keith's working hard, and to keep from thinking about Edie on that date, I'm going over the Uncle Ryan stories Dad told me today, trying to decide which ones I'll tell the guys later when we go out for a late-night breakfast. But in my head, imagining van Doren's face as I tell the stories, Uncle Ryan isn't coming off so good. He sounds kind of pathetic, acting crazy after drinking or messing up fun times by getting too drunk. I mean, I know Uncle Ryan was a good guy—Dad wouldn't love him the way he does if he wasn't—but he might not sound that way to other people if they hear too much.

At Denny's restaurant, we're in one of those circular booths, passing around the two coffees we ordered to share, and everyone's chattering about the show. Then van Doren gives us some details about playing the Whisky in June and Keith tells a Sascha/Karen story that has the guys laughing and telling him he's whipped. It's fun, but I'm clammed up, afraid to tell the Uncle Ryan stories and feeling guilty for not telling them. Then Uncle Ryan slides into the booth beside me, looks at the empty coffee cup by my spoon, and signals the waiter. "I think my cup has a hole in it," I hear myself say. The waiter steps over fast, his face concerned. I grin and hold up the cup. "It's been empty for like five minutes." The waiter rolls his eyes and tells me to hold my horses. Van Doren laughs. Then Keith and the rest of the guys laugh. And then me and Uncle Ryan do too.

■

As soon as Mr. Tomita drops his chalk on Monday, Edie stands up and says, "Come on."

We walk out the door together and toward the stairs. She wants to know all about the Filibuster show; she's sorry she missed it. Sorry she missed hearing me introduce them and says it must be a lot of fun.

She says we should get together to study for our next algebra test. "It's been a hard unit," she says, and I get the grin that makes the whole of me go warm every time I see it now. "You'll need the help."

"I will," I say.

She glances at the stairs but doesn't leave.

"Does this mean you solved for y?"

She shakes her head, but there's a smile with it. "It's a big one," she says. "We'll have to take our time and work on it together. Okay?"

It's not the answer I want, but at least there's something to build on, you know? And did I really expect her to just break up with Dylan? Maybe, but not really, now that I think about it. Who wants to be with a girl who would do that? "Okay," I say.

I know what she's going to say next, and I say it with her. "Now is the time to go." She bursts out laughing and I get a little glance back from her as she goes.

■

At lunch, I tell Keith about all of that and he says we should get together after school to start planning my next move. It's not a bad idea, I say, but we'll have to put it off until the next day. I've got somewhere to be today, somewhere Keith can't come with me. He's dying to know, but I won't say.

As soon as the bell rings in sixth period, I'm out the door. I don't even go to my locker. I want to run to Treat's house as fast as I can, and I do.

Mrs. D answers the door, smiling when she recognizes me. "I'm sorry, Reece," she says, "Treat's not home from school yet."

"That's okay," I say, and I'm pretty sure it sounds happier than it should. "I'm just wondering if my jacket is still here."

She steps back and opens the front door all the way to let me in. "Goodness, I'm not sure—"

"It's probably in the . . ." and I want to say "studio," because that's what it was, but I just point at the door to the garage. "You know, probably out there where we practiced."

She walks me to the door and opens it for me. "You can have a look around."

Treat's Bug is right in the middle now with the car cover over it, the >I< logo stretched across the roof, not a bit faded. The amps are stacked in a corner with the instruments. The chairs are folded up, leaning in another corner with the rolled-up carpet, and the computer boxes are stacked against only one wall now. It's weird, you know? It's all the same elements that made it a studio, but it feels totally different and hits me hard, like a little version of losing Uncle Ryan.

I'm thinking maybe I'll just go, but then I see this one computer monitor out, sitting on top of its box, and there's my Packy jacket in a pile behind it like a little car cover that slipped off. I pick it up and dust it off, and the weight of it is a handshake from someone coming off the plane, that person you haven't seen in forever, and everything's okay now because he's here.

Mrs. Dumovitch walks me to the front door, saying she's happy I found my jacket and that she thinks Cherise is a wonderful girl but misses seeing me and Keith. We're invited over anytime, she says, and you can tell she means that the way she lingers at the door as I cross the driveway.

It's warm now but I don't care. I slide my arms through the jacket, feel it tug around my shoulders and prop up my back. The patches are all here, stitched tight like they've always belonged, like they're supposed to be right alongside the Packy patch.

I head up the hill, thinking about tomorrow in the Bog when I tell Keith we're starting a band. He'll get excited and say DikNixon is back, but I'll tell him no. DikNixon is dead, and we're not going to be Dixon or the Pardon or Ford spelled *Fjord* so it looks like we're from Europe. We're moving on to the next thing. Our own thing.

ACKNOWLEDGMENTS

I could not be a writer without the encouragement and support, early on and still, of my parents, Kathleen and Robert, and my wife's parents, Joy and Mike Hensley. And I wouldn't be the writer I am without my wife, Julie Hensley, who not only told me early on that this was a book, but also what it was really about and what the title should be.

I'm so fortunate to have had early readers for this project, many of whom could see its potential before I could and pushed me forward: Lex Williford, Jewel Parker Rhodes, Bert Bender, Ron Carlson, and especially Mike McNally, whose influence is all over this book even if there's still some baseball in it.

Thanks to the Hall Farm Center for Arts & Education in Townsend, Vermont, for the time and beautiful space to write many of these chapters (and for the blueberries and beer). Thanks, too, to Kristen and Kara of Purdy's Coffee Company in Richmond, Kentucky, for providing ambience and lattes so conducive to writing.

Thanks to my agent, Mackenzie Brady Watson, whose editorial eye and enthusiasm have made this a better book. And thanks to everyone at Plume for their hard work, with special thanks to my editors, Matthew Daddona and Kate Napolitano, for their insight, their encouragement, and their ability to make the good, hard work of revision a joy (really).

And for various reasons, thanks to Bernice, Boyd the elder, both Daves, Derek, Jay, Jennifer, Jim, Kenny, Nancy, Toan, Wes, and Young.

Last of all, a sweeping, general thanks to all those bands (punk and otherwise) who hit the height of their fame in some backyard long ago, yet continue to inspire.